BROWNING ROAD

JEFF MARLOWE

BROWNING ROAD

www.jeffmarlowebooks.com

Library of Congress Control Number: 2021921066

ISBN: 978-1-7358917-3-6 (paperback)

ISBN: 978-1-7358917-4-3 (eBook)

Capablanca Books

Philadelphia, PA

PUBLISHER'S NOTE:

This is a work of fiction. Names, characters, places, and incidents either are the product of the author's imagination or are used fictitiously, and any resemblance to actual persons, living or dead, businesses, companies, events, or locales is entirely coincidental.

ALSO BY

Jeff Marlowe

Available by Capablanca Books

Never Going Home

www.jeffmarlowebooks.com

That was then, and that was us.

Chapter One

DON'T SELL TO NO BLACKS

"I told them not to sell to no blacks," my mother said to my father and brother; though not so much to me, and all with a not-so-subtle air of indulgence in her own pride. This was sadly typical. I was only seven at the time. Nonetheless, I could still see it. She went to the screen door and looked across the street to our neighbors, the Coyles, who had just put a for sale sign on the front lawn of their house that morning, and she smirked. Up until then, I didn't recall anyone moving from our block before, though it must have happened at some point. It was probably the same scenario we had that day. One by one they came visiting; some alone, some in pairs. Nothing arranged, but all the same consistent, and civil enough. The neighbors didn't crowd around the Coyle's house with torches and pitchforks like in the old Frankenstein movies, they just might as well have.

"What did they say?" my dad asked with our basset hound, Christy, at his feet. She was always wanting to be petted again, and he indulged. That dog didn't care how much she would trip over her own big ears, as long as there was someone to play with, and the tail kept whipping. Amazingly for that house, that was one happy animal. Old Joe Pszcynack only showed affection to the dog. That's why we needed her, despite my mother's initial objections to getting a pet of any kind. I'm glad we had the dog then; it was just never enough.

My mother closed the door entirely and put one hand on her overweight hip; she never exercised and was practically addicted to candy and it showed. Growing sideways and more frowning than smiling every single year, even back then. It never stopped the habits though. Some long for hollow sympathy over actual solutions.

"They said 'okay.' They knew we weren't fucking around," she explained. "I was over there with Arlene and she told them not to sell to no blacks either. We said we were sorry to see them go and wished them luck in their new home. Bob and Marion are retired, they worked until they were both fifty years old and put food on their table, so they earned it. The Cooks went by their house earlier and talked to them, Ernie and Grace Bergen walked over there, and they told me they told them not to sell to no blacks. The Lanzas told them not to sell to no blacks either."

The false look of confidence on her face was only reassured by the fact that pretty much everyone on the block said what she said, and more importantly, thought what she thought. All this, unfortunately, was always essential. If everyone is doing it, well then, it's not wrong. That's how it always worked, and principally how it still does. Lack of guilt by association. These people were raising children.

My mother turned from the door, as if anyone else could know what she was saying. It's not about what one says, but who hears it and when. Sensitive about sensitivity.

"Even Cathy and Jean and all the rest of my friends will ask if the

Coyles are selling to any blacks," she continued. "None of them have this kind of problem where they live. There's no blacks anywhere near their neighborhoods. But they would move if they did, it's not just me."

The friends. Very rarely was anything not about her clique of girlfriends. Even when they were not even there, they were there. Always. Anything and everything got back to them and all decisions and judgements were somehow weighed by their very existence. Barbara Pszcynack cared about what they might know, or more so, perceived.

"Well, they get the point," my dad said, looking out the window through the shades at the Coyles. "If it were anyone else leaving and them staying, they wouldn't want any niggers living here either. They can move if they want, but just don't fuck us over. Don't leave us to watch the damn neighborhood fall apart. We don't deserve it, we're good neighbors."

My dad didn't walk over to the Coyles house with them that day, even though he'd known them just as long as anyone. He simply didn't talk much. In fact, my friends often told me they never heard him speak a single word. What they didn't realize is that was actually a good thing.

"They are already busing the niggers up from 36th street to Joey and Jack's school," he says. "They belong in Camden. I saw one ride his bike down the street a few weeks ago; he should know better, the shit we have to put up with."

That man wore a steady frown on his face every day of his life, along with the constant shaking of his head, somehow in permanent disapproval. I can hardly remember seeing him do one or the other, not even one time. Everyone in that house understood the Coyle situation perfectly that day, except me. I actually got it, I did, though I just never accepted it the same way. Though that in turn was always an issue; it doesn't really work unless everyone agrees. Like it or not, they can always tell if you don't.

Charming fellow was my father. Everyday his beer gut somehow got bigger and the rings of graying hair on his head somehow got thinner. Round headed racism on wheels. He barely spoke half a sentence without using that particular word, which even then I knew not to say in front of black people, I didn't think it should be used at all. Though in my dad's lame defense, he would never say that if the right people were not listening. Regardless, the Coyles put their house up for sale that day. That's where it all began. We didn't move for a long while, much longer, actually. But it happened, they all saw it was coming. This was the state of Browning Road in the late eighties. This was Pennsauken, and this was its history.

I supposed this is when my parents considered selling our home, or "their" home as they put it so often. The house we lived in wasn't mine. I didn't own it, and even as a little kid, I had to be reminded of that, with all too much frequency. They didn't want to leave town; and they actually sank a lot of money into their house before the Coyle's departure. Most of it for converting our old musty basement into a really comfortable entertainment room which even had a small bar my dad loved. It's also where Christy loved to lay down and cool off in the summer.

That was that house and that's what was happening that day, more neighbors coming by the Coyles to ensure they were straightened out. I never took notice of time then, easy as it later became, at least in retrospect. It was the eighties. Better times. I didn't have to notice, I was living it, and enjoying it, such as it was. My light green house, the white shudders adorned with green grass and bushes where I found a bird's nest upon and once a garden snake under. I ran clean down the street that day. Whatever wildlife in that eighties suburbia continued to frolic under the breeze and sun while their human masters so pathetically endeavored to stop the clock hands from turning. That was somehow something I could notice. I suppose I hated change too.

I didn't want to move; this was my hometown. It's where I was born and therefore where I am from. The video store was in walking distance, so was the 7-11, and they sold comics. My friends were in that town and I didn't want to lose them, and certainly not over skin color alone. That might have been enough for all the so-called adults, but not for me. If we moved frankly at any time before I graduated high school, there would be no hometown at all. Not for me, anyway. Fractured. Displaced. That was real. No perception needed.

Pennsauken itself is a suburb of Philadelphia, where my parents are from, where my grandmother still lived, and my dad worked every day. It's in New Jersey but we always thought of it as Philly. We are into the Flyers, not the Devils, get it? New York City might as well be London, England for all we cared. Our town was always a predominantly one-color town, at least it was for many years. Incredible how "that's how it always was" really sticks. It was there. That was long before all the white flight.

Pennsauken is not only a quick drive to Philly, but the town itself borders Camden, New Jersey. Since apparently forever, Camden had the documented reputation for being the most dangerous city in

America for poverty and crime (drugs, prostitution, rape, you name it), high statistics all around. Dubious honor.

Even during Camden's highest crime eras, Pennsauken remained a predominantly white middle-class suburban town. I never asked my parents why they chose to move there from the city a year before I was born, and they never seemed comfortable enough to answer anyway. I figured it out over time. That's what happens when one thinks.

My own first real experience with these evidently important race issues was when I was in second grade. That was only a year pre-Coyle-sale, it just seemed so much longer. Joey was in fifth grade I think at that time; most if not all my classmates happened to be white before then. It was what it was, and we didn't ask questions, nor were we expected to. I remember while we were all waiting for our teachers to start the day, my friends and I, who all walked to Longfellow Elementary School, were watching the yellow buses arrive from all over town. The recently closed Amon Heights Elementary, closer to Camden in proximity, brought all of those displaced students to Longfellow; and my friends and I would call it "the black bus," having no idea we were being racist at the time. It was all done matter-of-factly.

In our defense, we never considered this a problem. Yet the bus from Amon was in fact all black students, with the exception of Brandy Welcher, she was in my grade. Brandy had a crush on me for years. Her younger sister was cuter though; it was just the way she wore that red hair. Even still, we noticed the predominant skin pigment on that bus, no one was blind. My brother and his friends hated this new dynamic, though felt no inclination to tell us why.

Everything was changing. Matters in Pennsauken were what they were. I had even more to lose but somehow was far less threatened than all the grown-ups on the block. Change always made "grown-ups" really cranky. Delicate to their own articulate encouragement, if they truly had any. Were they really superior?

Eventually my parents stopped coddling each other over the Coyle confrontation; my dad went back to the T.V., my mom to the phone to make sure all her friends knew this was happening and she had it under control. Joey was not taking any notice of me during that conversation. The for-sale sign on the lawn across the street was a serious matter, far above my relevance level. I escaped upstairs to my room, my own personal kingdom then, and forever after in my heart, admittedly. My mom hated how much time I spent in that room. It made her look bad.

But it was mine. I decorated it with lots of comic book posters, lots of comics to read, aging toys to play with but I grew up in the eighties and we had the best stuff as kids. We had a far worse economic condition later on as adults for sure, but for the culture, that was a great time to be a kid. I think I still have old G. I. Joe and He-Man toys in a box somewhere but back then they were front and center. My parents and brother looked down on me for being a kid, maybe more so for enjoying it sometimes. I suppose someone always has to be below. I would never remotely bend to any such will. That created a few problems.

Another reason I kept my room fairly clean for a kid was I needed room to play with all this stuff, to stretch out and read. I loved comic books but had real books too. I had the essentials and more, *Lord of the Rings, Dune, Choose Your Own Adventure,* so many greats.

I always preferred the books over the movies, even at that age; and my mom liked taking me to the library because it was free.

I also kept a row of cassette tapes on a table, all organized by favorites and release dates. I loved rock and roll like Bon Jovi and Guns N Roses (parents back then didn't get bent out of shape over content as much as they do now) and I even had some Michael Jackson tapes. My mom often told me not to play those when my dad was around. The King of Pop was of a certain color, after all.

I even kept the Fireball Island board game out of the box and on display in that room because it was just that awesome. My friends never wanted to play it as much as I did. I knew not to do so with Joey, he would break it if he lost, or if he simply felt like humiliating me for a lark. That was always possible, more likely, actually. Nothing like being expected to win and always failing. The worst thing I could do was not play a game that was rigged.

That was my own world, the room was the first and maybe best place in his own history that Jack Pszcynack could really call his own, even at that young age. I try to avoid even saying that word most of the time. I hate my last name. It's pronounced "Puh-shin-yack," I forever had to explain, the name being of Polish ancestry. That and the very fact that no one could ever pronounce it was and it is still a major cause of concern, and frankly pain. That was the life of having a weird name. Later on, I heard even hiring managers would throw away my resume because of the difficult pronunciation. They behave the way they do because they can, and probably liked that there was not a thing anyone could do about it. Yet the grandees remained infallibly sensitive to any inquiry, curiously enough.

In any case, I also spent the occasional time then cleaning the floor near my bed with rug cleaner I swiped from under the kitchen sink. That was necessary sometimes. After pulling some comics out to read, I would spray the area down, drying it with a towel. Had to be done. After I cleaned, I could hear some voices outside my window, murmurs really, nothing coherent. I looked out the window and saw our two doors down neighbors across the street, Mr. Myers and his wife, standing outside the Coyles house, talking with them on a familiar subject. I knew Mr. Myers' wife was a former nun, but was always discouraged in mentioning it. It was too interesting to speak of.

I must have only caught the tail end of their conversation, as Mr. Myers, quite seventy-something was walking towards me, back to his house. Yet he stopped himself and turned back to the rotund Mr. Coyle. I couldn't hear him, but his lips were easy to read and he was waving his hand side to side, palm down as if in dismissal of any other idea. I could "see" Mr. Myers clearly say to the Coyles, "Don't sell to no blacks." It couldn't be said just once, evidently.

Interesting that the Myers and Coyles had probably known each other for decades up to that point. They lived on Browning Road long before the time my parents arrived there from Philadelphia; so, this was also an end of an era for them, though the message remained clear. Oddly enough, Bob and Marion Coyle didn't move very far from Pennsauken at all. Though they were moving away, they were staying in New Jersey. Just a little further eastward to the Atlantic County area, to be closer to their daughter who lived there, as she only recently had their first grandchild.

I forget what Bob Coyle did for a living, he had been retired for at least a little while. I think he was a salesman of some sort; Marion

Coyle was a housewife. At the time of planting that infamous for sale sign, the Coyles were in their early fifties. This of course was back when a middle-class couple could retire in their fifties, something myself and my friends would not have when we reached their age, and even that with a seeming lack of survivor's guilt on the part of the haves.

The Coyles had the benefit of being born at the right time to be able to simply retire, put their house up for sale, and move closer to their grandchildren. Baby Boomer heaven, no false consolation for them, it was real. The Coyles' immediate descendants never had what they had. Less. I wonder if they ever felt bad about that. I wonder if it was ever given any thought. Doubtful, however sad.

In my room (I still called it mine), I always kept my door shut and often locked. It's not private otherwise. Christy was at my door, trying to shove her big basset nose underneath to at least smell what could be going on; she had the curiosity twice that of a cat, and was a better pet all around for it. I liked placing my fingers under the door to provoke her attention and I would always know she was wagging her white tipped tail, hoping to get inside and see what was going on. The dog was always welcome. If anyone else was home, the door would stay closed.

Ever absent minded, I forgot the towel was still on the floor, and walked back over it in my bare feet now wet from my steps. I cleaned that floor fairly often as I peed on it during the night. Such a petty thing, looking back, but I was scared to leave the room at night. The fear was working when it shouldn't. Yet keeping me afraid had more than one purpose.

The bathroom was across the hall at that house, next to my parents' room. From where Joey slept in his room, he had a clear view down the hall. Some late evening before the beginning of the exodus, I got up from bed one night to go to the bathroom. As if I tripped some alert wire he set, Joey noticed I was up and about and he wasn't. Even in the dark, I could still see via moonlight his skinny face with that near permanent venomous sneer, or more often with me, his never ceasing, vile gaze. Always the demonic scowl through his skinny, sharp teeth. I existed and he hated me for it. Nothing was ever done to address this, or even recognize it, and that was not right.

"What the hell are you doing?" he demanded. Yes, I could still see him in the darkness, his sheets up to his neck, furious with me as if he caught me in the act of robbing a bank, if not a murder. Smug scorn from an abusive criminal. Joey's vindictive eyes pierced into me, and I froze, overwhelmed with guilt; for what I did not know. Bullies never want you to know. More power that way.

"I have to go to the bathroom," I said to him, pointing to the door. What the hell was his problem? Kids like him do not provide explanations. He only shook his head at me in disapproval, the head shaking alone clearly informing me "no, you can't go to the bathroom. In fact, you're not."

I remember shaking my head back at him; the little monster immediately jumped out of bed and made it as if he was going to come after me if I disobeyed him. He did it all quietly, the malicious whispers so our parents would not hear. Art of the bully, and by that point he was a seasoned artist. I would never have anything he didn't. Not by one inch. Joey had no qualms about fighting. Bullies know how to win. He would hit me; and the lanky, egotistical asshole that he was, he would make it hurt. What no one once ever took into consideration was that the physical act of being punched, even in the face, is not what scares the victim. It's not the pain, it's the fear, the humiliation, the degradation from the bully that matters. They are the worst nightmares, and most consider them winners, even then. Too many actually like it, and will never admit it. Yet they do.

He stared down at me until I relented. I went back to bed, and still had to go in a big way so I ended up peeing on the floor next to my bed. That's how all this started, whenever I had to get up to go, I didn't. It was not every night, but Joey could have been shot with tranquilizers and would still wake up at the drop of a dime to stop me from being out of bed when he wasn't. I was not to ever get ahead of him, even to pee.

Me being up and about the house after bedtime, specifically his bedtime, even if just to go to the bathroom, meant that I was, however briefly, his superior; and he would never tolerate that. I can't have something that he has, and certainly not if he doesn't. I was not important enough to be up and about the house for any reason. I supposed he felt that, again, however briefly; me being out of bed and him not, made me "cooler" than him somehow. Even so, he won. That being the whole idea.

So, that's why I cleaned my floor with the door shut. You have to go somewhere. So, when I had to go, there I was. The rest of that day I continued to wonder why my family was so increasingly apprehensive because the Coyles were leaving, and I could vaguely overhear some voices from across the street. That same Saturday we had to head over to Philly to visit my grandmother, routine for the time. My grandmother, Marie, lost her husband some years before, now it was only her, so we visited often. Unless a major holiday, my dad stayed at home while we visited, also routine. My grandfather was fun, and actually friendly. He didn't make me feel like an intruder, a nuisance, or an expense. That was a man that could be loved, not feared. But he was gone, and all that was left by then was memories. Treasured, yes, but never good enough.

Kids, being kids, we took forever to get ready to go that day. I was ready first. That didn't matter. My mother didn't want to leave yet because Grace Bergen next door was out on her porch, watching the neighborhood. Barbara could not take a trip to the grocery store without Grace watching and asking, "Where are you going, Barbara?" She would not even step out of the house if Grace was on her porch.

Later, even after we had all moved, I used to refer to such nosy neighbor sensitivity as "Grace Bergen Syndrome." My mother always hated that phrase. In fact, she often denied this was ever a problem at all. For all its power, denial is sensitive to itself. Entirely on cue, Barbara told us we couldn't leave that day until Grace goes inside so we would just have to wait. I asked her why this was an issue. That happened. A seven-year-old boy asked his mother why they couldn't take a ride as planned because Grace Bergen was out on the porch, always there, old and limpy, irritating old voice, grey and retired as she was. This is what she did with her life. Outlandish. Or terrifying. Kind of both.

Yet ask and challenge, I did. My mother didn't answer, only shouted me down because the question alone was out of line enough as it was. I told her it was ridiculous, and she raised her hand up as if she would slap me but didn't. Not her way, but she certainly wanted to, which was just as bad. Barbara just shook her head at me, her favorite. Then she stared down at me until I stopped asking questions. Cheap ploy but it works, wretchedly. No consequences, though there actually were.

Eventually, Barbara was brave enough to venture outside, and as luck would have it, Grace was not on the porch. All was clear. I beat my brother outside after we were told to get ready to leave again, nearly an hour after we were told the first time. I got ahead of him, in a sense. Yet for the social experiment I chose to run, that was something else entirely.

Joey had not left the house yet, so my mother and I would have to wait for him. I know she wanted him to move it along, Grace could come back out at any time. Without ever being told that this was a rule, I was always expected to sit in the back whenever we drove somewhere. Joey always rode shotgun. The front seat was always his without fail. Not this time. I climbed into the front seat. It felt admittedly strange being there, but I liked it, and asked myself as to why I always had to sit in the back anyway. I knew it was an unpardonable crime.

My mother almost had a seizure. Her entire body twitching in discomfort, as if being strangled by invisible ghosts under her own skin; sheer terror in her eyes for that transgression. She didn't say anything at first. Joey was still inside. Barbara looked at me up and down in shock, her mouth gaping at me. Her breathing noticeably lost any of its normal rhythm. Grace Bergen was no longer on her mind at this point. Then her left eye started blinking rapidly.

"What are you doing, Jack?" she said now looking at our own house door, horrified that I dared or even thought of what I was doing.

"I can sit here," I told her. "I got here first and he's taking his sweet time. There is no reason I can't sit here. Incidentally, why does he always have to sit in the front? What's the big deal?"

My mother, an apparent adult, downed a hard swallow, she could have been sweating, not fearing for her life but getting there.

"I just don't want any fights, okay?" Is all she said in response. I relented, hating myself all the more for it. As I was getting up to get out of the car, my brother came out of the house.

"Get the hell out of there!" he said. Barbara turned away as if the boss was yelling at one of his subordinates at work. She didn't actually have a boss, and Joey was certainly not in charge. Could have fooled him.

"What the hell do you think you're doing?" Joey sneered. "Don't piss me off! You heard me, you little shit!" Joey was only at maybe fifty percent Joey as he settled down in the front seat, frowning and shaking his head at such an intrusion, and then started working the radio. Not saying a word, my mother put the car in reverse back down the driveway. The color of fear. Social experiment completed.

There were reasons in addition to the consequences. It was never mentioned. Not once in any given point in human history. Joey had severe psychological issues, however subtle. Perhaps it was narcissistic personality disorder, a chemical imbalance; whatever it was, he had a psychological problem, and that is why it was never treated. Unwritten rule there. Or maybe it was just because he was a bully. People like bullies. They will deny it, sure, and questioning said denial makes them very distraught. So, the solution: Do nothing. Ignore the consequences. I didn't. That never went well.

Grace Bergen came outside on her porch again with excitement in her face, yet didn't say anything. Grace only waved at us, Barbara giving her an awkward wave in return, fake smile and everything. As if it wasn't awkward enough, we finally left the house.

That was my social experiment. Effective exercise altogether. I suppose in a way, it was a success. By merely sitting in the front seat of the car I learned what I had already suspected. I was younger than Joey and therefore inferior. He was not yet eleven years old. My mother was terrified of a ten-year-old boy whose temper and ego dictated the very air we breathed, and I was accountable for crossing the lines he set without explanation. Worse yet, I was still asking questions.

As we drove off, I saw the Washington family who lived down the street knocking on the Coyle's door. That being Mrs. Washington and her hippy son, Larry. I would sometimes walk past their house and hear him playing his guitar. Never really felt welcome though. The more I think of it, they were pretty trashy people all around; and Larry stank of an odor I had not yet come to have known. We learn things as we get older, it gets more fascinating as we go along, especially when so contemptuously kept in the dark, seemingly of our youths alone.

The Washingtons looked at us driving by with what seemed slight apprehension. Could not imagine why. They were just visiting their soon to be departed neighbors. Nothing wrong with that. I could still see the chubby, and by that point, more than annoyed Bob Coyle open his door to greet yet another set of visitors. How often did the Washingtons visit the Coyles anyway? Yet there Larry and his mom were, at their door. I could not for the life of me imagine what they were going to ask of them.

Chapter Two

ESTU ME

It turned out that the Coyles didn't "sell to no blacks." They did, however, sell their home to a rich couple all the way up from New York City who liked to buy houses everywhere and the Coyles house was therefore bought, and turned into a rental property. Then the rich couple rented the Coyle's old house to a black family, the Petersons, our new neighbors. I thought all hell would break loose in my house but whatever my own family's rage, certainly the entire block's ire, was only exhibited by uncomfortable silence, and perhaps with begrudging acceptance.

Mr. Leon Peterson was actually a Camden city police officer, living within driving distance from Pennsauken with his wife and six-year-old son. Maybe it was the fact that he was a cop that lent Mr. Peterson at least some approval from his new neighbors; despite being the only black family on the block. Police command a certain modicum of respect, be it deserved or not, especially in those days. So being a cop, Leon Peterson and family became more or less accepted. He was a friendly man, nothing intimidating about him other than perhaps his profession. The Petersons would by then at least be accepted as the token black family, and that would have to be good enough.

That was the logic, after all. This was the entire reason the polite and separated mob approached the Coyle's house the day they put that for sale sign on their front lawn. If the Coyles had "sold to blacks," that would be, as my neighbors and certainly my own family perceived it, the death bell for their neighborhood. This train of logic (if there was any), was not pleasant. Bad enough that gainfully employed neighbors such as the Petersons were not welcome there, it was if one black family moved to the block, then that would signal other black families could do so as well; and the neighborhood in short time would be overrun. This was unacceptable to those that came before, or at least to those who had their own way up until then.

This is one of the essentials of white flight, doubly so for a town so close to Camden, New Jersey. There were established boundaries, and selling to a black family is a clear violation of security (largely emotional security) policies, however unwritten. If one moves in, others will come. Despite the convoluted racism, I didn't realize it then, but do now, how the browning of certain neighborhoods would, in effect, bring down home values; and even make them more difficult to sell. The neighbors really were protecting their interests that day. We lived then and even now in sick times. This is what we were. Living history.

A few years passed after the Coyles left our company and the Petersons took their place. Perhaps everyone hoped that this tokenism would hold. Life changed for me too. I had "graduated" from grade school, by then eleven years old, in middle school. No longer walking, but taking a long yellow school bus every day. Joey had moved up to high school and also had to use the bus, yet not as often.

Taking the bus to school and back every day brought with it its own perils and humiliations. Yet for some reason all throughout middle school and certainly high school, it just wasn't considered "cool" to take the bus; at least not in the morning. Joey made sure he would not fall victim to this in the summer before his freshman year. Even something so seemingly trivial had been well planned out. Perception of cool, and premeditated. I was despised for even pointing that out.

My best friend who also lived on Browning Road was Michael Del, who was in the same grade as me and we went to the same school all our lives. In addition to his cooler than us eighth-grader sister, Jennifer; there was older brother Kenny Del, the big man on campus and by that point a high school senior. Kenny had his own car and drove his girlfriend and a few friends to Pennsauken High School every morning. Again, for some reason it was the mornings, there was far less stigma at taking the bus home in the afternoon. I still do not know to this day why that was so. Yet I ask. Nevertheless, by offering a weekly payment of gas money, Joey was able to be in the Kenny car to school every morning, and his problem was solved, hades forbid.

Reputations really matter. Questions less so. I had to take the bus with Michael and his sister every day; at least I got to start off each of my days with friends. His cousin, Matt, also rode with us. He was the only son of Arlene, the neighbor my mother took a walk with to the Coyle's house that day; they all lived right there on the block, two houses from each other down the street. The two Dels.

Michael and I, being the same age, were close friends since before kindergarten, friends before any real memory. I always found it interesting that his house was only slightly larger than my own yet with three kids in the house, Michael shared a room with Kenny, and they got along just fine. I would always cry inside, not just then, always. There was another world away from my own brother who wouldn't let me out of my own room to take a piss.

Michael, lanky, dark haired, retainer in his mouth, and tall for his age like his brother, was like me into everything one and the same. He eventually grew to nearly seven feet tall and to just about everyone's consternation, never played basketball or was interested much in sports. He didn't have to be told how to live, not by them. Not then, anyway. Better times. So fortunate that he was a true friend, and within that perfect era. The eighties. Be it Phillies baseball, pro wrestling on T.V., GI Joe toys and cartoons, anything. It was in middle school that I discovered my love for comic books because of all the reading growing up. That and that Batman movie with Jack Nicolson as the Joker took us all by storm; I just had to get into the comic books to keep up with the adventures of the Caped Crusader after that. Hence Michael Del's own interest in comic books by then.

Wednesdays were when new books were released. I had to see if the next issue of the caped crusader was out, and other titles I was into: Wolverine, the GI Joe comic (essentially a twenty page story advertisement for the toys, but I didn't care); and many others as time went on. Kids can get addicted to these things like cigarettes. There was no comic book store in town at that time so we often took a walk to the 7-11 on Westfield Avenue, essentially Pennsauken's main street.

Being into comics and discussing them was the rising tide for many kids in school at the time. I had made friends with X-Men lover, Damon Bailey, a black kid who was in many of my classes and often was assigned to my "table" as that is how kids were organized by teachers for some reason.

The first time Damon and I really talked was in Longfellow elementary, in fifth grade. We were both drummers in the school band, and would sometimes talk in the back of the room. We quietly understood that if we were going to be in a school band playing (very badly) classical music, drums were about as cool as we were going to get.

One day our teacher needed more chairs in her room for some event she was doing so she asked Damon and I to head to the boiler room one morning to pick up extra chairs they had stored there. It was this hot, loud, industrial room that was like the basement of a big house. We had to ask the half deaf janitor for the chairs we were sent to get, and after him asking "huh" about twenty times, he eventually figured it out and went to the back of the room to get some from a large stack of chairs. Somewhat annoyed at taking a direct request from two kids; skin color notwithstanding. Then it happened.

"What are you doing here?" a piercing voice that made us both startle in inane fear, came from behind us. It was Miss Rule, who I actually had once as a teacher. Even then I always thought she was so young compared to all the other teachers in the school, but that's only because she was. She stood there in the boiler room with us, her face red with self-righteous fury, her one hand buried in her purse, and staying there. Somehow, I knew she could read my look, which clearly asked what the hell was the young, striking school teacher doing in the boiler room? We told her in weak voices that our teacher sent us here because she needs extra chairs.

"You don't belong in here! This is not a place for students! Get back to class now!" Is all she said in response as we scattered out the door like frightened mice, back into the hallway, and with no chairs. That failure's responsibility was on us, and we knew it. We told our teacher that Miss Rule made us leave the boiler room. Our teacher said nothing in response, and less in explanation. I found out later that Miss Rule liked to smoke there, if that was not already obvious, even to elementary school kids. Damon told me he heard those cigarettes were laced with cocaine. Miss Rule was later fired. They did not explain a single word to the students as to why, and felt even less inclination to do so.

On that day, I found out Damon was into comics, and then we would talk about them all the time together. It was almost like having our own comic book club at lunch hours, talking about all the stories while a good many kids would look at us like we were from Mars since they didn't read them, including Michael for a while. Comics were something "in" that he was not yet a part of; that and maybe he had a problem with Damon and I bonding over them. Damon even rode our bus in the morning, so comic books were often the first topic of the day.

Michael wanted to try out comics, perhaps to keep up somehow, so we trekked to Westfield Avenue. Michael didn't realize I invited Damon to join us. The truth was, Michael actually liked Damon, they were both into watching sports in a big way, and the only thing Michael seemed to dislike was his encyclopedic knowledge of comic books. Beyond that, Damon and he were at least school friends, we all were. I didn't really know how Michael's parents felt about black kids visiting our area of town, even if to simply meet at a 7-11 for sodas and comics. I can't imagine they were too keen on it. I was not as scared as they wanted me to be, yet I knew my own parents were hardly any different on the subject.

Michael's family, Arlene and Matt Del included, were Catholic like mine, at least in name anyway. Everyone had to believe (or say they believed) in something, as long as it wasn't atheism. Michael's father was a friendly, sometimes funny, though alcoholic mailman, and his mother was an extraordinarily overweight school nurse, but she didn't work at our school. Michael was always vocally happy about that. I didn't blame him.

An elephant in the room, yes, I knew Michael felt it weird, or at least alarming, that Damon walked all the way up from his house to join us for comic browsing. Damon often dressed in tattered blue jeans and a slightly torn white t-shirt (for all I knew, his only clothes). His curly hair almost dusty somehow as if greying; he was a little younger than me, yet older than us still. He was one of the friend-liest kids I knew at school. Eleven-year-old boys are hardly easy-going, but I always noticed that venerable consistency with him, and wished everyone could at least try not to be selfish, or irredeemable, ignorant shits. Too much to ask too often, yet not with him.

None of it really mattered that day, it was fun to buy comics with Damon as opposed to only talking about them. The store only had so much of a selection, and since we were kids, we could only hang out there for so long before the miserable clerk behind the counter would tell us to buy something or get out. Occasionally, she would try to get creative and say something along the lines of "you guys have five more minutes, then it's buy or bye-bye!" Anything to help her feel more important than she was, I suppose. I could never imagine how superior one could feel working at a convenience store; but then again, which likely only made her preeminence farce all the more volatile. We can't help the age we are, or gender, or anything. Nor should we apologize for any of it. We should not have to feel the worse or inferior for it. Maybe she knew we could see it. Problems. Nevertheless, we knew to keep it moving.

All three of us only had enough money to buy one or two comics anyway, with hopefully enough money to get a soda or gum, anything for the road. Damon and I had at it, discussing the ins and outs of all the different characters and where they were from, how their powers worked, their "real" names, the fact that nobody knew where Wolverine came from, all of it. Michael, trying his best to hide his own discomfort with any of the comic lore, stared at the rack for a little bit. He had to get something after all; and then out of nowhere he grabbed an issue of Captain America of all choices and stood up to pay the cranky clerk.

"Why Captain America?" I asked him. Damon took no notice as he read right there in the store.

"Because I heard Captain America was popular," Michael responded with his unfortunately typical air of confidence. As usual not looking at me, but the tactic was popular so there we were. I'm happy he at least tried to get into reading. He only kept at it for a couple of months, and later sold me his Captain America books for baseball card money. Cap somehow became my favorite character thereafter and I never missed a single issue up until the very month I graduated high school. It was all in his book's writing, and those stories kept going, and I didn't stop. Captain America was a man out of his time. That's why I kept reading all those years after. Michael never gave another thought to it.

It turned out Damon was into Marvel's wallcrawler, Spider-Man, telling us on the walk home that he's the super-hero he identifies with most. "He's one of the most realistic heroes out there," he explained. Talking almost as if he was somehow an academic authority on the subject of super-heroes; he was just awesome. He opened the book to us; the aging clerk girl rolled her eyes as we left. In retrospect, being young was always my favorite crime.

"I sometimes feel like Peter Parker," Damon went on. "Not really the powers of a spider, climbing up on walls and shit like that, that's cool, yes. But Peter Parker grew up without parents, he grew up poor, and never made any money off of his superpowers. He has to pay the bills, food, tuition, and he takes care of an elderly aunt who raised him, so he has it rough. He's got real problems. I identify with all of that, a lot more than you guys know."

I could see Michael watching Damon flip through his new comic book as we walked back home. I still do not understand to this day why Michael asked, but ask he did.

"Damon, does it ever bother you that there are hardly any black superheroes in comics?" he asked. "No one for you to identify with on a, well, identity level?"

Damon stopped and looked at Michael like he had palm trees suddenly growing out of the sides of his head.

"What the hell are you saying?" Damon responded, yet all the while keeping his welcoming cool about him. That would never go away.

"Why would anyone have to self-identify with any character, in a book or in a movie? Why would they have to share some kind of immutable characteristic in order to enjoy a film or show? Collective pride? Luke Skywalker doesn't 'look' like me, yet he's still awesome, and a realistic person for living in a crazy science fiction world. Daddy issues with him, for sure. What of Indiana Jones, or John Rambo? I love all that stuff. Are you really saying to me that a character or actor has to 'represent' me by 'looking' like me; because of skin pigment? That's ridiculous! Their character represents me; that's what I identify with. It would be damned arrogant to think Peter Parker needs to 'look' like me in order for me to enjoy, or 'identify' with his comics. That's totally absurd. If we ever get to the point in life where people start demanding creative decisions or casting to 'represent' them; then it's not representation, it is pure ego; and we should slap them upside their head if they do."

Damon never put out any bad vibes, even in the face of Michael's goofy question, who by then was faking a smile to hide his own embarrassment. It's good that he joined us, even for a failed new interest in comic books. Can't be left out. Michael was my best friend, to be sure, but when he was a goofball, he really was one. We all get like that from time to time, after all, we were buying and reading comic books. Hardly what the "cool kids" were into. Silly, maybe. But I had friends.

All that walking and talking, we eventually reached Browning Road, and had to go home. Damon said goodbye and continued walking probably ten blocks more to his neighborhood further south, thirty-something street he lived on. He didn't seem to mind. We only hung out with him every so often, I'm not going to doubt at least part of the reason for that is for fear of how our parents might react if we hung out with him indoors ever. Back then, even neighbors were watching.

The bus route that picked Michael and I up each morning did run through Damon's neighborhood first. We were the last stop before school. That was always something, riding a bus with a bunch of middle-schoolers, many of them from rougher neighborhoods than mine, and the attitudes to match. All the kids would glare at us when we got on the bus, it was not really a pleasant atmosphere by any means despite being a bus filled with middle-schoolers. Such was that time. Innocence well lost.

Sometimes, there would be people who would not let us sit in the free space next to them; I was not cool enough for them, or they "needed their space," was always a frequent argument, all just to be dicks; always such an ordeal. How could one ever expect more? Nevertheless, there was that one kid on the bus that I dreaded seeing every single day. The daily dose of fear, and a reminder that ignorance is not just bliss, it's appreciated.

Coletta. I knew she was in seventh grade, a year above us when I first heard her loud, and remarkably obnoxious voice throughout the bus rides to and from school; yet she was always worse in the mornings. Everything about her really spoke "big." Big hair, tall, big mouth, big earrings, big voice, and big body. She was not really fat, just noticeably large for her age, for a thirteen or fourteen-year-old, whatever she was, she could have passed for a thirty-something adult. She almost seemed built like a female professional wrestler who could pile drive any of us without breaking a sweat. Worse yet, she always looked like she wanted to do just that, which didn't help matters the more I thought of it, and I was thinking.

I could hear her talking above everyone else; this being an everyday occurrence, Coletta didn't seem to have any friends. She often sat in the front of the long yellow bus, sitting in the green chairs, talking in general, yet to no one specifically; she simply needed to be heard. Predictably, most of the kids on the bus, out of fear or likely their own arrogance, listened to her with attentive faces and Coletta certainly fed off that like a maggot feeding on rancid flesh. Though it was never enough.

One morning after Michael's Captain America comics discovery, we boarded the bus to the familiar scenario. Coletta was flapping her gums about something incoherent, and sitting sideways on her bus seat, her giant legs way out in the middle of the aisle. Michael climbed on the bus before me, somehow maneuvering his way past Coletta to find someone willing to offer him a seat. I tried not to accidentally touch Coletta, knowing that it was somehow my responsibility not to touch her even with her legs way out into the aisle as I passed. I failed. My leg brushed up against her. Contact.

Coletta reached out and grabbed my arm, the whole bus falling silent in anticipation of what the evident insufferable queen bee of the bus would do to me for such a transgression. Ensnared in the web of the charmless bully. Knowing that she would never suffer one ounce of accountability for herself. Brave new world. Her eyes bore into me and she squeezed my arm ever tighter. Almost like shriveled wood trapped in a steel wound up vice, or at least that was the nice way of putting it.

"Can you say excuse me?" she asked, looking at me like I was the rudest person ever to grace her majestic presence and how dare I brush up against her person. Again, everyone stared; I didn't doubt for a second who they thought the victim actually was. While Coletta clearly asked "excuse me," it sounded more like "estu me," her deliberately ghetto style accent somehow lending her more credibility she did not deserve yet was granted all the same.

"Yes," is all I responded, really kicking the hornet's nest then. She squeezed harder and shook my arm up and down like a rag doll.

"Can you say excuse me?" she asked again, and again it was "estu me."

"Yes," I responded, trying to keep walking forward; even when knowing I couldn't. Coletta stood up, raising her voice louder than I imagined possible. She was just getting started. My arm was getting numb.

"Can you say excuse me?" Though I still heard "estu me."

"Excuse me," I finally said; deliberately in a low voice, no longer looking at her. Certainly not wanting to.

Coletta let go and rolled her eyes at me in disgust, then turning her head away from what I clearly was. A moron. An intruder. Rude. How dare I? That girl was an artist, however immature, and that with dubious reverence.

I managed to find a seat next to Damon, across the aisle from Michael. The tension on the bus died down quickly enough but Michael was shaking his head at me.

"Why did you touch her like that, what's wrong with you,

Jack?"

"What?" I asked him. Michael still looked enormously dis-appointed in me. He pretty much was that whole day. I didn't quite understand it then, was he trying to avoid the bully by siding with her? Was he angry with me for questioning him? Even at that age, no one liked that. Never ask questions. Brilliant program. Damon looked at me for a bit on the ride to school, somewhat amused, and amused is usually a decent defense mechanism for most. Not so much with him.

"Coletta's my cousin, you know," Damon said in his usual reasonable tone. "She acts like that all the time, try not to take it personally."

"It's hard not to take it personal," I said. Furious, not so much over Coletta, but Michael; not to mention all the other idiots on that bus who really believed in their hearts that the repulsive bully was even remotely in the right.

"She'll forget about you by tomorrow, it's just her way." Is all Damon or anyone else had to say on the matter. As years went on, sometimes for fun, and frankly spite, I used the term "estu me" often later on with friends and various girlfriends. They all thought I was crazy. But I remembered. That was just my way. No one defended me to the likes of Coletta. Why all the admiration? They could not see anything I couldn't.

Tensions cooled between Michael and I almost immediately after that particular incident. I miss how easy that was in the pre-teen years. We were all far more resilient then. Better still as shortly thereafter I was invited to Michael's house for one of our infamous weekend sleepover nights. Yes, even middle school boys did that sort of thing. Sometimes Michael's father worked overnight so it was fun to have less supervision issues in the house, we were not bad kids, but fun is fun. With his parents not being around too often, and his older sister out on sleepovers of her own, it was really fun to be at his house. After all, it wasn't my house. It always felt good to get away.

Kenny Del was the oldest and coolest kid on the block, but he hung out with some rather shady characters. Kenny himself looked normal but the friends he hung out with were long-haired heavy metal fans whom Michael and I were outright terrified of. Maybe it was what we saw of heavy metal on T.V. or on album covers, but it was all scary. Michael and I were too young to go to concerts. We heard they were wild. Crazy crowds, violent fights, mosh pits, and we even heard people got trampled on at these shows. We also heard stories of drugs, topless girls, all of it. Rock n' Roll. Born too late. Why did it go away?

Kenny's friends all wore Metallica t-shirts, the unchallenged leaders of the metal world at that time; and they would blast the music from their cars whenever they came by, just to show off. It was effective, fascinating, if not entirely frightening; and we kept our distance. I still liked the music, being afraid of it only encouraged it more.

Another reason Kenny and his friends were cooler than us is because they were old enough to see rated R movies. Kenny even had some on V. H. S. format so Michael would ask him to let us borrow them. That was sleepovers at the Del's in general, playing video games or board games all night, and watching movies, oftentimes above our age grade. I was not yet old enough in my own mind then for the gory horror stuff, though that was to come. Kenny had other movies in his room, rightly hidden away but we knew they were there, just not for sleepover nights. Those movies were for when no one, and I mean no one else, was in the house to catch us watching them. Kenny was like most older brothers at the time, and had a stash of porn movies hidden away under his dresser. We still found them, naturally.

It was obvious sleepovers were no time to watch a porn movie and indulge our curiosity since Mrs. Del was home, but the fact that I knew they were in the house, and that Michael and I had watched them before, after school when no one was home, random curiosity. Many, in fact most, twelve-year-old boys watch porn, even at that early age and it wasn't considered wrong to watch them together, at least to satisfy our mutual curiosity to what sex was really all about. We would only stand in front of the T.V. in awe. It was somehow less scary and easier to just watch, and on top of that, Kenny always had his steady supply. How could we not look?

I was always tempted to ask Michael if we could smuggle another porn video away from his brother, but hardly ever ac-tually suggested it. Michael would sometimes call me a pervert for asking, anything to be superior on this matter; so, porn was only a very occasional viewing event. Then again, Michael was just as curious as the next guy so there was that. We were not to talk about it much in general, but these particular videos were teaching us something to be valued later on, even if we didn't know it at the time.

If we had the night, we usually stayed up often until dawn; Mrs. Del would typically fall asleep reading her Al-Anon books and then the living room was ours. Sure, we usually watched movies or T.V. shows but it was ours for the night. Whatever shenanigans we were up to, we would always finish the night (and often fell asleep on the chairs) watching *Stand by Me* on video; this was actually my first and favorite rated R movie I ever saw. By then it was a tradition to watch it on sleepovers.

The movie was four twelve-year-old kids going on a long walking journey to find a dead body, all the while talking about their remarkably (and often ignored) complex lives while cursing up a storm the whole way. These kids even smoked, which wasn't a thing for us, but still fun to watch. No parents, no older brothers, just them. However indirectly, that is who we were, living our own lives as friends at twelve and it was the whole world to us, not just the movie, but the attitude, the fun, and above all, the friendship.

I once asked Michael if he would ever be up for remaking the adventure in *Stand by Me*, walking on railroad tracks to somewhere far, the shore, anywhere really. He responded in a huff that "we could just drive there," apparently forgetting we weren't old enough to drive yet. Michael suggested things like asking Kenny to drive us, but he was missing the point; walking is better, this was us as friends and it would be fun, however a pipe dream it was. Since the movie had four boys, I asked Michael who else could go on this trip besides me, him, and Damon.

"We could just drive, and I'm not going with any of them," Michael said. He just didn't get it. I wanted to live in a way that our parents did not know everything we were doing and who we spent time with, and Damon was a good guy all around. A friend. Maybe Michael was racist. I think he was probably more concerned with not getting into any kind of trouble, and he knew our families didn't want Damon on the block, even with Mr. Peterson now living right across the street from me.

Stand by Me may have been my perception of the gold standard of friends. The last line in the movie is "I never had any friends later on in life like I did when I was twelve. Jesus, does anyone?" I just didn't know what I was in for. I loved my home on Browning Road in Pennsauken, even with the inexorable tensions with my family, exception the dog. I still didn't want too much to change. Yet I also never believed in cliques. It did not have to be just Michael and I, and that's it. I could say change is always scary to everyone but that's probably not truthful enough. Change is horrifying. The times and devices of all our lives were changing before our eyes; even if we didn't want it to happen. "Want." That word so often escaped me, and often guilted me away. I wasn't really aware then of what was happening in that town, on that block; I just knew I didn't want to lose my friends. I couldn't. I also didn't know that what I wanted simply didn't matter.

Chapter Three

SHATTERED

Michael and I didn't stay up all night for that particular sleepover; and we passed out on the couches somewhere near the end of *Stand by Me*. As much fun as I always had there, it was always awkward being there for the morning Del routine. The house was no longer left to ourselves, so I made some lame excuse and left. It was never taken personally so it was just as well. I soon found myself back at home, such as it was, and alone again.

At least there was the dog, I loved hanging out with Christy. As a curious basset hound, Christy had to be chained or on a leash all the time or she would smell a path all the way to Cape May and maybe beyond if she smelled more food anywhere else. I spent the rest of that morning on our blood red, wooden back stairs, watching Christy sniff around the backyard, myself eating crackers and resting on my feet on my skateboard because I was never good enough to skate beyond the patio, for fear of embarrassing myself on it around town, hell, even just down Browning Road. I knew there was always someone watching.

I could always practice on the back patio. Most houses on the block had them; large, white cement platforms up against the house, rock hard and adorned with picnic tables, garden hoses and grills. It was fun to try and skate around all the crap out there. Christy was sniffing around the clotheslines, that basset hound nose would find something somehow. Sometimes she would take a moment to look at me and wag her tail, maybe because I had food. The potential new meal was her priority, but she loved everyone all the same.

I hardly ever took notice of days like that late morning; the beautiful, sunny, and breezy day that it really was. For the weather. Merely sitting there and watching the dog nose around the clothesline posts was more than enough to take my mind away from any concern I could have at age eleven; and kids that age have more concerns we seem willing to credit them for. Even worse if they happen to question why.

As I sat there contemplating that and whatever else, my mother opened the back door right behind me, my back to her; she had opened the door with one plump hand, grasping a huge bundle of clothes by ten hangers with the other. She must have seen me, if I was really there to begin with. I didn't turn around or move immediately, only about to.

"Jack, move." I heard her say. I was still watching the dog, not yet moving to any initial command.

"Look at the dog," I said. "She's sniffing around the clothesline, she would nibble on the clothes if she wanted to, she's never done that before but she could, because she's Christy."

"I don't care, Jack. Move." My mother kept going, nonstop to the point of falling over me, letting go of all the clothes in her hand, her large body somehow turning over, one-foot landing on my skateboard. It went flying across the patio as my mother collapsed; chubby, lumpy elbow first onto the hostile, unwelcoming surface. She didn't scream but her teeth gritted in agony at what I feared was a broken arm, yet later learned was a severely shattered elbow.

My back turned into an upside-down anxiety well, over my shoulders and into my hands to the point I could barely move to help my mother to her feet. I could not help myself but to only say, "I'm sorry; are you okay, mom? I didn't see you!"

"Oh, Barbara, are you hurt?" I heard loudly from across the fence we shared with the Bergens. It was Grace, that day sitting on a chair and reading in her backyard. Jesus Christ, was that old bat ever not exactly where you didn't want her to be? Grace rapidly limped through the gate of her creaky fence to join us on the patio. My mother was gritting her teeth, saying in choked tears, that she could not feel her arm. She sat there on the patio, head down at being embarrassed before Grace Bergen. Who else was watching? Then Barbara started crying like a five-year-old girl, high pitched and cutting through my heart like someone threw a bucket of arctic ice-water over me. I had nothing to offer but guilt and fear. Grace ignored me.

Hearing the commotion, Joey came outside to see my mother lying on the patio, crying, with Grace telling her she will take her to the hospital. He immediately looked down at me, shaking his head in disapproval. Then the frown. Priority one, never failing.

"Where is your father?" Grace asked Joey, not making any eye contact with me. I knew her question didn't help matters much.

"He's out," Joey said to her with some apprehension. He knew. "He's over in Philly today with his friends." Old Joe was in Philly every weekend, usually, only coming home to sleep. Sundays were barbeque and game days. Not home. Another thing we were never supposed to talk about.

"Call him, I'm taking your mother to the hospital, tell him we will take her to Garden State Hospital," Grace said, helping my mother across the patio, past my skateboard and over to the Bergens' car. Christy was shaking at this point, always the keen eye for when anything goes wrong. Joey unhooked the dog's chain and brought her into the house. His vulgar gaze turned to me as he passed, twisting his frown in every way for relish.

"Look what you did, you idiot! I hope you are happy with yourself, dad's going to kill you when he finds out."

A shiver went through my spine, shuddering down to my butt. That is where shit comes from. The blame had now officially been placed. All was in order.

"Don't just stand there!" Joey shouted at me, somehow piercing even more. Christy ran into the house, smart dog, for being so afraid.

"Go over and make sure mom is okay," the older son said while trying to appear in charge. "Or don't you fucking care at all?"

I walked out front to see Grace Bergen and her ancient husband help my mother into their car. Barbara angrily waved me over, so I ran to her.

"Go inside and get my purse, the Bergens are taking me to the hospital and I need it. Hurry up."

"I don't know where it is, or which one." Not realizing how dangerous my honesty was becoming. My mother, gripping her right arm with the better one gritted and showed her teeth to me like a wounded pig, near squealing in disgust with me. The rage stopped her dead in her tracks when Mr. Peterson came by to check on things.

"Do you need my help?" he asked to no one in particular. He was not in his cop's uniform that day, just happened to be outside. Mr. Bergen just looked at him, not angry, though not smiling, while Grace waved him off with a quick, "we'll take care of her," and closed the car door. Joey, still frowning at me, came out of the house with my mother's purse, raining fury at me for having to do my job I just couldn't. Mr. Peterson backed off and watched the Bergen's drive away.

"Do you boys need help, does your father know?" Joey refused to look at Mr. Peterson, then told me to come back into the house. I looked Mr. Peterson in the eye, not yet crying. Back inside, Joey was pacing around the kitchen, hands on his hips, head still shaking nonstop. Opportunities.

"I called dad and told him what you did," he said, still looking down at me. Then with a snake-like hiss he said, "Dad's going to kill you." He actually loved this. Probably happier than a pig in shit that no one could possibly blame him for anything. Jack's fault.

"And don't tell him that Mr. Peterson asked to help!" Joey screamed. "Dad's already pissed off that those niggers live across the street from us; don't tell him that he spoke to us, Jack, or he's going to kick your ass even more!"

I sat there on the couch, trembling, Christy was curled up in her bed doing the same. Joey went upstairs to his room, for what I never knew, he always enjoyed berating me whenever I was in trouble, and without pause. I could do nothing but wait. I could faintly hear my brother upstairs saying something along the lines of "that fucking little moron, always causing trouble; he never learns!" Joey stayed upstairs until our dad came home, then made sure he was the first person Old Joe saw when he came in, his story first. As if there would be any other. I could not control the tears.

My father marched into the living room, red in the face, still wearing the sunglasses he uses for driving. He was too important for any of this, and older. Even from older pictures we had in drawers, this overgrown man-child was always in a perpetual state of middle-age. Slightly overweight, not fat but always in the process of getting there; his face and arms also in that "teacher tan" state; not entirely bald but slightly greying rims of hair. He never looked directly at me, at least it always seemed that way, far more so that day. Like a higher up manager, too important to be bothered with a low-level employee, and beyond annoyed for having to take any time out of his precious day for anyone inferior to his feeble grace.

"What happened?" he asked my brother, who was already pointing at me.

"Mom went outside to hang up clothes, he got in the way and she tripped over him. It looks like she broke her arm." Joey hung on every one of his own words, making sure to keep his arm extended and forefinger directly pointed at me for the entire explanation. Old Joe put his hands on his hips and executed one of his perfect frowns. He needed me to know how upset he was with me. I looked up at him with pathetic watery eyes.

"It all happened so fast," I choked. I was only given half a second for that before I was drowned out by the real volume here.

"Oh, enough! I'm sick of all your goddamned crying! Grow the hell up!"

I fell silent, so did Joey. Although he looked up at our father, I didn't. I wouldn't again. Old Joe shook his head and waved us on, asking Joey what hospital they took her to, probably embarrassed that neighbors he didn't like (however white) were taking his spouse for treatment and he wasn't. That was my fault too, obviously. We got into old Joe's silver Plymouth, my brother sitting in the front passenger seat, naturally.

"Are you sure Garden State's the hospital they took her to?" he asked Joey.

"That's where they said they were taking her, I don't know," is all my brother said, again happy his own ass was covered; though not mine. Old Joe Pszcynack hated the answer "I don't know." As if that is an admission of weakness, and ineptitude. Everyone should be more concerned how they are perceived, somehow proud of a lifelong playground. He stared at me through the rear-view mirror at this most recent disapproval. It was still on me, and there were no qualms of kicking me when I was down.

My brother looked at him as we drove off, a sick contented blend of dread and reassurance. He rode that shotgun seat with somehow even more subtle pride than usual. No, it wasn't subtle, it was beaming pride. Afraid of old Joe as he was, Joey probably didn't have the digestive issues I had on that drive with old Joe Pszcynack raging at every stop and turn.

"All the things I do for you," old Joe said, spit escaping his mouth as he lashed. "I pay the fucking mortgage, I pay for your food, your bullshit toys, all of it!" He then looked into the rear-view mirror at me yet again, tan sunglasses blazing. "Don't you understand that? I pay for the food on your plate every day! What have you got to say about that, huh? This is how I'm repaid, is it? All I do is get up every day, work, work, work; and then I have to come home and deal with this shit!"

Almost in mid-sentence, he slammed on the brakes. I'm not sure if someone cut him off or likely he almost rear ended someone. He drove his way. He owned the road too, evidently. Old Joe slammed his red greasy palm on the horn, keeping it there blasting for over five seconds. Then he picked up speed. Even though younger than him and inferior, I knew he was always one of those asshole aggressive drivers that would give me hell on "their" road every day from the day I turned seventeen until I would ever have the pleasure to never drive again. This is that jerk on the road, this is what's going on inside his car. Everyone I ever crossed on the road hence was old Joe incarnated; and somehow, that's how they liked it.

"It's bad enough I sank my own hard-earned money into the house, and what I get in return is niggers living across the street from me! What the fuck was wrong with the Coyles? We were good neighbors, and we didn't deserve this kind of shit! Fuck them!" He slammed the brakes and honked the horn a second time, this time longer. I stopped counting the seconds after that.

At another red light he slammed his hands on the steering wheel and heaved a heavy sigh, turning his head in my direction completely disgusted for what was curled up in the back of his bought and paid for car. It was his. For all my shaking, he knew I hated him for it. For all of it. For him.

"Did she trip over you or the fucking skateboard?" The middle-aged lout froze himself within his own frown, my brother eagerly awaiting a question put to the accused.

"Just me," I lied. I didn't remove that skateboard from its resting place on the patio for months, and never used it again to any recollection. Yet I wasn't going to give him the satisfaction of feeling superior any more than he already had. Enough was enough for this arrogant brat. The skateboard to him was an inanimate object that could provide him control; something he could take from me as punishment for what I had done wrong. He had to be in control. He had to be, somehow. Yet I resisted it, even in terrified silence. How dare I? He was looking for it after all. En Garde.

I tried to show the level of fear I knew he wanted, but I am a bad liar. Another problem. I knew this was an accident, even during that nightmare of a car ride. I also knew it just didn't matter. He turned his head back to the road in disappointment. After all, there must be punishment. Otherwise, how would I ever respect him? The truth really was, I never did again after that morning. I never did at all, really. He drove on.

After more incessant honking and turning around to glare at me through his sunglasses at every stop, old Joe got us to the parking lot of Garden State Hospital. I had been here only once before. The day I was born. No room for nostalgia beyond that, my family always saw hospitals as almost like police stations. If you were there, something was wrong. Someone was to blame. Someone else to perceive, to know what you are under the skin.

"Just stay here!" he screamed at us, slamming the door to the point of making the entire car quake on its shocks. I had no illusions as to who would be accountable had the windows broke. He was finally gone, the worst thing about sitting there for that fifteen minutes or so was knowing even at that age what the problem was and knowing he was going to come back.

"Oh my god, Jack," Joey said to me; for some reason also not looking me directly in the eye. "Dad's going to kill you! Do you have any idea how bad this is? You shouldn't have done this. Dad is going to kill you." He looked halfway afraid when he said that. He was in fact pleased.

"Could you just be quiet?" I asked him. Then he decided to look right at me.

"No!" he screamed. "Dad's going to kill you!" No challenge permitted. Superior. I supposed he was learning.

I knew my luck had far run out by then and what I feared would happen did happen. Old Joe angrily opened the driver's side door, sat down and shook his head down at the steering wheel, then looked up at what I don't know.

"She's not in there," he said, Joey looking at him as if he was certain he was about to witness a murder. Afraid yet excited. Old Joe didn't move for a moment. He then simply turned around and gave me "the look." The look was intended to express his disapproval, and the look itself somehow had some purpose other than coaxing his own ego, and it was expected that one should never want to get the look. I spent the following decades questioning it randomly to family members and friends; nearly all of them usually gave me blank stares in return. That only raised more questions. The way we handle bullies, it only proves we are insignificant, self-worshiping assholes. I would do better. Even if it killed me.

Old Joe Pszcynack, he didn't like when things didn't go his way. This was his playpen. He would not be compromised by circumstance. He wasn't in control of this situation. His children might not have suspected it then, but anyone else easily could have. Perception.

That was unacceptable. There was nothing he could do. We drove back home empty handed.

Back to Browning Road, old Joe was never one to miss an opportunity such as Mr. Peterson not being outside his house at that moment.

"Are the niggers outside?" he snarled. "I've had enough shit thrown at me today, I don't need a reminder of who ruined the neighborhood, I don't care that he's a cop. If he was decent cop, he should be smart enough to know he doesn't fucking belong here and now that there's one black family on the block, that just means there is more to come. Because they think it will be okay to move here. Motherfucker!" He slammed his fists on the steering wheel, near breaking it in half.

"He's probably inside, or not home," Joey said to him like a feeble sidekick to an equally lame super-villain. He knew as well as anyone, it was better Mr. Peterson was not around. He also knew old Joe was too chicken-shit a racist to say anything to the man's face. The Bergen's were not home either; and we still didn't know what hospital they took Barbara to. No matter, there was some other business to attend to.

"Get the hell up in your room and read some goddamn schoolbooks!" my father screamed at me as we walked up our short driveway, Christy barking in excitement that someone was home. "Your teacher sent me a letter telling my you're stupid! Don't tell me you don't have any homework! I better not catch you reading the goddamn comic books! Get the schoolbooks and read them!" Those last two words sounded like "read-um," old Joe still let's his thick northeast Philly accent escape him. Especially when he was mad, which was quite often. I was responsible for this. I realized then that he could never be.

By then I was in my room again, the door most certainly shut, where it belonged. That "stupid" remark he made was in reference to a couple months before this offense; when my English teacher decided to send a letter home to my parents, explaining that I was not applying myself and deliberately not doing my work when I easily could. Most of which was true, although nowhere in the letter was the word "stupid" used. That's all old Joe Pszcynack could read of it though, or care to remember. That was all he needed.

Just about everyone in class didn't trust Miss Mackies, oddly because she wore a wig, and it was obvious. I always wondered what was under that thing but for all I knew she was a cancer survivor or something that caused her to wear it, none of which was any of my business. Mackies, to me, looked like an evil, older version of Carol Brady; dressed every day for seventies sitcom reruns. The kids always seemed to make a big deal out of simply the wig then. Middle School indeed. I didn't trust her because she reminded me of what was waiting at home.

Mackies loved to lecture students, myself above all it seemed then. This was probably because she knew I didn't like her, and I would subconsciously (to the point of consciously) not do much if any work for her as the idea of making such a narcissistic, authoritative teacher such as her happy made me sick. If she wanted something, it was wrong. I suppose I just enjoyed it when she didn't "win." I could not do that at home, so school became a precocious outlet for some release. Hence, the near failing English grade that year.

After one class, Mackies decided to give me one of her classic "don't forget I am superior to you" lectures and told me she was sending a letter home explaining my lack of effort and that thin rail of a wigged excuse for a teacher even made an offhanded quip to me that she felt sorry for me for the likely "child abuse" that would follow as a consequence. As I was being lectured and continuously unimpressed with the teacher's ego, she was showing me her record book to elaborate how poorly I was doing in her class, and I could not help myself to notice the grades listed next to Tumisha Porter's name, right above mine.

Tumisha was a particularly portly young girl in my English class, notable from being somewhere south of Damon and Coletta's neighborhood. I never knew exactly where she lived, only noticing how much more disengaged with Mackies' class (probably all of her classes) than I could ever hope or care to be. I looked at her grade list and saw straight F's across the board; Tumisha literally did nothing in that class whatsoever, showed no interest, and hardly talked to anyone. The girl just stared as class went on, sometimes drawing rap logos in her notebook, not much else. The resulting grades were hardly any surprise.

After Mackies ended her tirade with the ever cover-your-ass question of "Do you have any questions for me?" I asked her why she never lectured Tumisha as her grades were clearly terrible, far worse than mine. And certainly something should be done for a student falling behind so miserably. The teachers never talked to her about it, so why lecture me so much? Later in life, I eventually understood the reason why. I just never agreed with it.

When I asked Mackies why nothing was being done about Tumisha, she slammed her fist on her desk, her wig not moving a millimeter. "Don't concern yourself with Tumisha or any other student! Concentrate on your own work! You can do better, you just won't, that's what the real problem here is. You are making a conscious decision to not do your work and that's why you are having these problems. When someone tells you to do something, do it!"

I could have easily kept delving into the matter, and had every reason to. Yet I didn't. They won again. All I could do was ask more questions. It's one of the few things I'm good at, even back in sixth grade English class, it was that. Still, if they didn't want me to take notice of any of their bullshit, I can't imagine why they always made that so easy to do.

No one cared that Tumisha was doing so horribly in school; least of all her own teachers. My parents had other concerns. They were embarrassed the letter arrived at home, very afraid Mackies might think they were not raising me right, or disciplining me enough. Bad public relations, hence old Joe's "stupid" comment; however useful to only him, and however immature. I didn't actually matter.

Nevertheless, he succeeded in scaring me half to death that I literally sat on my floor that day and tried to read my English textbook with wells of tears in my eyes. It wasn't fear alone. Barbara was hurt, and my fault or not, it was perceived as such. My brother's taunts about old Joe killing me may not have been literal, but I got the gist of it and more and he knew it. That was real enough. Far more than only fear.

My room, though a refuge, quite pathetically only protected me from the wolves and their erroneous resentments by a wooden door; and one that the owners of said door loved to remind me that they themselves owned, not me. Was I renting that room? Was I to repay them for it at some unspecified time? It always felt so. I suppose that was the idea. Perpetual debt. Perpetual advantage. How can one love someone they also fear?

I wasn't really reading as much as holding and crying into that English book. I never wanted to leave that room; even given I was in the belly of the rotten beast and there was no way out of that situation. Notwithstanding, him using the word "stupid" cut me worse than anything, not just for the lie but for the notion I had no basis to criticize, no grounds to challenge him. After all, who is older here? Who pays? Who is inferior?

I never knew where old Joe went when he left the house. Probably nowhere. He was not one to look or feel helpless, he probably just drove around to make it look like he was doing something important until he knew where Barbara was. Then he could tell everyone he always knew where after the fact. Charming. I knew he had been drinking that day; but he might as well have been drinking herbal tea, he was the same person either way; never antagonized. That is power, and that was real. Acknowledged, reluctantly, but hardly respected, at least not by me.

Astonishingly, Joey didn't take the advantage to taunt me again as soon as old Joe left but then I heard the Bergens pull up into their driveway. Only two car doors shut.

"Joseph." I heard Mr. Bergen call from outside the house. He didn't knock. Ernie Bergen was a cigar chomping retired fireman who probably didn't ask for Joey's name because he thought Barbara's fall was my fault, just that Joey was the elder child and evidently wiser for that reason. I didn't respect Ernie Bergen much after that. Probably a bitter old man because his parents named him Ernie.

I could hear Joey go outside and mutter with the old man a bit, after a while he ran upstairs and opened my door. I was far too terrified to lock it, not that that would have stopped him.

"The Bergens had to take her to a different hospital, that's what they decided to do on the way. Mom had them call grandma and she's on her way here now. Her arm is broken." Joey then paused for a minute so as to see my reaction. I didn't give him one.

"Mom's in the hospital and they have to keep her there overnight!" he emphasized "overnight" with an elongated hiss, satisfying certainly to himself.

"Dad's going to kill you!" Again, the hissing sound. I gave him no reaction, still. I was not sure what he was after, exactly. What reaction would make him happy? Not just looking at him, which is all I did. How dare I? Joey shook his head at me in displeasure, as if I was responsible to him, or he raised me better than this. Utter disappointment and I deserved whatever punishment I got. He left my room, he had to be there to tell our grandmother that Barbara tripped over me and I broke her arm.

I faintly heard the front door open again, Christy went wild because she loved when my grandmother, Marie, would visit. That dog loved everyone without the reservations that were so abundant. I was still sobbing into my textbook when I heard Joey say, "Jack's fault" and my grandmother telling him to stop saying that. He wouldn't. Marie, younger then of course, but still the aging widowed grandmother lightly tapped on my door. She looked down at me through her thick eyeglasses, easily the least menacing creature in that house beyond the family dog. I can give her credit for handling that situation a lot better than some, but it was never enough.

The short, grey-haired savior, such as she was, gently walked into my room. She only spoke a calm "Jack," to me, nothing more at first. I threw my textbook across the room in unfettered fury, Marie didn't like that, though she knew it wasn't because of her. I bawled into my hands, then my grandmother kneeled on the floor and hugged me giving me that "shhhh" sound in a vain attempt to calm me down. If her husband, Frank, or "Pop" as he was better known were still alive, maybe none of this would have happened. Or so, I dreamed.

Grandfather Frank, or Pop, he was something else. Old, yes, but completely into the popular culture of his time. He saw the greatest movies in the theaters, saw the best baseball games in town, he knew everything about actors and other famous people like a living ency-clopedia. And would later sit with me and watch all the old school horror films with me. Never failing, he would take his false teeth out and growl like Count Dracula. Like all the old greats, he was unfor-tunately long gone. Lost to time. Here we were.

"I know you are upset, Jack," she said as I continued to cry. "Your mom is going to be fine. Don't hate your father, he cares about you, that's why he takes care of you. He pays for your food, and he works hard and puts a roof over your head. He's allowed to be upset once in a while. He loves your mother. That's why he's upset, that's all." She continued to hug me and looked away as she spoke.

I refused to give in to her. I wouldn't. This was wrong. That's what it was.

My grandmother stayed with us the rest of the day. She let me stay in my room. Old Joe eventually found out what hospital the Bergen's took her to and saw her. When he finally came back, I heard him say "where is he?" My grandmother told him I would not leave my room. I thought he would bound right upstairs to cover that development, but he didn't. Not for a while. I heard other mutterings from the three apparent adults in the kitchen: Old Joe, Joey, and Marie. I heard something along the lines of "how she fell" and "being overweight caused a problem" and "worst shattered elbow they've seen in twenty years." I might have heard the word "nigger" a few times, maybe not; though that was certainly never outside the realm of possibility.

Eventually old Joe came to my door and opened it, he didn't knock. After all, that was his door. His room. At least I wasn't crying by then. Well prepared, I had my English book in my hand. Ready. I didn't love him anymore, if I ever did. The book issue was gone from his mind, if it was ever really important to him to begin with. He looked like he didn't want to say a single word to me at all. That was only because he didn't.

"The doctor said it wasn't your fault," he said as he looked down on me. "So, all that stuff I said, just forget it."

I lightly nodded, that would have to be good enough. His precious time. Apparently still annoyed, he turned away. I didn't leave, I simply sat there where I was, staring at the four walls, hating myself for everything I was, where I came from, and likely where I was heading. I could not move. Some time passed by, I have no idea how much, really, but it was enough. I heard him come to the door again.

"I said to forget it!" Joe "senior" said, almost at the same level of rage he had on that car ride. Me sitting there meant that I wasn't over it. I could have been holding a grudge. I could have believed he was accountable for himself. He would not tolerate that. Not one bit. I got up and walked around the house, only to come right back up again, even ignoring Christy. I stayed in my room until the next day. Before bed, Joey came by and ducked his head into my room one last time.

"They know it's your fault, Jack. Dad's going to kill you." I looked at my brother with a face that clearly said, "not until I kill you first." He didn't shove or throw punches at me like he normally would whenever I challenged him. He simply left, satisfied he got the last word in. It was hardly the last thought in.

The worst thing anyone can do to another is question them on their bullshit, especially when centered in the very storm of it. Sad revelation that no one but me had half a mind to really care about that. I was living in Pennsauken, New Jersey. There was a black family living across the street and I didn't care any longer. I didn't to begin with. Nor should I have. That block of a neighborhood, that town, undeniably that very world I was coming to live in had a lot more issues that needed addressing beyond petty racism or nosy neighbors; and for that endeavor, we were not giving one ounce of attention. Not even a thought. I was a kid, and thinking was not what those kids were into. What was the opposite? There I was.

Chapter Four

THE MERRY MONTH OF MAY

It does not always heal all wounds. Time can often seem to only provide more shelves for us to store our memories upon, and attempt to cover that up with whatever we can. It wasn't easy in the months following the arm breaking and brief hospitalization. Grandmother Marie practically moved in with us for a time, taking care of things and still working a jaded effort to get me to forget what happened, to forget what was said, or at the very least not let on what I really thought. That failed.

Barbara had to go through a few months of physical therapy to get back to where she was before the fall, but she got there. Only there. Old Joe didn't harangue me on the subject any longer, and in short time he was fine with me avoiding everyone and staying in my room in general. We never spoke, and it was good. Joey still gave the occasional reminder that while I may not have intentionally harmed her, it was still my fault and apparently, they told my brother exactly that multiple times behind my back, according to him. No reason to believe his slithering tongue, but it was not outside the full expanse of possibility either.

The shattered elbow healed with a permanent scar from the surgery. Barbara would not be going skiing anytime soon after that, but it was not as if major physical activity was a thing even before that fall. The guilt was always there, even though it was an accident, that family was just very big on blame, to assign "fault" was of the utmost importance. People really are sensitive to any kind of liability or accountability, and if there is an opportunity to seize the moment and proclaim, "that's not my fault," then they will take it. I had no such luxury, and it was known. They still complained about black people all the time for some reason.

In the two years that followed, even beyond, if I ever brought up that incident, how I felt about it, how it affected all of us, what it did to my mental well-being in general, I was often met with the most infallible of deflections which was to be implied, or outright stated and that was that I needed to "get over it." That is what it comes down to; the problem is not what happened that day, the problem is not how my family handled it. The problem is not how I felt and still felt about what happened. The problem was that I would not get over it; and thus, the blame again was shifted over to me, the youngest and therefore least mature of all Pszcynacks. How could I ever challenge any of this?

There were new milestones upon us by then. Interestingly, no more neighbors had left and there remained only one token black family on the block. The Petersons probably knew by then what the issue was with everyone. They likely knew on day one. I had reached eighth grade and Joey, now seventeen, had a job, his driver's license, and a literal hell on wheels attitude to compliment all of the above.

He now worked at Rickles, the local hardware store in town. Old Joe was into hardware and worked at a chemical plant all our lives, so Joey fit right in with this. Hardware meets hard ass. Perfect training. Somehow his employers never caught on as to how much merchandise he would steal from the store and later sell from the back of his car. I would sometimes find dozens of brand-new drills and other such tools in our shed in the backyard, or under his bed whenever I felt like rummaging around the house when I was bored. He did the same to me, nothing interesting to find. All the hidden movies were still at Michael's house anyway.

Joey got himself a used white Mazda car which he had the words "SPEED DEMON" stenciled across the top of its windshield. By the time his driver's license turned four months old, he already had three tickets on his record; two for speeding and one for playing his radio too loud. He was only getting started.

At seventeen, Joey really was moving into the world fast, and that quite literally. A year before he went on a date with a girl. I never got the girl's name, but it was only once he took her somewhere. Barbara actually had to drive them to the restaurant or wherever they went and Joey almost began throwing punches when I snorted at him in derision when I overheard their plans. Barbara yelled at me, explaining she did not want any fights. I was to be quiet, only me. In any case, there was no way I would ever let myself suffer the humility of having such a chauffeur; but it all made me wonder what was in store for me in coming years. What kind of girls would I meet? What would they want in a boyfriend?

Kel was in and out of the picture in a blink of an eye; forgettable, yes, but to me, it was interesting and even terrifying to know that any girl would ever be interested in my brother. After all, such an abusive, racist, and altogether repulsive character could hardly attract even a halfway decent girlfriend. Girls would prefer a nice guy, or so I presumed. Welcoming guys, caring, personable, and with good friends. Joey barely had any at all. How could any of them be interested in Joey or anyone remotely his type as a boyfriend? They couldn't. This is what I wanted to believe at fourteen.

I was too young to date but I wanted to know what I was in for. Three years goes by fast. What would lay ahead? Some of the girls that would hang around Kenny Del and his friends would often give me pause. Not so much Kenny himself, I always found him a good person all around, and his girlfriend was never mean or dismissive to us. But admittedly, it all made me a bit uncomfortable since I knew they were having regular sex. As long as the Del parents were not home, Kenny would have his door shut while Michael and I were in the house and we could hear his bed rocking and his girlfriend screaming her head off, in that delightful way. Michael and I would often only gawk at the sounds. We didn't know if we were invisible or just irrelevant. This was almost too real for us, but no less fascinating. It turned out sex was real.

Knowing what was happening was more than just watching porn at the Del's house, which was still a thing. Kenny still kept a renewed stash of videos in his dresser; and we found as we got older, we were by no means any less interested in the world of sex. It was becoming real, at least around us, and there was no stopping it. Nevertheless, it was the girls that hung around Kenny's heavy metal friends that gave me the creeps. They dressed just like the girls I saw on T.V., groupies hanging out backstage for a chance to meet or even have sex with a rock star, and it wasn't considered wrong, it was fun. Except this particular sex wasn't backstage, this was right down the street at the Del's house. We kept our mouths shut but eyes wide open.

One May afternoon, my brother was out working, as was old Joe; which made it all the better day. I was watching a music video on T.V. which was from Metallica, and the video depicted a hospital room where nurses took care of an injured veteran with a bag over his face. The patient was using Morse code to beg the nurses to kill him, to put him out of his misery. I couldn't watch it and at the time could not understand why so many people liked this band so much. I always found horror more entertaining when it was more classical. Nice to know there were people out there more disturbed than me, I supposed.

Christy was sitting next to me that day, panting heavily, and rightly so considering how hot it was. I was sweating as well. Exceptionally hot for May. I changed the channel to see the weather report and the weatherman was explaining it had not been this hot in the Philadelphia area since late August of 1981. He expected that a lot of homes will have their air conditioners on which was all but unheard of in May. What they didn't know.

Barbara walked by my room, herself visibly uncomfortable in the heat, her dark red hair slightly wet from sweating.

"Are your windows open, Jack?" she asked.

"They've been open all day. Can we turn the air conditioning on?"

"No!" she screamed with her face transforming into fear as if I sat in the front car seat or something. "It's May!" she continued. "You don't turn on the air conditioning in May!" Obvious eyes rolling at me by then. It would have bothered me less had I not seen it coming.

I looked at her with the inquisitive look everyone hated. "But the weatherman said it's not been this hot since August of 1981, didn't you hear him?"

"But it's May!"

"I know that, but it's not been this hot since August of years ago, we're both sweating, Christy needs about a gallon of water. We should turn the A.C. on."

"But it's May!" she said again, sounding more desperate with each repetition, and there were many.

"It's really hot," I continued. "We can turn it on for a little bit, and cool down the house. It's not going to cool down with just the widows open. You can turn on the A.C."

"It's May!" she said, this time in near tears. "You don't turn on the air conditioning in May, that's for the summer, when it's really hot. I know my friends have their air conditioning on. None of the neighbors have theirs on, so we are not turning on ours. Don't give me a hard time, Jack. It's bad enough I had to go through all that therapy. None of my friends had to go through what I did; they didn't suffer like that. Do you think that's fair?"

I didn't answer, and she just walked away. A few minutes later, I heard her muttering on the phone. I was not sure who she was talking to until Barbara said loudly, "Arlene, you are putting your air conditioning on in May, how dare you!" Entirely in a sarcastic and friendly tone, with just the right pinch of fear. She murmured along and Christy and I continued to roast in the heat, and no, and that air conditioning was never turned on. It was May.

Barbara was just as uncomfortable as the dog and I were, probably more so given her size at that point. Exercise and diet habits never changed. Still, she would not turn the A.C. on. This was not because of some crazy routine of not using the A.C. until June every single year. But that the electric bill would go up, and old Joe would get all pissed off at her for running the A.C. in an off month, especially when he himself was not yet home. He would not care if he was there anyway. The way he saw it, we can live without air conditioning at any time, he grew up that way, after all. Cheap when convenient. He didn't "need" all those drinks.

Air conditioning was not a necessity, odd coming from a man who watched as much T.V. as he did. Vacations were expensive and not a necessity, Christmas was expensive, and what did we do to earn any of those gifts anyway? My November birthday was too close to Christmas; that was on me. Money was always such an issue, and it never made anyone happy. No one could let that go, and they didn't want to.

After her call, Barbara marched past my room again, not talking to me but speaking out loud so I could hear her. This had its purpose. Why complain at all without the benefit of an audience?

"I can't believe Arlene! She's got a lot of nerve turning on her air conditioning while the rest of us on the street have to sit inside and roast like pigs. I can't believe she would turn on her air conditioning. Damn her!"

Barbara was friends with Arlene Del, not as much as she was with her seven or so high school clique friends, but they talked fairly often. Arlene and her son, Matt, lived only two houses down from us and Arlene was Michael's aunt by marriage. She and Matt both had her full-blooded Italian look about them even though the Del family was actually Irish.

While Michael was into sports much more than I was at this point (myself reading even more comics and never getting enough of the Captain America books by that time), he was never as much of a "jock" as his cousin. Matt, only one grade above us, loved sports. That was fine as everyone was expected to be into sports. Especially boys, we were supposed to be obsessed with Philly sports teams, not reading comic books or playing with toys; so, Matthew fit into the Browning Road atmosphere just fine. Well, not exactly.

Matt Del was that stereotypical white kid who wanted to be black. He loved sports and he worshiped many professional athletes. Professional athletes to the stature of Reggie White of the Eagles, Juan Samuel of the Phillies, the by then retired Dr. Julius Erving of the Sixers, along with Charles Barkley; and the list went on. More so, he listened to black music; rap, of course, never the Temptations, Chuck Berry, or Luther Vandross. Always rap.

He wasn't dating yet but if he was, he likely would have dated black girls. That would have gone over wonderfully. However, he did hang out with black guys. All of Matt's core friends were black. Maybe Matt knew what the unwritten rules were regarding such activity for the residents of Browning Road, but if he knew, he clearly could not have cared less.

It was that same lovely burning hot day that Matt decided to invite a bunch of his friends to his house and play tag football. Tag football was always played right in the middle of the street; whenever a car came by someone would say "car!" and the game would suspend for a few seconds, then promptly resume. I wasn't invited to play, and I didn't want to be, yet I did see them playing outside. It was a different spectacle to behold but I saw little harm to any of it. I knew they were older than me, and for that reason I was not cool enough for them and I knew damn well to keep my distance. Besides, they would never talk comics. They were not cool enough for me.

Old Joe usually got home sometime after five each day. It was near summer, so the sun was still out, not that we needed a reminder given the heat. It was just me and my parents that night, Joey worked the store until closing. I happened to be in the kitchen when old Joe got home. He was certainly never one to miss any apposite moment to slam the door and that's exactly what he did when he came home. The clicking of Christy's dog nails on the kitchen floor that led to the side door entrance became more frequent as she knew old Joe was home. Normally pushing her nose outside before he could even get in, Christy slowly retreated when he came inside the house.

"What the hell is going on out there?" he snapped, looking only at Barbara, who was walking down the hallway into the kitchen. Christy was still wagging her tail because the old man was home, yet not going as berserk in excitement like she normally did, an acute concern and caution in her basset eyes. No barking. Too smart for her own good, perhaps.

"What's wrong?" Barbara asked. Looking at him in that half fear, all apprehension, look she always gives him in any given situation. Old Joe sat down at the kitchen table, not slamming his fists but resting one; almost ready to break something, and wanting to.

"I just got off work, I'm driving home, and I get to my own block and I see Matt Del playing football in the street with a bunch of fucking niggers! What the hell is wrong with Arlene? How can she just let her kid do that? Fucking niggers! Doesn't she have any goddamn sense at all?"

Barbara and I just stared at him. Pathetic as it was, staring is often an effective defense mechanism. A way to avoid being held accountable for anything you might say, as you are not saying anything at all; and that's exactly what she and I were doing as old Joe sat there in the kitchen, still sweating because of the heat. The wisest of all available options, immature though it was. No one was going to ask to turn the A.C. at that point. Old Joe didn't like all the silence either; not that anything would make him happy anyway. He knew how to address his own concerns.

"Call up Fox and McCormick!" he said to Barbara, not looking her in the eye but jabbing his thumb in the air towards the telephone on the wall. "We're putting the damn house up for sale now!"

Barbara remained silent, again, just stared at him as I did. She didn't pick up the phone, but did go in one of the drawers for the phone book. Fox & McCormick was the big realtor in town back then. After the Coyles left, I remember overhearing my parents talking about realtors. The exit strategy if the neighborhood would get too unaccommodating for them, and it was taken very seriously.

Then it had all come to pass. I can just imagine the look on old Joe's face as he drove up to a tag football game in the street two doors down from his own house. In his mind he probably wanted to stop, get out and tear Matt and Arlene Del a new asshole for allowing a few black kids from Matt's grade to play football. He didn't do that, but his blood must have run cold as he passed them, and they looked back at the aging, angry white man in return, just with far less vitriol. I wondered if any of them really knew how mad and aging that particular white man really was. I wondered, as they played tag football in the middle of Browning Road, if they knew what their own part in history actually was. Black kids playing football in the street. That's all it took for the white flight engines to ignite. Nothing more.

While the Coyles had the distinction of being the last family on Browning Road to leave for "legitimate" reasons, merely retiring and moving closer to their grandchildren; the Pszcynacks were the first to leave for racism, and for that alone. The first out of the gate for the white flight. The honor was ours. Barbara called Fox & McCormick the very next day and within less than a week, a for sale sign was planted on our front lawn for everyone to see.

There were no mobs this time, no teams of neighbors knocking on our door, no one telling us not to "sell to no blacks." None of that. What happened was that on the day the sale sign appeared on our lawn, Barbara came back from shopping or somewhere and saw Mr. Graff, our next-door neighbor on the other side, talking in front of his house with old Mr. Myers. One can only guess what they were discussing. Barbara got out of her car and walked right over to them. While Mr. Myers was a clone of Dick Van Dyke, and even talked like him, Jerry Graff was short, slightly overweight with a gigantic and always crusty nose; nothing appealing in any way about him, but he made up for it in his own temper. We could hear him yelling at his wife and daughters at the top of his lungs for hours on end. Yelling about nothing and anything in between. He never carried the attitude outside for everyone else to see but if he was concerned about appearances like everyone else, he was not doing a very good job at it.

I could hear Mr. Graff ask, "You selling?" With Barbara quickly responding that she wanted to find a bigger house and that my grandmother was going to move in with us. I knew that wasn't happening. I knew what she was downplaying. It was always fine to be racist, though not to be perceived as such. Not by anyone. Even other racists, evidently.

For me, the worst of it was Michael knocking on my door later that day. The look he gave me when I came to the door said it all. This was it. It was all ending soon. I can't begin to say how many times we would walk up to the front doors of our houses over the years and ask, "Can Jack play?" or "Can Michael come out?" as this was how kids made plans in those days. Days well gone by.

We walked around the block for the hell of it. I told him I didn't know where we were moving to, not far I didn't think, but I didn't know where. He thought it odd that we were moving but didn't know where we were going yet. He was right. Michael didn't say he would miss me, but this was a huge change for us, that being an understatement. What was going to happen to my friends now that I was moving? What was to become of my life? How much, if at all, did anyone care about any of those questions?

Michael delved in search of all details he could get about why my family was moving away. I never heard his parents go on and on the way my family did with the racism thing but I can't imagine, given his parents' age in general, that they would be too happy with more black people on the street. They just didn't get as enraged by it as old Joe, I guess. That or it was an unwritten rule to keep racism in the family itself. My parents never went on their tirades or dropped the "N" word when there were other people about, or friends visiting. Appearances indeed.

Even still, our house was going to sell sooner or later, and I would have to move. I didn't want to leave but the neighborhood and town were changing. If more kids like Damon would be moving to Browning Road, that would be most welcome. But what about kids like Coletta? Even worse, what about kids like that when they got older? It seems so few of us get better with time; I know that's not true across the board, but it is a major recurrence and there's no reason to ignore it. I didn't tell Michael that the reason my parents put the house up for sale was because my dad drove by Matt Del playing football with black kids. I don't know if that's because I felt weird or guilty as a consequence of it.

"Fights have broken out at school," I said to Michael. "On the bus, there's the Coletta issue, who knows when she will start more trouble than she already has. There are reports of more crimes happening, even around here. We live close to a bad city. This neighborhood, this block itself, it could all go bad."

Michael didn't look right at me. I wasn't surprised he ignored the remark about Coletta. After all, she could possibly find out what we said, and he couldn't have any of that. I didn't know if I was being racist, the neighborhood we lived in could conceivably get pretty bad. After all, we were right up against Camden, the worst city in the country and for all we knew, the world.

"That's not going to happen," Michael said, a confident, dismissive look written all over his features. We walked on.

"It might," I said as we continued.

"It's not going to happen?"

"Why? What makes you say that?"

"Because. It's not going to happen."

"If you think things are changing now, what makes you think

they will stop?"

"It doesn't matter, because it's not going to happen."

I allowed him that last word for all the good it did for either of us. It was just always so hard to accommodate denial. I would miss this town being ours. I knew he was angry with me. This was change, like it or not. Friends were always important, at least to me, and they were to him too arguably more so right then and there. But he was staying. Not me.

I learned the hard way that people, and not just middle school kids, expect to know where you are moving to when you say you are going to move. Neighbors would ask me where we were moving to if I was walking the dog. I didn't know where. I thought I should have just answered them honestly. No such luck. At school, Damon was no different on the subject, despite how much he had changed in only the passing of a couple of years. He still hung out with us, still loved to read and discuss comic books with me, but he was a "player" guy by then. Always wearing sunglasses, except when the teachers told him to take them off in class. He even had a girlfriend now, a white girl named Jami who I've known since the first day of kindergarten. Damon said it was something else to be dating a white girl if you were black. He smiled when he told me that. I didn't know why.

"How the hell can you be moving somewhere when you don't even know where you are going?" he asked me at lunch one day. He did look cool then in the sunglasses, maybe a little goofy looking back on it. At least his girlfriend didn't sit with us, that was not a thing when we were that young.

"Well, we have to sell the house first," I told him. "Then we can have an idea of where we can move. It's not going to be far; no one is changing jobs or anything and they won't want to move back to Philadelphia, they hate the idea of living in the city."

"Sounds like they are flying," he said, not looking that upset with me, but not smiling either. I wanted to sink into my chair.

"Don't sweat it, Jack. I feel bad for you. It's not like this is your decision, anyway. You are the one who is going to have to suffer the most. I'm sorry, since you are not even in high school yet, hopefully you can move before next school year because it would only get worse later, I think."

I never thought about that. He was right, of course, but I refused to really register any of it in my mind at that point. I wanted time to freeze. In a new school, there would be no Damon, no Michael, would anyone else want to talk about comics? I would not be one of theirs, wherever I ended up and life in Pennsauken would still go on. It was my hometown. I wouldn't have a hometown any longer.

"You crazy white people," Damon continued. "You see a black person move in or even walk down the damn street and you want to move away. Thinking it will only get worse or that all of us are as bad as Coletta or some such. That's a pipe dream. Did you know that most of our family is from Camden? A lot of them still live there. That's not easy. Everyone thinks Camden is ghetto, and they are right, mostly, but the problem is those that behave ghetto, not so much where they live.

"Did you know that a lot of Camden kids actually fake their address so they can go to Pennsauken schools? No one wants to realize that, and less give any thought as to why that is. Black people living there are scared. That's why they are moving to even as close as Pennsauken. Camden is all drugs, gangs, and drive-bys. Who can blame them for coming here if that's all they can even afford? At least the basketball team will get better overnight, right? Most people just want to live in peace. I don't see how that could be exclusively a color issue. But I somehow know that it is."

I didn't say anything, only wishing I did and I wasn't going to get all mushy on him and tell him how much I would miss him. Damon was never into that, no one was, really. I wasn't popular enough to have too many kids ask me about the move, a fact I was actually thankful for, but the sale sign was still sticking out of the front lawn like a giant zit, and word always got around, especially when I didn't want it to.

It felt like the beginning of the end. Probably because it was. I went to bed that night staring at the ceiling. All my comic book and Phillies posters were still on the wall. The posters and even the beige painted walls would be gone soon enough. The light would shine through a different window. Reading while laying down on a different floor. All my own ambience gone forever. The door was closed. I felt like jumping out the window and running away. It was more than tempting. I usually stayed up reading comics with a flashlight if I could not sleep. I couldn't even do that. None of this would be a part of me for much longer. That room was my world, my escape, but they were taking that away from me because a bunch of kids were playing football in the street. It was that petty. I knew that, even then. No one was listening. I knew that too.

Maybe the house would not sell, and they would give it up, this whole moving idea. Barbara was already planning on viewing new houses, she just didn't tell me where or felt any need to explain at all. Consistency even in chaos. I grew up in this one town, this one block, this one house. This was going to be someone else's room and my cheap parents would probably end up getting something smaller, and I would have no say in any of the above. No choice. Dead end street coming, and fast.

I felt like going outside and tearing that Fox & McCormick sign right out of the ground. I could have. I didn't. This was all out of my hands; yet somehow all on my lap. I was the only one who was moving. Silent hero at best. Nobody cared, and I was given a front row seat for this performance as if I need any reminders. Watching was my only option. I was of little consequence, less consideration. Expendable. Irrelevant. Discarded.

Chapter Five

STREAKING

Christy eventually got tired of barking at all the strangers visiting the house by the fourth or fifth showing. This was happening. The Pszcynack's house, that family with the name no one could pronounce, their house was for sale. Almost immediately, a parade of potential buyers began arriving to tour the house. Every single time, we had to help Barbara clean the house, to make sure the beds were made, and answer prepared questions if they were asked of us. I didn't participate, though if someone asked me where we were moving, or why, I told them I didn't know. Barbara hated that. She wanted to sell the house, and honesty was simply not going to do that. There were a lot of people interested, a lot of new faces inside the house, and they were all black.

Never had there been so many, or any, such people in the house as this. My parents hated if the buyers touched anything, and they did touch; flushing the toilets to see if they worked, turning the faucets on and off, light switches, all of it. It was new to all of us, disturbing, yet this only served to strengthen

Barbara and old Joe's resolve to move. They had to leave, as it was not really even their home any longer. There were black people marching through their house.

The disinterest was welcomed with open arms by that point. As if, yes, they hated the fact that black people were walking about the house almost every day, but this made it all the easier for them to lose any real emotional attachment to the house, to the town, to all of it. They lived here for over fourteen years themselves by that point. If they ever had any attachment to begin with, it was flimsy at best, as all it took was for the block to get just the slightest bit darker for them to let it all go. I didn't quite grasp then and there what was really going on. I just happened to remember everything.

Old Joe and my brother were hardly ever home when these tours took place, which was probably just as well. Barbara would tell me not to stare at the buyers, and to make myself scarce and not answer any of their questions, let her do that. She knew exactly what my state of mind was. Clearly what I thought mattered little, if at all. I never got the lecture about how this was for my own good and moving to a better neighborhood would be best for me. No one asked me anything at all.

Christy had some fun with this. If anything, she liked the opportunity to be petted or play with someone new; especially if any potential buyers brought their kids along, they loved that basset hound charm. Yet even the dog's adorable charisma didn't matter compared to what would happen soon after the placement of the new for sale sign.

The Graff's next door had a German Shepard, Stormy, who would always bark at the visitors checking out the backyard or the side of our house where he could see them. I was always terrified of that dog. Mr. Graff once quipped to us after a group of visitors left that Stormy had always hated black people and that's why he barked at them and it was good they kept him on a chain. Perhaps his dog being racist somehow made Jerry Graff less so. Yet still, that was as far as all the neighbors' criticism of our own drawn out house sale went. No mobs, no "don't sell to no blacks." The Coyles never existed. What was important then was not tomorrow, evidently.

It never came up in conversation, not once, but I was half if not entirely expecting the neighbors to make some level of stink over all of this. We did it to them. Barbara did not pass up the opportunity to knock on the Coyle's door when they put up their house for sale. It would be nice to say they were taking the time to say goodbye, but the real purpose, the motive of every single neighbor was to ensure that they would direct Bob Coyle's decision of who to sell his house to; as he should take into consideration the needs and feelings of his soon to be former neighbors. It didn't work out too well, but Mr. Coyle complied, kind of anyway. He cared enough, or maybe it really was fear.

The Pszcynacks didn't care. As a family, well, everyone except me, we wanted to leave. To get out of Pennsauken was all that could ever matter, the fate of our Browning Road neighbors simply of no concern, outside of how we were perceived of course. There was no amount of guilt expressed over this and no one demanded to whom or what color the house be sold to. I guess this is where the wall started showing its cracks. There were more black people in the schools, more in the stores, or at the mall, anywhere. The only means of action was to leave, and stop trying to save a town from what it could not be saved from. True to the point, my parents, being the first to leave for these reasons, thought themselves victims, and if not that, true heroes for deciding to leave when they did. You look out for your own, as they saw it. What is "your own?" I hated myself many times for never knowing.

Selling the house, the process of selling the house that is, was not going to be as easy as my parents and grandmother hoped it would be. Marie worked in real estate all her life, buying and selling houses where to her what black athletes were to Matt Del. This was her mojo. She taught her daughter a lot. The knowledge gained did not really come in too handy. For instance, I learned from Marie and Barbara that if one was viewing a house for sale, it was a faux pas to ask the following question:

"Why are you moving?"

That's what Primus, a tall, rather lanky Caribbean islander asked Barbara. When Primus toured the house, only myself, Barbara, and Marie were there that day; and I immediately liked him because he liked Christy and pet her, asking for her name. I honestly enjoyed his island accent and he was just an all-around pleasant man, more than a breath of fresh air for that house. When he asked that question, the one he evidently shouldn't have asked, Barbara again gave him the go to response that Marie was moving in with us and we needed a bigger house. Primus seemed to accept that lame excuse with his good nature and thanked us for a wonderful showing and the chance to meet the dog. He didn't end up buying the house for whatever his reasons.

Probably more damning to Barbara and Marie, beyond Primus

asking the "why are you moving" inquiry they hated, was that nearly everyone who toured the house asked exactly the same question. I think all of them asked, and why wouldn't they? Is not the reason a person or family is selling their house and moving away from their neighborhood a perfectly reasonable question for a potential buyer to ask? Not a practical morsel of information to have? Evidently not.

"Why do they keep asking me why we are moving?" Barbara asked no one in particular after Primus left. "They are not supposed to ask that when they tour a house, that's none of their fucking business! He wants to know why we are moving? 'Look in the mirror!' That's what I should have told him!" She jabbed her finger right into the front hallway mirror, threatening her own image with that brand of ample assurance. No one likes questions, your bullshit can be exposed that way. This would never change.

Primus of course was long out of ear shot when Barbara had her quarrel with the mirror. Marie deflected with the idea that most home buyers never bought a home before and do not understand all the etiquette. I always found my grandmother to be a lot less brazen with the bigotry nuance, but she was of that generation that had absolutely no problem with any of it. Instead of the mirror, they should have been berating the clock on the wall after Primus left.

Why were they so damned racist? Why all the vitriol? Damon said they were "flying" but where to and exactly why? Furthermore, they moved to this area, this town of Pennsauken, when they were expecting me in the late seventies. They knew the town was right up against Camden, which was a more than run down town even then. What did they expect?

Back then, during the early white flight era, I was far better at asking questions than discovering answers for them. So I went to sleep that night pondering whatever I could, trying to keep my mind off all the nonsense and on more important matters like Captain America's dealings with the Red Skull or when the Riddler would appear in the Batman books again. There are worse things to fall asleep to. I hardly ever got up in the middle of the night by that age. Sometimes in the quiet of the house, I could hear Christy snoring her heavy snore from her bed by the front door. She could go on all night sometimes. I eventually nodded off and didn't hear a single thing.

The next morning, I woke up to more than just some commotion from next door at the Graff's house. This was fairly common, as Mr. Graff liked to scream and yell all the time, even at breakfast if he felt the need. That morning he was arguing with the police parked in front of his house. I looked out my window and saw Mr. Graff and his wife, both in bathrobes, talking to the police, one of whom was writing everything down, and two officers standing behind Mr. Graff as if they were going to arrest him for some reason. Old man Graff didn't look too happy, and as the police talked to him, I could hear him say, "I didn't do anything, you can't arrest me. Find the little shit who broke into my house!"

I had to admit this was more than half fascinating, and I could hear my parents not arguing, yet talking loudly in the kitchen about something that happened in the middle of the night at the Graff's house. Barbara, sounding exhausted at explaining what happened to Old Joe and my brother for probably the fifth time, kept going on. I came downstairs to where everyone was, Christy gave me her typical good morning welcome of wagging her tail at me and then sat her fat basset behind down to watch this new drama unfold.

"I came downstairs last night because I heard the Graff's dog barking his head off," Barbara explained. "They keep him chained up in their backyard all the time. Christy didn't move, she was dead asleep and snoring really loud, she didn't even hear me walk past her. The man ran away before I got to see anything through the window, but someone broke into the Graff's house last night."

This was a new turn of events. I could not remember ever once before hearing of a break in anywhere on the block. The Graff's had a rusty old door on the side of their attached garage, anyone could have got it open. Looks like that is exactly what happened that night.

"Jane Graff heard Stormy barking and came down to see what was the matter. Then she saw a little black man crouching down in the garage, and he was looking right at her. His eyes were almost glowing in the dark. Jane started screaming and saying, 'what are you doing in here' and 'go away' really loud. Then her husband ran down the stairs and chased the burglar out. He chased him all the way down the street but couldn't catch him, he was too fast for Jerry. Then Jane called the cops, and they are still out there."

Barbara looked through the shades on the living room widows, annoyed that there were cops in her neighborhood for any reason at all. Again, I don't remember there ever having been cops summoned to any house even once for as long as I can remember. Barbara was probably of the same mindset, so this was a first for everyone. Though some things never change.

Christy began walking around the kitchen and living room, knowing there was some commotion and only wanting some pets and attention while everyone was home at once. Barbara looked down and shook her head at our dog in unabashed disappointment.

"Can you believe her?" Barbara asked old Joe, pointing down at Christy, who looked up at them with the most realistic "what the hell" expression a basset could give.

"Their big German Shepard was barking his head off last night because the damn black broke into their house. Jane was screaming and hollering and here Christy was, sleeping in her bed, her nose buried under her big ears and snoring her head off." Barbara turned away from our dog, disgusted in any living being that was not herself.

Old Joe looked down and shook his head at Christy, giving the dog the same mighty frown he was giving me the day Barbara broke her arm. Seriously. They were somehow, no, not somehow, actually casting blame upon the dog for sleeping through a break in at our neighbors' house. Joey didn't refute any of these accusations against a basset hound, even though he loved that dog as much as me, and in fact it was he who begged my parents and grandmother to get the dog all those years ago when we were little. At least they were not blaming him. C.Y.A. even if an animal had to take the blame. Classic.

Mr. Graff was still being interrogated by the cops. We didn't know why. Barbara, who had talked to Jane Graff earlier that morning, explained everything.

"The cops were almost about to arrest him," she said, pointing her finger to the window.

"Why him?" Old Joe asked, with my brother's, (and admittedly my own) interest peaked at this idea.

"He sleeps in the nude," she said. "So, when he heard his wife screaming, he ran down and chased the damn nigger out of the house and all the way down the street stark naked. He just couldn't catch him and he got away. They said they could arrest him for indecent exposure."

Joey busted out laughing in the kitchen in front of everyone. I had to admit I smiled too, and even Old Joe gave one of his rare grins. This should be in the real study of the history of this town. Know that a middle-aged man chased a would-be burglar down the street in the nude; probably screaming all kinds of profanities at him until eventually wheezing and giving up as Mr. Graff was far too out of shape to catch anyone running away. Justice would not be served but he himself was nearly arrested for indecent exposure. I can't imagine how that would have played out in the local courts.

This actually happened. This was our town's history. An aging, overweight man who enjoys screaming at his family over breakfast woke up in the middle of the night, then while completely naked, bare feet grinding in into the cracked sidewalk, somehow ignoring the pain, his fat gut and big untanned ass flailing under the night sky; he chased a black man down the street to no avail. One had to admire his conviction.

"He was still naked when the police arrived," my mom continued. "He was so angry at what happened that he didn't even bother to get dressed. The cops must think he's crazy."

"How many cops came?" my dad asked. It actually took me another few years to understand why this question was relevant at all. Why would the amount of police officers who responded to a call be of consequence? There are reasons, sadly. Perception is everything, and some questions were always more predictable than others.

"The cops are angry because this is their jurisdiction," old Joe later explained. "Graff made an ass of himself chasing that nigger down the street, but the real problem is Camden is leaking into Pennsauken and now the cops have to deal with that. They used to know never to come into this neighborhood, then idiots like Arlene's kid brings them over to play football in the street, and now we have them breaking into our houses. We were smart to put up the house for sale, it's only going to get worse."

For my own part, I had far less pride, even the thinly veiled kind, in the moving endeavors as he did but then Barbara, still doing her own pondering, had to fight some new tears back. Looking away and into the window like a nervous cat while wringing her hands, having no idea what to say or do, only that she couldn't have this whatsoever. It's not happening. All of a sudden, the old naked man running down the street stopped being funny.

"This is going to be in the newspaper," she said while briefly face-palming and shaking her head at the window, damning the Graffs for having their home broken into.

"My friends are going to read about this, and they will know it was on Browning Road. Now I'll have to explain to them what happened, and they will know I live on a crime street; fucking Graffs and the damned dog, goddamn it!"

Incredible. I had always revered, almost respected, Barbara's fortune to have the same group of girlfriends she has had since she was in first grade some forty years prior to the old running naked man. I could only hope to have friends with that much longevity in my own life and had no idea where Michael and I would be when we were in our mid-forties. That's just him and I. Barbara is a member of a clique of about seven girlfriends, always up in each other's business and it became painfully apparent to me at a much younger age than I was that Barbara's happiness, her mental well-being, and just her altogether perception of herself was entirely dependent on how she is perceived by those girlfriends. Or rather, how she perceived they perceived her.

This incident would be an embarrassment to Barbara. After all, her friends' neighborhoods didn't get broken into last night, and none of them live adjacent to Camden, New Jersey, if that is in fact where that burglar came from. Everything is a competition with those girlfriends she is apparently so close to. Having to explain why she bothered to move to this town in the first place had now become a liability, in addition to not knowing where we were moving to. For that clique of girlfriends, I wondered if their husbands spent so much arbitrary time away from their wives and kids. Is our level of happiness in life really only measured as to how others are doing, for better or worse, than ourselves?

Curious, yet it seemed of little matter. The fact that Jerry Graff was butt naked in his pursuit of the perpetrator would likely be left out of the newspaper's crime reports, yet that was not helping Barbara's cause in the slightest. Three or so of the girls actually did call Barbara's several days later when they read about it. I would hear no end to it. Things were not going in a favorable direction.

"Everyone is going to put their house up for sale now," she said, tears now visibly welling up within her eyes; almost breathing heavily while she went on. "They're all going to put their houses up for sale and now I won't be able to sell my house because they will see all the for-sale signs on the block and know that the neighborhood is going to shit!" Her sobbing continued. Old Joe did not say a word to her, but I knew he agreed. All they could do was hope they could sell that house before then. Hope alone.

Incidentally, Barbara was right. Within less than two weeks of the naked run down, there were more for sale signs planted on lawns down Browning Road, four of them in addition to ours. Arlene Del's included. Michael was staying right here on Browning Road yet not his cousin Matt, the very kid who sparked old Joe's racist-fueled rage just for playing football in the street. He would be leaving as well, and their house was nicer than ours. A big addition with skylights was put on Arlene's house some years prior that made them the minor envy of town. I knew it would probably sell before ours did, even given the fact I was still trying to block out the idea of any house selling, or anyone moving. We all could have stayed, or so I wanted to believe.

Old Joe was remarkably silent on the matter, though likely still proud of himself for being the first to at the very least attempt to move. This began an apparently permanent panic attack for Barbara, after all, she had told her friends that she was moving the day she put the house up for sale and this was going to take a lot longer, and the burden of explanation as to why would always be on her until the damned house was sold. Delightful delay.

What we, or certainly I, were witnessing were only the beginnings of a new family obsession. They (hardly we) not only wanted to get out of Pennsauken, they absolutely needed to; and if they ever found a house that they liked, the Browning Road home had to be sold first before they could make any such purchase. None of this was going to be easy. I was in no rush. Just as well it would be harder to move. I may have been just a guest in that house, a freeloader who lived there rent free but it was my home, and my hometown. Even as everyone was bent out of shape; worried, and somehow even more racist than before, it was nice to see the little guy take a "win." It was never going to be enough.

Chapter Six

THE PRETTIEST GIRL IN THE ROOM

I've always asked a lot of questions, most of them without ever being given any real answer. Questions are often abhorrent, just not with good reason, and without actually calling them that. People get noticeably cranky when we question wherever our world is at any given time. As if wanting to know more about the world we lived in then and live in now is a bad thing. Then again, no one said intelligence made anyone happier.

I learned very early on what an unfortunate disadvantage I was placed in, being the youngest human being in my family. Quite simply, it's that easy to be, or at the very least perceived to be, superior to another based on the number of years one has existed by comparison. I was younger, and therefore was always at least one step behind, often a number of steps by design. There was nothing I could do about that. One can't argue on behalf of their own age to someone older, and that's the way so many like it. Splendid perpetuity.

An opportune advantage to this system, if there was ever any to be found, was having an older brother by three years; rotten, shamelessly arrogant, and verbally (sometimes physically) abusive though he was. No matter how different Joey and I were, as we grew ever older, I was able to see three years into the future at all times. With him attending middle school first, I was somewhat more prepared for the little nightmare that would be for me. He got his driver's license before me, almost immediately collecting several speeding tickets or reckless driving citations somehow to everyone's surprise but my own. Still, him being older, I was able to see a bit more into what driving would be all about for me soon enough. There were a lot more assholes on the road than I ever realized.

We are always concerned with what lies ahead and for better and frequently for worse, my older brother provided a window of sorts for what was to come. Albeit the timing was often far too immaculate for my own wellbeing. There was always that one subject of analysis that exceeded all others, something we could never get off our minds, not that we often wanted to. I had my first crush on a girl all the way back in kindergarten; a blonde named Michelle Lofner. It was only a crush, of course, yet that is when I first realized my male given member would never give me any recess. Not that I ever gave it much respite in return.

The other half of my species always mattered, even when I didn't want them to. Each day was always like a new experiment to study. One afternoon Barbara and Marie were preparing the house for yet another showing, this time with an additional caveat. Sadly (for everyone but me), the family that was to tour our house was actually going to take advantage of time and circumstance by visiting all five houses for sale on the block in one day. Sometimes I wondered if even Barbara wondered what the hell was the point of it all. My fool's hope, nothing more.

Later, Joey came back from a morning shift at his hardware store, walking through the kitchen door with that arrogant smirk on his face because he knew what was coming. And it was not as if Barbara could wait even a second to indulge in the hapless news, though she would never once submit to calling it that.

"Joseph has a girlfriend," Barbara said to my grandmother with a disturbingly eager and shit-eating grin across her face. Marie made that "ohhhh" sound that I could never figure out why so many people used when this type of news was released. Can't change the channel in this case. Why do they not realize how ridiculous that sound makes them appear? Why do they never care who they could hurt in doing so?

"He found out that a girl at school liked him. He bought her a flower and gave it to her and asked her out and she said 'yes.'"

"Ain't I slick?" Joey asked with his snake-like tongue sticking through his 'always needed braces but his parents were too cheap for that' teeth.

Barbara smiled like the sun. Marie walked over to Joey and gave him a kiss on the cheek.

"I heard she is very pretty, I can't wait to meet her, Joseph," she said while holding his hand. I didn't smile. I left the room. That was not in their interest. Joey was not only coming to an apparent crossroads in life with his first official girlfriend, he was doing those two in particular an invaluable service. Such dubious wealth must never be lost, and certainly not disparaged.

Joey walked away and up to his room with an "aw shucks" aura about him. Johnny Confidence undeniably. I met this new girlfriend of his. When he had her over the house for the first time, I was (naturally) in my room when I heard all the introductory commotions. And that same ingratiating noise that was like nails on a chalkboard mixed with stabbing an ominous alley cat with red hot fire pokers. Through all that, I could hear the girl's voice going on and on about how cute Christy was, so for that I took the time to step in and meet her. What I met was cruelly veiled dishonesty incarnate.

The new girlfriend was one Christina Columbus, always referred to only as Tina. I never saw her in school before, but she was two grades above me, and lived on the other side of town near the middle school. She was Italian, though very pale skin so probably not full-blooded Italian. Very short, even for her age, with long curly brunette hair. She even smelled good, hard as it was to admit. Really the carbon footprint pretty girl. The type any guy could fall for with even one sideways glance. That beautiful face, diamond blue eyes, enough for anyone to drown in if they looked long enough, and that would never take long. She would be getting by well in life. Mostly because so few would ever ask why.

Yes, she was a pretty girl. Definitely the type of girl I would like to date in about three years from then. Yet this was a problem. If one of the prettiest girls in school, perhaps the prettiest, is attracted to a guy like Joey, what will this do for my own chances some short years later? I kind of looked like Joey, sharing some remote facial features, but that's as far a stretch as our similarities went. So, what of me? What about good guys like Michael or any other of my friends? The good guys, at the clear risk of sounding conceited, we had less the ego. Would we be disregarded? I knew this phenomenon was not happenstance, and furthermore, I knew Joey. I had been studying him for years and was still hard at work at it. There has to be a reason for this behavior, questions as to why she chose him. None of those answers would likely be pleasing.

My brother dating that girl was no good for anyone, including him, let alone my own future experiences. As I watched that girl petting the dog, I could not take my mind off how damn attractive she was. Guys liked looking at her. Nothing wrong with that at all on its own but why was she interested in such a jerk? Jerk was the nicest word I could think of to describe him.

Was it too early or perhaps too selfish of me to say, even to myself, that I wanted to date an attractive girl when the time came? Would they not be interested in me and be more drawn to the Joeys of my age? This could be a serious problem, and even a serious epidemic for a very long time, perhaps indefinitely. At the very least, I had to ask why.

I knew even then how easy it was to blame Joey for lying, for putting up a front only to be discovered later how wrong everyone was about this. It would have been easy to blame society for favoring that egomaniac and disregarding everything that came along with it. Only because the pretty girl was pretty, and they liked having that around and knew damn well the consequences of that specific criticism. No one would question the girl for her behavior; and given that, I found myself even less comfortable with the situation as a consequence.

The nonsense party raged on and up quite rapidly once Tina was a mainstay in that ridiculous production. Joey and his girlfriend never missed a day together. He would very rarely, if ever, take her out to dinner somewhere, or a movie; really nowhere except usually hanging out in his bedroom all the time. Apparently, her mother insisted on guests always sitting in the living room to talk with the whole family and allowed them not even the slightest privacy. The Columbus house rule was hardly accommodating to the evident power couple's tortuous agenda. It was different within the Pszcynack walls.

At first, the door was kept open. In time, it was always closed. I figured out years later why he didn't take her anywhere; and it wasn't just the sex alone. In those days, I had simply not understood the isolation angle going on with them. There were painful lessons to come.

Our house was shown that day with the usual parade through every room and occasional awkward stares and predictable questions. We were the first house on the block that the new family hit. Their realtor, a younger looking man than the usual realtor type, explained that they would be visiting all the houses but as the family left, he pulled Barbara aside and said he would be right along down the street shortly. Once he made sure his clients could not hear him, it was time to take care of a problem. His problem. Captain narcissist realtor rolled his eyes and shook his head at Barbara.

"Why are there so many sale signs on this street?" he asked, literally disappointed if not embarrassed at the fact that there were so many options on the block.

"I don't know," she replied, staring at him blankly for at least a minute.

In his still berating tone, the realtor said, "No one is ever going to be able to sell a house on this street if there are so many for sale signs up at once. Can't you talk to your neighbors and ask them to space it out a bit? I can't sell a house here if my clients have these many options. It looks bad."

He never got an answer to that. It's true I was never on board with this entire moving operation, yet it disgusted me to listen to that asshole berate anyone over something that could not be controlled. If everyone wanted to get hysterical and leave, if they were really that disturbed by the darkening pigments, however immature they may have been; well, that's what they did indeed do. Embarrassing to see so many sale signs, yet clearly it was not going to stop our neighbors. If anything it probably made them even more racist.

I may not have understood that people were worried about the home values dropping, and they were, however pathetically. But how could that realtor put all the responsibility for the shit show on Barbara or anyone's shoulders? Was anyone going to fold at this point? The family that visited that day didn't buy our house, or any on the block for that matter. We never saw that guy again to any worth of recollection. He can take credit for the fact that I never took an interest in real estate at any time thereafter. Every action has a reaction.

Some things never changed, and the riding the bus to school issue swung back upon all of us again by the time Tina graced us with her existence. Barbara heard through Arlene Del and a few other sources that fights were breaking out on the school buses more often. This was actually quite true, though Barbara's solution was to demand that Joey drive me to school every morning (only the mornings), and he begrudgingly agreed. Probably because old Joe demanded this as well. Not to mention Joey was just as racist as any of them were. I had to admit that I would not miss Coletta and her inescapable mouth every day. Michael still rode the bus, and Damon never asked me why the change, I think he was getting tired of inquiries at this point and guys with girlfriends tend to think less, more power to him there.

Joey's girlfriend lived in a somewhat "better" part of town but the problem of students feeling like they were too cool to take a big yellow bus in the mornings knew no divisions. Why this was a thing only at sunrise, I will never know, though I would have liked an answer there too. Thus, Joey had to pick his girlfriend up at her house at 7:30am every single day for a ride. His little Mazda had only two seats, the back hatch covering a small platform over the speakers he installed. And Tina, small as she was, climbed back there every day and sat Indian style until I was dropped off at school.

This went on for barely a week until her parents complained that this was not safe, and she would have to take the bus instead. This would not be allowed and Joey easily finagled an arrangement with Barbara to let him drive her most definitely uncool old Buick, a car with actual seats in the back, to school every morning while Barbara could drive the white Mazda to work or wherever she needed to go each day. Joey did not want Tina to ride the bus to school and without question, Barbara relented. Barbara must have looked fascinating driving a little white Mazda with the words "SPEED DEMON" on the windshield to her part time job working as a receptionist for a doctor's office. All for the sake of a girl not taking a bus to school. What would they not have done for the pretty face?

There always seemed to be more and more showings, yet no bids on the house, and certainly no sale. Friends and random people at school would still ask me where I was moving to, and infallibly, my response was always that I did not yet know, which created more confusion and more questions. What the hell were we doing? That question should have been stenciled on our house as well as on the windshield of Joey's car.

The girlfriend was not over at the house on the nights that Joey was working a late shift at the hardware store. Michael and I were still hanging out as usual yet there were less and less instances of him (or I) ringing each other's doorbell's at random times throughout the day just to see if we could hang out, or play as we used to call it when we were little. I still thought Michael was at least somewhat angry with me that the sale sign was on the lawn to begin with. Hard to take, and hard to blame him. So sometimes I just had to entertain myself. One night while Joey was working and both my parents were home, a comfortable day of no house showings or Tina grandstanding, the doorbell rang so I answered it.

A tall, slightly overweight man with a dirty blonde balding hairline along with a sneering mustache was standing there looking down at me through the screen; as if slightly disappointed that a kid answered the door. Not really caring, he reached into his jacket pocket and pulled out a police identification card and badge.

"My name is Detective Jay Henry, from the Pennsauken Police Department, I am looking for a Joseph Pszcynack, who owns a white Mazda and lives at this address." He butchered the last name of course. Even I knew better than to correct him. This was a cop, and he was at my house. Why did they always have mustaches?

"Joey is not here right now," is all I said to him, gawking at him the whole time.

"Are your parent's home? Can I talk to them?"

"Okay," is all I said, knowing how important this must have been, we never had a cop knock on our door, and he must have been there for a good reason. I called to Barbara and she came down from where she was upstairs, Old Joe was watching T.V. in the converted basement they had finished years before. The detective explained to my mom that he was here for Joey, she immediately called down to the basement that a police officer was here to talk to them. They all gathered in the kitchen while I stood on the stairs and watched.

"An elderly man who lives here in Pennsauken filed a complaint with our department," Detective Henry explained. "He says a teen-ager followed him home a few nights ago, he was in a white Mazda with the words "SPEED DEMON" on the windshield. The teenager followed the victim all the way to his house and got out of his car, yelling at the elderly man that he had cut him off on the road. The old man refused to argue with the teenager and warned him that he would call the police, at which point the teenager shoved the man right on his front doorstep, before getting back into his white Mazda and driving off. The man wasn't injured save for a couple of bruises and broken grocery bottles."

My parents only stared at the detective in return. Old Joe frowned with his arms folded over his chest. Barbara, with a slightly cracking voice asked, "How can you be so certain it was Joseph who pushed this man?"

Detective Henry all but rolled his eyes.

"The victim didn't get a license plate number, but he did iden-tify that the young man was driving a white Mazda with the words "SPEED DEMON" written on the windshield. He called the po-lice, and the next day he came down to the station to file a formal complaint. Now we didn't know who this kid was, but we do keep current copies of the high school yearbooks with us. We allowed the man to flip through all the pictures and he identified your son as the man who pushed him."

More silence. That tactic never works, but it's always used. I felt sad only for that reason. I believed all of this immediately, of course. Joey and his self-worshiping temper, high on himself because by then he had a hot girlfriend, who probably knows about this assault crap yet is still dating him. He gets cut off by an old man on the road, and Joey had to be right or "win" so much that he followed the old man home and shoved him to the ground because he threatened to call the cops. Joey probably "felt threatened" which is likely the excuse he would have used had he been home when the detective came to the door. Any sensible person would call the cops. Feeling "threatened" is a go-to response to shift the blame, and ultimately avoid accountability. This, sadly, seems to be everyone's prime directive.

"Did the old man identify anyone else in the yearbook?" Barbara asked. "It could have been any teenager that shoved him."

The detective nearly laughed at her, while old Joe gave her a darting look, still not saying a word. His usual rants might not go over too well with a policeman in the house.

"No," the detective replied. "Joseph was the only student that the victim identified, we verified that he is the owner of a white Mazda that fits the description we were given of his vehicle."

Barbara swallowed nothing in her throat hard, placing her hand over her heart. "Well, Joseph is not here right now. He works a good job at a hardware store and he's closing the store tonight. Are you bringing official charges against him?" She had that 'don't upset his poor mother' look on her face, though hardly her best performance that night. Guilt has its limitations, despite any and all overuse.

"Well, that is up to the victim," Detective Henry explained. "I am running an investigation to verify it was in fact Joseph who followed and assaulted this man. It's up to the victim after the investigation closes if he wants to file formal criminal charges or not. I will leave you my card, please have your son give me a call."

Old Joe looked down at the kitchen floor. "We'll talk to him." Is all he said and with that the detective left. Old Joe immediately picked up the phone to call Rickles, he gave Joey a tongue lashing and told him to come home immediately. He even gave him Detective Henry's phone number right then and there and demanded Joey call him before he came home. By this time, I was up in my room, and could hear my parents muttering at each other that Joey did not consider what people will think of them (not us), and that the cops will see our odd last name on a piece of paper at the station and know who we were, and what Joey had done. Not to mention they are trying to sell the "goddamn house," and this was not helping matters any.

They stayed in the kitchen for over an hour, mulling over this new fiasco. I wondered if Joey was going to be arrested or jailed for this, admittedly not feeling too particularly bad about such a prospect. I heard Joey pull up into our driveway, I peered through my window shades, somehow cognizant of the idea I did not want him to see me look. I did notice that the "SPEED DEMON" words that were across the top of his windshield were now gone. Joey never mentioned them again and my parents didn't ask him why they were removed.

I heard Joey slowly come in through the kitchen door, another chance for Christy to greet him, only to back off because she knew this was another such day. Dead silence for over a minute. I could hear old Joe say loudly, "Did you push the guy or not?"

"No!" I could not see Joey, but something told me he didn't look old Joe in the eye when he said that. Then again, he was a remarkably good liar. Nothing to admire. Barbara said nothing.

"Then how come when the old man went to the police and flipped through the yearbook, he picked out your picture?"

"I don't know!" is all Joey said. Denial. It's unstoppable. Insatiable.

"Did you talk to the detective?"

"Yeah."

"What did he tell you?"

"He told me that an old man got pushed and picked my picture out of the yearbook. I don't know why, maybe I look like the guy who did it."

"He said the kid who pushed him was driving a white Mazda. Then he picked your picture out of the yearbook, and you're telling me it wasn't you? Why did he choose your picture and not some nigger's or something?"

"I don't know!"

"Does Tina know?" I heard Barbara ask.

"No, why would she know? I didn't push the guy in the first place."

"Well, they seem to think you did," I could hear old Joe say. "You better watch your ass; the old man can still press charges if he wants to. I don't want any more fucking cops coming to my house, understand? We're trying to sell this place, and this doesn't help that. Don't you understand how hard this is on me? I'm going out on a limb in my forties to sell here and buy another house. Now the cops think we are criminals. He's got nerve, they knock on our door but don't do anything about the fucking niggers breaking into houses. I know you have speeding tickets, one day you're going to fuck up and I won't be here to save you."

"Okay," Joey said, and this was the final word they had on this matter. It was never brought up again. Repudiation. What better way to resolve anything?

It turned out that the old man never followed through with any criminal charges. Perhaps he had a heart he should not have had, or perhaps he just didn't want any more aggravation. Maybe he was afraid. If someone has the nerve to follow and shove a complete stranger in front of his house for apparently being cut off, well, it's entirely possible that such a person could do worse; or seek retaliation because he called the police. And not to mention, Joey knew where the old man lived.

Something like that was in my brother's personality; that old man showed evident disrespect for pursuing criminal charges, after all. A detective coming to the house was enough to sway Joey not to seek revenge for someone seeking justice for a crime. Oddly, later in life, Joey wanted to be a cop, and even looked into police academy training. Thankfully that never happened.

If anything, my parents were probably relieved it was a plain clothed detective that rang our doorbell, not anyone in uniform. The neighbors might see that. What would they think? Priorities and so forth. Not to mention, even if Joey was never arrested for this, the Pszcynack name was in the police system somewhere; cops are human beings, and they can make judgements of their own. No one can pronounce our ridiculous name, but they could easily remember it.

The next day, old Joe was out over in Philly as he often was, drinking a bit more and more as time in Pennsauken dragged on. I forget if Barbara was home. She didn't talk about her husband's drinking or alienation either. Little matter, Joey came into my room and said with a tongue lash, "Jack, when the cop rang the doorbell last night, why didn't you just tell him I was not home? Why did you tell mom there was a cop at the door?"

"He asked for mom when he knocked," is all I said to him.

"You should have told him no one else was home, then he would have just gone away. Why the hell did you tell him mom and dad were home?"

His eyes were piercing into me like knives, shaking his head in that ceaseless disappointment. I was to blame again. Heavy responsibilities. I didn't answer him. Nothing would have made him happy anyway. I didn't know it was my job to cover my brother's abusive ass when he got in trouble like that. Apparently, that job that I didn't know I had was so damned important that he, or anyone for that matter, didn't even have to tell me it was my responsibility. It was something I was simply supposed to know without ever being told. I was always exceptionally good at breaking all the unwritten rules. After all, they were never actually spoken.

"You're a fucking moron!" were Joey's last words before he walked away in complete contempt of my deplorable ignorance to his demands, to what served him. I didn't know who the boss was, and I didn't care.

All the same, he would not find me guilty. Had I any idea whatsoever that a detective was going to come by the house that night, I would have deliberately made sure that Joey was found and answered for what he did. Justice by proxy, but justice all the same. The urge to protect him never came into the furthest fathoms of my mind. No one likes cops coming to their door. It scared me a bit, and my parents had their reputation to consider but wrong is wrong. Later on, I was always nervous around aggressive drivers on the road for fear they would be so pissed off at me, they would follow me home. I was probably more often right than not. But this didn't happen to me. But it happened to an old man in my hometown.

The goofy car trading between Barbara and Joey continued unabated. Even after a blatant crime, that girl could just not take the bus in the mornings. I wondered if Tina, Joey's dubious girlfriend and the center of Barbara's devotion more than I first realized, thought of this. She probably knew it all happened. Did she think Joey was the victim here? Poor boyfriend. Yet did I digress? Maybe this turned her on even more. What was it about the wrong type of guy? Was this the sort of girl in my own future? Or of Michael's? Even Damon's? I didn't feel bad asking all those questions. Yet somehow that just made everyone else feel worse.

SUBPRIME

It was a Latino family that toured the house twice. They looked like a family anyway, and they had two little kids with them. Barbara looked down her own nose (not just due to pigment this time) when their realtor explained to her the couple buying the house were not married. I never got all the details, I just remembered that Barbara was excited that they were really interested in the house. It seemed as though our home on Browning Road was finally being sold, the move becoming all the more real; a reminder that this was inevitable, no matter how much I tried not to think about it.

My family was pretty much racist to anyone not white, or not their specific white, on occasion. Black people always bore the brunt of their quiet wrath, but Latinos were up there too. That was only half the superiority there, even in the early nineties, it was still considered taboo to be divorced or to cohabitate with a boyfriend or girlfriend. I'm sure those things were more rampant than I realized, even Michael's parents separated a number of times due to his father's alcoholism. The couple who bought the house (I never got their names and I doubt my parents cared as long as the house sold), they were rather hands off, letting their realtor handle all of the sale work. I don't know if they spoke much English, I never heard them speak once even when they were there. Yet this house was their selection, even with all the other options on the block.

I suspected such old values that brought the vitriol with unmarried couples, and wondered how much the Latino man spent time at home and how strange, if not wrong, it would be that this new family would be calling this house that was my home, theirs. If they only knew the everyday dealings the so-called superior and married white people were having at this time with cops visiting the house not a few weeks before this couple placed in their bid. At least my parents could say they were married, that was a power in and of itself, however lame it was.

Even still, the sale was going through like clockwork; the bid went in, the house was decreed "sold" even with a sold notification draped on top of that damned Fox & McCormick tumor on the front lawn. My parents even got rid of the aging couch in the living room, thinking they were just going to buy a new one for the next house. This left the living room almost barren save for a lamp they couldn't let go of and the fake fireplace mantle against the wall that was actually included as part of the sale. The biggest room in the house was now only an expanse of dirty green carpet that Christy loved to run around and give herself back rubs like it was an indoor front lawn. At least the dog was finding something to enjoy. It gave me less grief to see the house was looking like crap as opposed to how much it was making me believe all of this was just that.

Almost overnight, my parents found a new house in Mt. Laurel, NJ, not terribly far away from Pennsauken but white enough to move to for the convenience and affordability they were looking for. They toured it once, along with Joey and, of course, inviting his girlfriend with them. Always around and growing ever more important was she, and only sixteen at that. Tina was generally quiet, what could they have seen in her other than she was pretty? Maybe that was all they needed. It still didn't explain why she was dating my brother. Why him? What was wrong with the other guys? Above all, why couldn't I ask?

I contemplated this even on the trip to Mt. Laurel; hopelessly wishing she wouldn't be there as much. Whatever we despise is often right in our face. I supposed that was part of the idea. Still, the next tour of this new house was to be the last. My parents had to put in their own bid by then, though they couldn't do that without selling in Pennsauken. I was always explaining that to everyone; true to form, they were never satisfied. To my surprise, my parents invited me with them on this new house tour. If that wasn't a sure sign of confidence in this move, then there was never going to be one. Another grim milestone they could see right on my face.

The new house was decent sized, not too much bigger than the one we had; some shops but no actual comic book store to walk to; at least there was a 7-11 nearby for the monthly books. I had no idea what else to expect. It was hardly my concern, ultimately. Remarkable that the old couple who lived there were nice enough to answer any questions, and even went for a walk down the street because they believed it was best to give buyers privacy for their own tour and discussions.

Barbara did ask them why they were moving. Retiring to Florida, they said. I believed them, they looked old enough, older than the Coyles who left under far more intense scrutiny. I didn't understand then how much easier it was for a boomer couple or anyone older to retire then and didn't know I was likely never to have such wealth of opportunities when I reached their age, or even beyond. They had theirs, and it was all the more valued for the fact that we didn't. Everything handed to one generation. Golden age indeed.

I liked the new house well enough, I refused to entirely accept that this would be my new home; moot point however, considering the source. Yet this is what had come to pass; on the day we were to complete the sale in Pennsauken, we were to move to the new house and before then it was time to start packing. My parents bought about a hundred brown boxes in which we were to store everything, including clothing for the movers to take. I proceeded with less enthusiasm than my parents wanted. This was supposed to be their best decision ever, and any lack of fervor to the contrary would not be welcome. They could see it on me. Even body language hurts, perhaps even more so.

When Michael found out, he gave me a going away present; a copy of one of my favorite books at the time, *The Outsiders*. He even gave me my first trade paperback comic book in the form of one of the Batman story arcs going on at the time. I suppose this was sweet considering he was no longer into comic books. Those were just another fad to him, I liked to stick things out, and they were great stories at that time. Comic books were becoming almost like cigarettes to me and I was gleefully addicted to the habit.

I had Michael's phone number, and we agreed to talk every day or at least as much as we could when I moved. I still felt some bitterness about him because I was leaving, yet when it was actually happening, I suppose we both reached a certain level of acceptance. The following year, we would both start high school, from what we heard from his older sister and brother, Pennsauken was notorious for splitting friends up with classes anyway, especially if they lived on the same block. I was never quite sure why that was a thing, but it was. Getting older was inevitable, I just really wanted Michael with me for the whole ride. Hell, Barbara was with her friends since she was around seven years old, I only wanted the same. This was not going to be easier.

I still felt like a hypocrite with my undying dedication to friends. I didn't exchange phone numbers with Damon. We never called each other even after meeting years ago as drummers in school band. We had never been to each other's houses and the comic book meetups were few and far between by moving time. He still read them, but girls were clearly his new fixation by then, even before high school started and he still wore those sunglasses all the time. Have to admit, they were befitting of how cool he really was. Terrible that we were not going to hang out much anymore if at all; and I made it all the worse for not doing anything about that. Was I ranking friends? Was Damon not important enough? He knew why we were moving more than anyone.

By the time the dreaded Latino couple was bidding on the house, the school year was about to end, less work and more just running out the clock just like every other year. Damon told me he was sorry to see me go but he saw it coming; and wished me luck.

"At least you are moving now," he said. "High school will be a new start for everyone; and you will be joining other nervous freshmen in your new high school; you'll get to join them in all the endearing apprehension. You'll probably find that most schools are all the same anyway, regardless of the increasing shade of color; and you'll always have something smart to say. Even if nobody really wants to hear it."

Damon was usually the epitome of cool, all the same, something about his tone was off when he said that, as if he wanted to tell me something but couldn't. He might have been hurt that I was leaving but it was never like him to get caught up in his thoughts the way Michael sometimes could, and I always certainly did. He was above all the petty racism, but this was something else. Something worse.

"Oh yeah, I forgot to mention," he said, looking over my head, with a concentrated nonchalance. Perhaps a bit too concentrated. Damon was only just a bit less cool right then; yet even that little bit of a loss would mean more than a bit of trouble.

"Me and the guys were hanging out in the courtyard after school," he explained. "We were actually talking to Joscelyn, you know, Tina Columbus' little sister; and she was asking if we were friends with you and if we knew that your older brother was dating Tina."

This was never going to go well, I knew Joey's girlfriend had a younger sister in middle school, but I never wanted to meet her, and would generally ignore her if I saw her in a class or in the halls. Barbara always wanted me to make the effort to get to know her, which is probably another reason I never did. Even still, the elephant in the room was finally being noticed.

"We said we were friends with you but that you and your brother don't hang out much," Damon continued. "Also, that we didn't get the impression that the two of you were close at all. Joscelyn asked why we hang out with you, and I said we had a lot in common and that you read a lot and your brother is probably more of the jock type even though he's not on any sports teams at school. Everyone knows he works at Rickles. Some of the guys said out loud they wondered why Tina would be with him. What does she see in him? Seems wrong. Anyway, Joscelyn is the cute type who knows she is too hot for us, so she didn't hang around long. Your brother Joey actually showed up with his girlfriend to give her sister a ride home."

This type of thing would drive my parents crazy, and Barbara particularly. If they found out that people know Joey and I did not get along, that would make them look bad. Everyone on Browning Road knew that we fought a lot as kids, that's probably another reason my family wanted to move. To somehow erase a bad reputation along with the rampant racist issues, though none of the above were going away. Even still, I had no problems bashing my own brother in front of my close friends, making fun of him and asking questions. The guys always got a kick out of it; most likely because they really knew I was never lying. It was little wonder that anyone could figure out not all was well even with the move upon us. No brakes on the bullshit train.

"Your brother overheard us talking," Damon revealed. "He thought we were questioning why a girl like her would even be dating a guy like him. I just said we were joking around and that you have been dogging on him all year." Damon's tone was sadly a forced sense of humor, and even more forced smile. He never lied well and it showed. Perhaps he was not lying, exactly, but he was clearly trying to downplay the situation under the shield of laughs and smiles.

I really loved Damon as a friend, but even he was not above such tactics to avoid accountability. It appears Joey didn't start a fight with him, but if they were making comments about his girlfriend, especially comments that outright said or even implied there was something fundamentally wrong with his relationship, then there was nothing but trouble abound by that time.

I could question Damon all I wanted but he wasn't wrong. He probably didn't realize what a sensitive powder keg of an issue this all was, Joey dating that girl. Whomever asked questions of this was to be burned at the stake for heresy, far worse actually. Joey must have threatened him somehow and Damon likely tried to downplay it to Joey as much as he did with me. I know Joey would never have bought any sense of humor, even a false one, and let alone from a black kid. Damon and I never talked about this particular subject later on; it never came up even once again. It would have only hurt things, another sad example of my brother's relationship with that girl being completely destructive. Yet somehow it was becoming the greatest relationship on the face of the planet. Too much to ask that it would have ended then and there. Maybe too much to ask at any time.

Joey never had too many friends, less so as he got older, and even less after he met Tina. The latter fact was hardly shocking. He stopped talking to Kenny Del when he didn't need his services driving to school each day. The only two friends he kept through most of high school were Carl Schimer and Terry Pamaul. Carl used to be a regular visitor to our house, they were both into hockey and professional wrestling. But we never saw Terry much, his family was from India after all. I was actually surprised Joey was friends with him for so long for only that reason. Old Joe hated Terry, and had no issue sharing that as he was sufficiently feared. No objections to Tina, though, and she certainly provided Joey with much more notoriety. That was completely acceptable.

Later that night, Joey banged on my door and demanded I help him and my dad unload a new extension ladder from Carl's truck to be taken to the backyard. I was not remotely interested but was reprimanded not to ever use it. I thought it odd that he bought a new ladder considering we were moving soon and we didn't need one. Then I realized that he worked with Carl at Rickles and that enquiring as to how he may have "paid" for it was a complete error on my part.

"Don't ever touch it, it's expensive," Joey demanded of me with his finger in my face; still that abysmal little kid who would not let me go to the bathroom in the middle of the night, somehow by then looking all more evil with age, even though only a teenager. The worst.

"Two, your friends today told me that they thought it was wrong that I was dating Tina and that she's too good looking for me. Do you know what the hell all that was about?"

Dead silence. A misplaced faith in himself that he was right, and certainly by comparison. Fear. Even with my complete contempt for him, his girlfriend, or his stolen ladder. Our parents were home, and it was likely he would not throw a punch at me but then again, he was never above that. This was Tina we were talking about. Such a prized treasure.

But the question was at hand. I looked right at him, which was probably exactly what he didn't want me to do. "Well, they can have their opinion." Is all I said to him. He gritted his teeth at me as if I broke his arm and couldn't find his purse.

"Well, you tell that nigger friend of yours that Carl and I will be paying him as his asshole crew a visit tomorrow. You better watch yourself too, maybe you'll get a visit too." He walked away from me for a few moments, but he was hardly satiated enough to allow me to forget even for a second. He was back in my doorway.

"You're the one who's fucked anyway, Jack. We're moving soon, and you're the one who has to go to a new school next year, it's not fair to you and I love it. I have one more year of high school left but mom and dad are letting me just commute from Mt. Laurel to Pennsauken each day, it's my senior year, so that's it. They are letting me. I told them to anyway. You have to deal with being away from your friends and being in a new school, you're going to have to deal with it. Not me." He gave me one of his signature shit-eating grins and left, disgusted with me again. The overvalued confidence authorized. Abusive and criminal. Undiagnosed disorder. Pure narcissism. This is what the pretty girls wanted?

Damon told me about all the kids from Camden faking their address so they could go to Pennsauken schools. This increased the number of black kids in class and in town, but Camden was by far and beyond worse. Lying and cheating for their own safety. Now my brother was going to be an "illegal" student going to Pennsauken schools, no different from them. He would probably still have to give his girlfriend a ride every morning. That irrational relationship wasn't just wrong, it was relentless. Nothing to respect, let alone accommodate. The key was to not talk about any of it. That's how we get by, and why I never really did. Denial was not for me, it's simply too dishonest.

Luckily, Joey's threat was only a bluff. I could overhear him from time to time complaining to Carl about his encounter with Damon, never to his girlfriend though. Maybe Joey thought Damon was not worth the trouble, more likely he was afraid Damon had older friends or cousins or what have you, and stirring up trouble with all the black kids at school was hardly in my brother's interest. The racism may have been rampant, but they all knew it was better left behind closed doors. So Joey contented himself with gloating over his circumstances compared to my own and enjoying that threat to me all the while. No reprisal. No comeuppance. This is what they wanted, just never spoke of it. He knew I never forgot anything, and that in turn can be used to certain advantages. I always felt like we were all on our own, even within our own home. I always wished I was wrong.

Compensation, that's almost as sensitive a subject as the beautiful girlfriend. It's what we have, what we "earn." If you have less, they have more after all. I suspected something was up, just from hearing late night murmurs between my parents, or my mom talking softly on the phone with the door closed. They were happy to be moving, but it didn't really seem like such a smooth ride. If something was amiss, why tell me? I didn't believe it the day it happened, but Barbara called home from work one morning later that month and told me to take the "Sold" label off the Fox & McCormick sign. By then, summer break had already started. I asked what was happening, obviously I should have known better. Almost as if relevance was a bottomless pit.

It turned out the Latino (she had to remind everyone about their race) couple who was to buy our house had some credit issues they either managed to hide or simply did not disclose to their realtor. Those issues did not remain hidden. Whatever it was could not be resolved and they could not buy our house; all this amongst a lot of phone calls back and forth between my parents, the realtors, and even lawyers apparently. The sale of the Pennsauken house, and thus our purchase and exodus to the Mt. Laurel house all fell through; and all less than a week before moving day. The living room was still barren, and remained that way. There were still boxes everywhere. Most of those were Barbara's boxes of stuff as I took my merry old time packing my things and Joey was always far too busy with his girlfriend to bother.

Barbara spent a lot of time explaining what happened on the phone to her friends, as well as the occasional neighbor asking what happened. As if Grace Bergen had any shame not to. Why was the house "sold" and then suddenly not so? Oddly, all such questions were answered with the truth, the couple that wanted to buy the house had bad credit and should not have attempted to buy a home until they got their finances set. They went ahead in the hopes no one would realize their credit issues. They failed, and thus the sale fell through.

I remember hearing Barbara crying on the phone to my grandmother shortly after the sale fell through. She was complaining through sobs and tears that this makes her and old Joe look like idiots. Anyone could see that the house was sold, and then not sold. So, was this because the Pszcynacks had bad credit? Did we fuck up?

It was getting harder to sell any house on Browning Road or in

Pennsauken in general by that point, what with all the sale signs on our block alone. Not to mention in the news there had been a lot of talk of a looming recession and that meant less home buyers. The sale of the house fell through because the buyers had bad credit. The consequences on the homeowners were there to be had regardless. We could not afford to move if the house could not sell, and at that point, half of it was already packed up to go and we were not leaving.

I didn't know what to say to my parents or anyone for that matter. I still bore the inconvenience of explaining to my own friends why we still have not moved, and why we again did not know we were moving to. Nothing had changed. I never wanted to move in the first place, so this was a good thing as far as my own concerns, which mattered enough at least to me.

Barbara refused to unpack most of her boxes, and would get all but enraged at the suggestion that we get another couch for the living room as opposed to leaving the largest room in the house so barren. Amazing how some subjects can so easily become off limits. None of this affected Joey's relationship and time spent with his girlfriend in any real way, shape, or form. Imagine that.

This was supposed to be easier, and if anything, my parents were supposed to be the heroes in this particular drama. The brave forty-something year old couple who put their house up for sale to get away from the darkening neighborhood they themselves chose to live in for nearly fifteen years. The neighborhoods were not supposed to change to begin with. They didn't before, why now? How could anyone see them in any negative light of any kind? Bad credit, visiting detectives, and naked break-ins were not supposed to happen. This should have been easier or at the very least, quieter. Zero average.

As elated as I was to stay, there was this pall of depression about the house thanks to that sale falling through. Barbara moped around a lot more, only really smiling on the rare instance there was a new house tour, or whenever Tina was there, which was becoming every single night by that point. Old Joe was spending less and less time at home, especially on weekends; at his favorite bar that was in Northeast Philadelphia where he was originally from. Even he took a lot of solace from spending time in the past. The present was just not providing the returns anyone wanted. I didn't miss him, but the fact was he was spending less time with us and no one questioned why.

I didn't expect that the Mt. Laurel house we almost moved to would be any kind of utopia. Maybe everyone else did, yet it was amazing the lengths and personal fortitude anyone was willing to go through simply not to see a darker skinned person outside their windows; or playing in the street. They sure were proud of themselves, that was immutable. Even the fact that Joey shoved a man for evidently cutting him off no matter how old he was, nothing would change. Change is admitting fault. This required a maturity that was just not there. Not in the upside down house.

Maybe all of the above would not go away if the racism issue was somehow taken care of. Maybe it didn't matter to them if it didn't. Nevertheless, we were still on Browning Road; still in Pennsauken, walking distance to Longfellow School and Westfield Avenue. Everything the same, yet nothing close. More new neighbors were moving in; none of them were of the desired pigment; and our house remained available for sale. Such tribulations of the victims. Come what may, whatever was in those four walls by that time, that was not going anywhere.

Chapter Eight

POLACK

The young couple walked around the house with their noses in the air. Their realtor struggled to smile; she probably had years of experience but absolutely no training or understanding on her part could ever counter such unease. In this house, she was hardly the first. After they left, Barbara found out that the couple was not interested in bidding and they did not like the barren living room and having to maneuver around all the boxes. It just created too many questions. So they were in and out quick. Barbara didn't care though, even if the realtors wanted her to clear the boxes out and restore the living room to a more appealing state, she was just not going to budge. She wanted to leave and removing the boxes and getting a new couch was out of the question; entirely contrary to the whole point. There was only one direction, even though that last couple was the first tour we had in what seemed like forever.

Nearly a whole year had passed since that Latino couple "ruined my life" as Barbara put it. Speak for yourself, it was all okay with me. A nasty recession was in full swing, and there were so few people touring the house that it got to the point where I forgot it was even still for sale. I even heard my parents talking from time to time that old Joe could have been laid off from his job, yet they refused to speak of it if they knew I was in earshot. Too young to understand apparently, even though it made perfect sense to me at fifteen. Teenagers understand far more than they let on, more so when disregarded. They are at a disadvantage nonetheless, not being in the big club. Excluded.

The neighborhood did change a bit regardless of economic turmoil. Arlene and Matt Del's house was the first to sell, and they sold it to a black family we never saw much. I guessed they worked all the time. The house was still the nicest on the block. That burned certain asses. The house on the other side of Grace Bergen was sold to a friendly black couple; I never saw the husband or knew their last name but Miss Elektra (she insisted we called her that, and I liked the name Elektra) sometimes came by to say hello to Grace or Barbara. Community, such as it was. She even baked cookies once, which were awesome. Obviously, most of the "old school" neighbors didn't reciprocate much, and I knew Barbara's fake smile and laugh when I heard it. She was still there in town, but not there.

Mr. Peterson and his family left their house. They didn't renew their lease. Somehow that man did not feel welcome here, he just never said it, which was really too bad because he was a really nice man for a cop. No ego that I could ever surmise. New renters came into that house once occupied by Bob Coyle's fat ass, we never saw anyone living there who looked any older than maybe twenty. Mostly teenagers who didn't go to school and spent a lot of time outside the house, smoking, apparently. They had a lot of visitors.

I watched Grace Bergen talking to Barbara across the fence, saying she thinks the new tenants were dealing drugs from the house. There was no actual proof of this, and the police never came to their house. It was no account of my youth that I knew damn well that Grace, as well as my parents, would never call the cops on anyone. They did only live right across the street, yet just like the naked break in, it's bad for everyone if police are on the block for any reason at all. I supposed some things never changed.

Somehow, I made it to Pennsauken High School. Well, I made it because our house could not sell, nevertheless, the guys and I were officially freshmen. Michael and I were never the coolest kids in school and I never wanted to be. Despite my avid comic reading, we were not considered nerds or geeks in high school, simply not important enough to whatever the "in" kids were into, and I never cared much for what that may have been. Such indifference only made my existence increasingly incongruous. This would change for the worse in time. The costs of not dancing to their tune.

Despite a peculiar increase in the interest in girls for both of us, Michael was just as single as I or any of the rest of us of the guys at the time, even with the escalating fascination with sex. Since we grew up on the same block, Michael did take some level of fascination whenever I would tell him I heard my brother and his girlfriend screwing next door to my room. They would only do that when both my parents were gone (at least that loudly) and didn't seem to care that I could hear them. They would play loud music though she would keep screaming even between songs, so the music shield was altogether pointless. Though it did bring an entirely new meaning to the concept of heavy metal.

By then there was never a day that had gone by when Tina would not be there. After all, my parents let them hang out in his room all the time without interruption, her parents never allowed it. Hence, she practically lived with my brother right next door to my room. Maybe my parents liked being reminded that she was there. Disturbing to think there was any girl out there that would have sex my brother, let alone date him in the first place. From what it seemed to all of us, Damon was getting as much sex as my brother, for all we knew, maybe even more. That and Damon was not the appeased asshole my brother was on a daily basis. I never stopped noticing; my parents had no issue along with blissfully blind eyes. Tina was always there. Questionable confidence.

They really loved her. Quiet though she was, it was obvious Tina was not the female equivalent of her boyfriend. Still no excuse for dating Joey Pszcynack. What was I in for if this is what the girls I would like wanted? Damon was handsome I supposed, certainly suave, and despite coming from a "worse" part of Pennsauken all his life, he didn't have cops knocking on his door because he shoved an innocent old man on his ass. That subject was still completely off limits. The police backed off of that incident but at the very least it would be dishonest to forget; and if not, downright irresponsible. Yet it was Joey who got to bang one of the prettiest girls in school on a near daily basis. Where was the justice?

My parents' "house pain" continued unabated, at least in Barbara's own misery that the house was not even showing, let alone selling. For old Joe, it was the two of them spending less time together, notwithstanding with his not-quite-yet-alcoholic drinking escapades. Though even with old Joe not being around too much; there was a certain community with keeping one Tina Columbus happy.

Anyone could find it bizarre and maybe even pointless to compare my friend Damon Bailey to Joey, yet Damon was always out and about with whatever girlfriend he had at the time. Usually with white girls but he never pigeonholed himself to that brand of girlfriend. Rarely was Damon seen around without one of his girls, whereas Joey was hardly ever seen in public with Tina at all. He kept their relationship almost entirely within the confines of our house, and more specifically, his room.

I overheard my parents talking one night after Joey left to take his girlfriend home. I didn't want to listen, but they were verifying one of my own theories, not to mention fears, of any potential forthcoming relationships.

"Why do they always have to be here?" old Joe asked. That sullen though piercing voice travelling through the ceiling. I was only surprised it was not another opportunity for him to use the "N" word, his favorite. So versatile.

"I don't know," said Barbara. "He always has her cooped up in here, can't he take her out to Bennigan's, or out to a movie, or somewhere? She's a really sweet girl, why does he keep her inside all the time? Take her out on the town. There's things to do. He should treat her to something, she's too good not to."

What my parents didn't realize, and something I had long suspected, even well into later life, was that there was actually a method to my brother's madness. I didn't entirely realize or embrace it then, but one of the major reasons to keep Tina indoors every single night was that she really was that attractive. I don't know if this ever happened to my brother, maybe it did, but there were other guys out and about, sometimes even seemingly more than the number of girls available by comparison. An attractive girl like Tina would, in short time, attract other guys, even if her boyfriend is standing right next to her. Half of those potential interlopers probably questioned why she is with that inexcusable, skinny shitbag with little to no friends, and the other half could not have cared less anyway. She would be presented with options.

Tina was a beautiful girl, however questionable, and Joey knew what he had, and that he likely would not have anything better ever again. He would not risk it. No harm would ever come to his relationship with that girl, and certainly no challenge. Damon could go out with his girls every night, or at least every weekend night. Not Joey. He could not allow that. Why risk it? Shelter her, hide her from the world. Tina could not be seen in public, and too many guys, or any guy at all giving her attention was no good for her own sense of confidence, let alone her questionable relationship with Joey.

The solution was simply to keep her inside all the time. That way there would be no such problems. Brilliant. Barbara justified it all by saying at least it kept them out of trouble. She didn't want to lose Tina either. Unhealthy. Yet all the same, Tina wasn't with Joey every night entirely. Not every night. After all, this was his senior year and the graduation walk was less than a month away. Though not for him.

I never realized what a good sleeper I must have been, so much happened at that house in the middle of the night, now that I look back on it. Only a couple of days before graduation; my grandmother had a party set up for Joey being the first grandchild to graduate high school; inviting all kinds of people; cousins I had not seen in who knows how long, what few friends Joey had at the time, Barbara's clique of girlfriends with their husbands, and of course, Tina. I was hardly "invited" so much as expected to be there. This would be good public relations, after all. It didn't matter. None of that happened. Joey was arrested at Pennsauken High School.

Honestly inexplicable that Barbara told me any of this when I woke up that morning, yet I noticed my brother and Old Joe were missing, I didn't even ask her where they could be. Not there was good enough. Most of the time I was kept in the dark; I was younger and therefore was not perceived as deserving any explanation. Maybe they just didn't want me to have any "edge" over my brother or anyone by being in the know. Or maybe they knew how different we were still becoming. That was a problem too.

Whichever the case, Barbara described to me what happened late the night before, that Joey was arrested along with Carl at the high school. They went with a lot of graduating seniors, all dressed in black with the intent to spray-paint the walls and apparently even the hall lockers with "Class of 93 Forever" or some such nonsense. They must have alerted security as the cops came to investigate and the kids all ran away. Joey and Carl were busted before they got to their car and were subsequently arrested and locked up for a night, completely responsible for themselves, as they were over eighteen. Eighteen. That number can hurt. It got even better.

"Joseph called us in the middle of the night from the police station," Barbara explained. "Your father is over there now talking to the police. There was another girl that was arrested with them. The only other kid that didn't get away and she was not even a senior, she's not graduating with them. Why the hell was she even there? She's just a junior who is in Tina's class. Do you know a girl named Gabby Cereni?"

Yes, I knew Gabby Cereni. She was a girl Damon, and frankly all of us would call "hot," popular for sure and who wasn't friends with Tina that I knew of, but empirically rivaled in attraction. Tina was more of a book and study girl herself, "smart" yet still dating a moron. Not many people asked why.

For Gabby, she was not a senior yet, though plenty cool and "in" enough to hang out with them. She was always in the school paper, at every event, junior prom queen or some such. In any case, I was not surprised she was there at the break in, and was actually rather amused that she got arrested. Balance and all that. It's disregarded far too much.

"The three of them will probably have to appear in court," Barbara continued, a look of pure disgust in her face which she tried to hide behind a veil of surprise. As if something like this could never happen. "I just spoke with the principal of the school, he said Gabby was terrified because she was caught, and agreed to give the names of all the kids who were at the school with your brother and Carl. Thank god Tina was not there. At least we still have her."

Yes, "we" have her. How was this a positive entity? This moron gets arrested for vandalism but in a way, that was all still okay, as he was dating the sweet (evidently, at least) girlfriend. What would he have to do to supersede this, kill someone? It's true that Tina was not there at the school amongst all the other perpetrators, but would this change anything? She was still Joey's girlfriend, all my parents and particularly Barbara seemed to care about, and she still liked my brother. Probably more so after that incident. All this amidst the prolonged relocation to whatever town we would move to. I still didn't know where. Nothing stops.

I would be remiss to not mention, or at the very least forget, that it was the principal of the entire high school that called home this time. Not some vice principal or discipline type school guy. No, it was the head of the whole damned school, Mr. Chapman. I'm not sure why the principal would take it upon himself to make such a call, but Barbara was given the whole account as to who was there, who was punished, who was not, everything. It appeared only the three students who were actually caught were going to face any consequences. All the others, nothing. No accountability. Brave new world.

"The principal was given the list of names of all the kids who broke in," Barbara continued. "This is so embarrassing. Joseph was the one who was caught and the principal of the school calls me to tell me all this. He said he couldn't believe the names on that list. Jack, do you know Debbie Lambuchi, Summer Styles, and a lot of other girls they are close with, and even that big baseball pitcher, Bobby Thomas? Mr. Chapman has all their damn names, graduation is in a few days, and none of them are being punished. All big high school stars, valedictorians, they are going to ignore all of it, and Joseph can't walk with them because he was caught. This is unbelievable."

Misery loves company, though it simply was not getting it. By then, I found it all the easier to let the sympathy grabs bounce right off of me. What would Barbara do even if sympathy was granted? What would change? Hardly the point, but I wasn't giving in. What was far more interesting was hardly the canceled family party, but the predictable reaction of the principal, along with Barbara and all the other "adults" in town upon hearing who was involved in the failed spray paint break-in. Rarely was I indulged in, hardly ever asked for an opinion. I recognized at least some form of justice regardless, no need to play it any other way than it was.

"Why are you and the principals and apparently everyone at all surprised?" I asked her. Barbara was still standing at the kitchen counter trying to appear busy, alert and near the phone, probably waiting for the next call to come in where she needed to play that hard level defense. Her fat fingers dug into the wooden counter when I asked, she didn't really look at me. Almost across my head, and not at the sleeping dog on the floor.

"What do you mean?" she asked.

"Who else would do something like this other than all the popular kids? Who else but the sports heroes and prom queens? Why would you be surprised? That is obviously who would be there. All dressed in black, pretending to be criminals when they actually were if you think about it; then running when the cops came. Why be this dense? Denial doesn't work."

Barbara only stared at me, first with a severe look of confusion, quickly morphing into a familiar look of disappointment. I didn't see any reason to let up.

"Joey was never that popular in school, everyone knows him as he's been in Pennsauken schools since kindergarten. Why was he there?"

I was seriously tempted to get into the reviled "he's dating Tina" issue, yet for whatever reason, I didn't mention it. She wouldn't listen anyway. Not a chance. Barbara rolled her eyes and turned away, remembering who she was talking to, and in what direction.

"I've got news for you," she said, tone shifting into more ostensible authority. "Joseph won't walk for graduation, not Carl either. They said he can come to the school to pick up his diploma, but he's suspended for the rest of the year. Don't mention this to your grandmother, I still don't know what I'm going to tell her."

Barbara shook her head with her hand on her temple, followed by a heavy sigh. Theatre. I was not sure if she was fishing for more sympathy, or simply more stressed that she would have to tap the bullshit well again. She was getting better with all the practice.

I was not entirely sure why I was supposed to feel bad about any of this. It was good he was rebuked for one of his crimes for a change. I didn't think he would learn his lesson though. Pipe dreams there. His reputation at school may have gotten worse but in a sick way, it actually got better. The bad boy. That's why the girl liked him. That type of guy. It would all make sense to them even though it didn't at all.

"You know he had this coming," I said. She stared, naturally. Defenses up, bulletproof, and ready. "He's been out of control lately; they didn't need to break into the high school. But they had to leave their mark before they graduated. They would somehow be less cool if they didn't and you are not kidding anyone, this would never have been an issue at all if he had not actually been caught."

Barbara, still feigning confusion, the skin on her face all the more that shade of red, refused to say anything right away. Playing the cards. After an awkward pause she said, "What do you mean?" This with even more head shaking and squinting her eyes at me. Jack makes no sense, and he needed to know that. Chess tactics, and that in a rigged game. Worse yet, they just were not working.

"He committed a crime," I replied. "Breaking and entering, or vandalism, whatever he did and now he's paying for it. Presuming you might feel so, you are right, they should all be punished and none of those goofballs should walk, and they should all be arrested. But they won't. The school needs them. They need the sports stars, the so-called smart kids, they need to show off. None of them are so great when you look under the hood. Sadly, no one wants to do so. The reason they discarded Joey and Carl is because they were over eighteen, and above all, they were actually caught. They don't need him now, if they ever did. I seriously doubt a damn thing will happen to Gabby Cereni and believe me, with her, I would have paid to see her arrested."

By then Barbara was looking at me as if I was a walking and talking slasher movie. The poker face remained. "Well, her parents are probably embarrassed," she said, looking away again. "I feel sorry for her mother. Don't you understand that people can form opinions, Jack? Even of you? I won't be able to show my face when I go out shopping, the families that are still here on the block will know. You will have a reputation too if this gets out too much. Don't you realize what people can think of you?"

As if I didn't notice. I knew what they were thinking. That was my reputation. That was even worse. But I noticed. The last name we had was ridiculous enough. Not many people had that name; and no one could pronounce it to begin with. How's that for embarrassing? Hell, I had just started high school; there was a long way to go with that. I considered changing my last name more than once.

Yet for Joey? My idiot, abusive brother with all the charm of a rotten door knob? His "reputation" was rising all the more. Most of the guys I knew questioned why an asshole like him could be dating a girl like Tina, as if it was my responsibility to explain why. After all, no one else seemed to want to.

What was it with them? It was as if I had to think certain thoughts, act a certain way, and above all, say certain things aloud. That mattered the most, obviously. Yet I didn't. I wasn't trying to be contrary for the sake of it. I was, however, a bad liar. If something didn't seem right, there was a reason, and it wasn't right, any of it. Quite the learning experience. There was something worse than liars, and that was bullshiters.

Not to mention, my parents would most certainly have to lie to my grandmother. How the hell were they going to bullshit their way out of this one? The commencement ceremony was too full, and they had to cut down on attendees for fire laws? Joey was sick? That's a classic. Or better yet, Tina's family wanted to throw a party instead and Joey had to be there. Can't argue with her wishes, yes? That would probably work.

"You really think you should lie to grandma?" I asked. "She's not going to buy it if you tell her Joey is sick, he is when you think about it, and anyone can figure out something is up. You shouldn't lie."

"This will upset her," Barbara said, seeming near exhausted but she would always find more fuel. "Is that what you want, Jack? You'll hurt her feelings. It's not right that she has to be brought into this. There's nothing wrong with your brother, damn it, now get over it."

"What's he doing next? He's not going to college, and even if he did, he would never go far away. Any guesses as to why? He'll just work at Rickles, where he steals from by the way. I guess that doesn't matter unless he's caught. As long as he's dating that girl, none of that will matter because she makes you look good, and looking good is obviously all that matters."

Barbara slammed her fist on the counter, trying to speak a certain word very loudly, yet catching herself by biting her lip and making a loud hissing noise that started with the same first letter as Frank. Her eyes just bored into me, as if the staring alone was enough to get her point across. I didn't know what her point was. I've heard the phrase "respect your elders" far more than once by that point in life; they never did elaborate as to what "respect" was, nor did anyone ever seem to feel the need to elucidate such a bias. That was the campaign. Yet there was still more to say here.

"Whatever happened with that cop who knocked on our door?" I asked her. "You never talk about that. Is that all resolved by not speaking of it? He hurt an old man, just for cutting him off. That is wrong, and you know it."

Barbara turned her back to me again, pretending to be doing something at the kitchen counter. Busy is a mind game. With her ample backside towards me, she said, "You don't know that for sure, they were never able to prove that he did that."

"Oh Please! You know it was him who did it. The old man said a kid who looks like Joey followed him home in a white Mazda that had "SPEED DEMON" stenciled on the windshield and then shoved him to the ground. Then he looks through the yearbook and pick's Joey's picture out of all of them. How could it have been anyone but him?"

Barbara coiled around, shoving her finger in my face, making sure to look down on me; even though by that age I was actually a little taller than her. That was a problem too.

"You ungrateful little shit!" she screamed. "Who the fuck do you think pays for this roof over your head, and the food you eat? What the hell have you done? You can't get straight A's in school, but you can read the goddamn comics? We're trying to move out of this fucking town to get you away from all the damned blacks. You want to stay here with all the crime and disgusting people in school? I know you hang out with that black kid sometimes, don't think we don't notice that, Jack. I'm sick of watching you walk around here with a chip on your shoulder; always behind a closed door like you are better than everyone else. Fucking snotnose! Clean up your attitude, stop reading the damn comics, and say hi to Tina once in a while!" She accentuated "Tina" in that tirade.

Barbara looked away again. Now I was staring. I knew what was important, I wished I didn't know why. Tina was everything. The bad guy can't be all that bad if he's with the prettiest girl in school. As long as he's dating her, he must be doing something right and his parents have done something right by proxy. Fuck that entire move, and fuck that ridiculous relationship. I would not be dishonest, less so when it was demanded of me.

"I don't want to move," I said to her face. "This is my hometown. I like my friends. I know you hate him because he's black, but Damon is better than Joey in every way shape or form, even on his worst day. That's honesty, and you are taking me away from that. If we move, I will be the only one moving, and you know it. You clearly don't care. So you can be as racist as you want to be, I know it makes you feel better, and I know why."

"You don't know what you are talking about!" Her eyes still rolling in contempt. "Get around the block a few times in life! You want to live here with all the blacks, then stay here, be my guest. We will be getting a new house; it will be better than this one. So, do me a favor, if you are staying here, you pay the mortgage, and keep the dog with you. I don't want her ruining my new house. She's a pain in the ass!"

Amazing that the lines that we could cross were guarded by a fat little basset hound.

"You're not getting rid of the dog if we move!" I screamed. "You try it and I'll break your other arm, and this time it won't be an accident! What will your friends think about that?"

Barbara stormed out of the kitchen to head upstairs, squeezing her fists while parading past me. Yet before she got halfway down the hallway she turned around and marched back at me. Again, finger in my face. I never understood how that gives anyone power, or any advantage, but somehow it does, or at least they think it does. Not to mention, I was still younger than her.

"I've had about enough of your polack shit! If you think I have to live here and look at your little Pszcynack puss, you have another thing coming! I don't deserve this shit! Fucking polack!" With that she left the room, this time not turning back, leaving me in the kitchen with a confused little basset hound looking up at me.

Words hurt, even when we won't admit it. I had heard that word before then. "Polack." She paused somewhat before she said it, as if the word was somehow just as bad as "nigger," the more frequently used slur at the time. Polack is derogatory for people of Polish decent, which I was. I was Polish. She wasn't. Old Joe was, and I looked like him.

Yes, I looked like him, damn near the spitting image of him my entire life. Only in image. But that was good enough. If I made a face at Barbara, she was seeing him. If I copped an attitude, she saw him. She hated him, if she ever loved him to begin with. She saw it in me. Difference was, she could talk down to me. Not him.

Old Joe and my brother retuned home later; the "polack" issue was never brought up, though I felt like I had too. I couldn't and hated myself for not pressing it. New emotions. New reactions. We would take that with us. As it turned out, Joey's arrest was as far as that break in adventure was going to go. No charges. He could pick up his diploma at the high school office, but he was not allowed to walk with his class at graduation. Marie was lied to as planned, oddly she didn't ask any questions. She probably knew something was up, but agendas are sensitive entities. It would have been harder to charade if my grandfather was still there. I missed him. Despite his fixation on pop music, horror movies and fictional characters, he was by far and beyond more real of a person by any comparison.

Old Joe, still berating my brother, not so much for what he did but for getting caught, and for involving the police a second time, referred to that incident as "strike two." He never mentioned it specifically, they still would never talk about it, but "strike one" was when the detective knocked on the door. Police attention. These were the embarrassments they could not accept.

"He's over eighteen," I heard old Joe explain to Barbara. "We are not responsible for him anymore, the fact that he still lives under this roof is a privilege, it's still me who pays for his fucking food here. If he screws up one more time, he's kicked out, gone. That's not his room he's sleeping in, that's my room. I shouldn't even be this good to him. He should be kissing my ass for what I do for him and his lazy brother. How would they even eat without me? Defiant little shits!"

Verification. We had not even moved yet. But that was Joey's consequence. A warning. Things continued on as normal, his precious girlfriend was still there every night without fail. They never talked about any of this. Cereni was kicked off the honors society and a number of other popular school organizations she was a member of. She even called our house once to talk to Joey, probably to make sure there was no more cop trouble. Bizarre she even graced us with a call. She didn't care about us before, and certainly not me, but she had to take care of herself. So much in common. I heard that in the following Fall, the school let her back in all the organizations she was removed from and it's as if that little break in and arrest never happened. They could not resist. Damn beautiful girl, after all.

Despite my time in Pennsauken winding down, I enjoyed the confines of my room even more. The door was always closed. I wished it was soundproof. Books, comics, even some old toys. All my life was there. It felt good being on another floor, behind a locked door. That was my kingdom, for however much longer it would last. I couldn't see any of them. Sometimes I would blast the radio so as not to hear anything. To further keep my distance from what was under my feet. I couldn't get away. I didn't want to, as if I was in love with my own cell.

Chapter Nine

OWNED

Her name was Rosie Quann. That's who bought our house in Pennsauken. What old school neighbors remained by that point probably cursed at us behind closed doors for another black person moving into town. Rosie was single, forty-something, rather heavy-set, originally from Camden and worked as a phone operator in Philadelphia. This was all I happened to hear, I was not privy to direct information, no matter how much I stockpiled it. When Rosie first toured the house, I wanted to like her because she was friendly to me and she liked Christy and that was always a plus. Friendly as she was, Rosie was not without her own self-indulgence. If she was not imitating Christy's loud barks and howls, she was going around the house talking about how "blessed" she felt to find a home that she liked. Bless this, blessed that. There was no need to see a "god" hovering and watching over everything, especially not there. She also thought Tina was cute when she met her on one of the house tours. Clearly, not everything was blessed.

Rosie placed her bid after her house tours, the Pszcynacks

accepted and the house would be closing soon. My parents and their realtor actually set up a meeting to discuss all the details with her. I just couldn't see my parents, certainly not old Joe, sitting down to talk on any kind of subject with a charmingly domineering black girl and however nice she was, Rosie was tough as nails. My parents knew it. That was something to look forward to. For me, I saw her as the girl who was going to be living in my home for the next few decades at least. I had no doubt she never gave me a second thought. Irrelevant.

At least by then, I finally had an answer to the question everyone stopped asking me almost a year before. I knew where we were moving to. I did not get, or rather was not granted, the opportunity to tour the new house this time. For whatever their reasons, my parents and grandmother chose the new house without including either myself or Joey, and oddly not even his girlfriend. It was all kept rather quiet, methodical even. Exclusive. The new house was not twenty minutes away from where I grew up on Browning Road, in Moorestown, New Jersey. No, not far. It might as well have been an entire universe away.

Right before the Rosie meeting to finalize the Pennsauken sale, Barbara, with a curious shit-eating grin across her face; with almost the same eager longing she presented when she first told me Joey was dating Tina, took me for a "drive-by" viewing of our soon to be home in Moorestown, though not inside. That's all I was worth, that or this was another way to cover their cheap asses. As soon as I saw the new house, I knew why they didn't include me on their initial tours.

The Moorestown house was perched on a corner location,

nearly engulfed by a long driveway and an extremely large front yard that could have fit about four of the same house upon its grounds. The house was a white and brown one-story rancher that reminded me of a trailer sitting in a park all by itself. It was that small, and they were going to cram five people and a dog into that little excuse for a house.

This was going to be my new home and my futile family, along with that girl every damn night, would be living right on top of one another in this one floor cell block on a yard that had enough trees and bushes to be named its own forest. Not to mention, it was me who would have to rake the mountains of leaves in the coming fall, which was less than two months away at that point. There was no stopping this and it was decided for me. It was all I could do not to puke right there in the passenger seat, and for the nausea alone, I was defying expectations. Specious for my own thoughts, and still younger.

"It's really small." Is all I said with a look of dread on my face. That being exactly what Barbara did not want to hear or see.

"It's not small," she said almost before I finished my own sentence. "It's a rancher, that's all. There will be less climbing of stairs and everything is on one floor, isn't that nice?"

She was dead serious. Her eyes presented her with what she wanted to see, and to challenge that illusion would not be tolerated.

"It's really small," I said again. "Look at it."

"It's fine," she replied, practically sweating by then in revulsion at anything I had to say on the matter.

She cut off the desperate silence as we drove away. "Don't fret, Jack. This is a nice neighborhood. You will still have your own room, so will Joseph. It's big enough for everyone and Tina can still visit too. You will have to take the bus to school, the bus stop is around the corner. There are no sidewalks in this part of the town. It gives it a more country setting, isn't that cute?" Grinning. Smiling like the Cheshire Cat. She knew she was lying, and that's why she smiled.

I could only offer more silence. No accommodation to offer. I simply could not tell her what she wanted to hear. I was growing honest by my early teen years. Reprehensible.

"I don't know what the hell your problem is, Jack! You should be doing cartwheels." That was said with a completely straight face.

Faith. Accepting something as fact even in the absence of evidence, or even with evidence to the contrary. I could not offer that either. If they could not see how damned small this new house was, they were deliberately blind. Again, I was forgetting that none of them were about the honesty. There was plenty to ignore, plenty to bullshit away. I hadn't even thought about the new school. I could taste the denial bone too; I just didn't have much use for choking on it. Moorestown was a rather "rich" area of southern New Jersey; some Philadelphia professional athletes even lived there though we would not be moving anywhere near them. I didn't get the "rich" ideas much then. At the time, I was naïve enough to assume people were people and that was it. No concept of wealth inequality and its consequences, just all the time in the world to immerse in it.

At least the house was a decent walking distance to a comic book store Michael and I visited once because they actually had a selection as opposed to convenience store racks. An interest in reading would soon be distorted into a new drug of choice. I would be spending more than just a little bit of time at Comic World than that glorified trailer.

Yet we were moving. We came home later that day and old Joe was in the kitchen with Joey, his only friend Carl, and of course, Tina. Old Joe looking somewhat distraught over something yet almost as if he didn't really care any longer. Carl had been there more so lately, helping move some of the larger items where needed. In some productions, an "outsider" was welcome in the dubious discussions within that bright eighties style kitchen. As a family, we hardly ever gathered anywhere else in the house. I might as well have not even been there.

Barbara entered the house with a "what now" look on her face. Things were going too perfectly, no tolerance for any problems. But apparently, for the first time ever, the Pszcynacks were a victim of an actual crime. Well, not really.

"We didn't even realize it, but the ladder is gone. We were going to move it from behind the shed and it wasn't there," old Joe said. "For all we knew, it's been missing for days and no one noticed. Goddamn niggers, I swear. We were right to move away from here. I don't care what anyone says. They just had to steal from me right before I left. I would have broke their skulls in if I caught them. Fucking animals."

Barbara did what she did so well and shook her head, staring out the window at the shed. They had come for her. This was not a failed break in followed by a naked pursuit down the street, this was a successful robbery. Black people, more than only one, intruded upon her house and stole her property. They didn't call the cops, probably because we were only days until moving. Yet this was the first verifiable theft on the block, and it happened to us. The fact that the ladder was stolen from Rickles in the first place was immaterial altogether.

The truth was, black people did not steal the ladder. It was two white guys who took it; the same guys who originally stole it from their hardware store and were sitting in that very kitchen with the "victims." A couple days before, everyone was out, and I was coming back from comic shopping when I saw Joey and Carl load the ladder onto a flatbed truck that was borrowed from Carl's father. As they were tying it down, I heard Joey say they could get good money for selling it. When I walked up the driveway Joey told me, as if annoyed for having to take the time to do so, not to mention what they were doing. I was never much of a rat; it was pointless after all. That and I generally disliked talking to anyone at home by that point in time, so I didn't bother. There I was, complicit in another lie; and how many, I had simply lost count by then.

One would have thought Barbara would want to keep this incident, such as it was, quiet; but she actually didn't. Everyone had to know. She was on the phone with her friends left and right, saying that black people, "niggers," as they loved to put it, had stolen the ladder. That this was the last and final straw, and how glad she was, indeed how smart she and her husband were, to sell that house. Shrewd businessmen. They should be in magazines.

Barbara told Grace Bergen, Michael's mom, all of them. Even on the phone with Cathy or Jean, or Peggy, or whichever one of the cliques. She spoke so loudly, as if wanting to be heard. That clique was everything at the end of the day, or even at the beginning of it. That theft being a "win" somehow, they had to know.

"We didn't even know it was gone for a couple of days," she explained to the girls. "We kept it behind the shed, it was a nice ladder, but they didn't have to break into anything, they just walked into the backyard and took it. Probably while we were asleep. Of course, the damn lazy dog slept through the whole thing. All she had to do was bark once and they might have left. I should feel violated because they stole from us, but am so glad we made the right decision to move away from here. We deserve better than these people."

Again with blaming the dog. That basset hound had more charm than any of them. Though with moving, I could not ignore the notion she would want to get rid of Christy altogether. That would not work out well for anyone. I know they didn't care to believe it, but I had my own lines, and they were coming up fast.

"My mom actually did the right thing," Barbara continued squawking to her friends. "We're not calling the cops since we are moving now, but she went over to the new neighborhood and started knocking on all the doors, asking everyone if there were any blacks who lived in the area. Moorestown is nice, but we want to make sure we are not jumping into the same situation again. They all told her there were none and that we will like it in the new neighborhood, so that's a relief."

All white. That's all that mattered to any of them. Even my grandmother, not surprising given her age. Still wrong, not to mention obnoxious. Knocking on doors to literally ask if any black people lived around the new neighborhood. As if not being around an opposite pigment would solve all or any of their problems. We would be literally living on top of each other in that new house, walking over each other's footsteps. In each other's faces. A nightmare personified. They had to see that coming. They didn't. Denial. It negates the side effects of all the bullshit and that cure sells very well. I didn't spend much of that time smiling. Rosie Quann changed that for me, however briefly.

Rosie was larger in size up close, sitting at that kitchen table with her realtor. Black and short braided hair, she grinned all the time and spoke with her hands in motion with every sentence. She used the word "sike" a lot; but despite all the joking and laughing and my parents obviously fake smiles, Rosie was not playing around. Despite whatever she paid for the Browning Road house, which was probably a great deal for anyone around that time, Rosie wanted everything else as well, and she got it.

She was plenty smart enough to know what white flight was, and what these goofy white folks were flying from. She was not there that day just to buy the Pszcynack house, she was there to own them. Superior. I wondered how much my parents gave any thought to what, or in this case, how that word's definition was.

"The township actually has a law that there has to be railings on the front and side steps, can you install those before we sign?" Now she was all business. She knew.

Awkward pause from my parents at first. Then they agreed. They had to sell.

"There is debris in the backyard that the inspector said had to be removed." Rosie pointed out.

Again, an awkward pause. Not too long. My parents agreed.

"The stump between this house and the house where that older couple lives is not going to just rot away, can you have a stump removal team come to get rid of it?"

They agreed. They had to sell or wait another year or longer.

"The closet door in the small bedroom is off of its rails and won't move. That has to be fixed too."

I didn't even think about that. That was my room, I just never moved the closet doors from where they were. My parents turned and frowned at me for that one. At least one person wasn't their superior here. I begged to differ. Still, for Rosie, they agreed. It went on like this forever it seemed. When Rosie got them to agree to leaving the kitchen microwave as part of the sale, I laughed out loud. No one looked at me. My brother and his girl were not there for that meeting, which helped. Barbara simply stared down at the kitchen table, in defeat yes, but never to admit it. The mirror.

Old Joe kept up the fake smile with this guest in the house, but he also raised his hand slightly at Rosie, as if to say "enough is enough, let's sign." It's not as if one of his racist tirades were going to help matters here. Rare for him to swallow his pride. He had to sell. Something else to repress and take out on his own family later.

Rosie could have probably kept it up all day, they were powerless before her. Goofy white racists desperate to sell their home, all because Browning Road was literally getting browner. Eventually it ended, and they all signed.

I would forever miss that house. But now it was Rosie's house. She owned it, and she had owned them. After the new homeowner (the owner of my house) left, my parents shook their heads, probably still feeling superior to Rosie because she was black of skin. Not ever willing to admit to themselves how they let this telephone operator from Camden make them her little bitch.

Grace Bergen saw Rosie drive away from where she parked outside. We took Christy outside to do what she does, Grace loved our dog like everyone else, she was a cute basset hound, after all, yet Grace so often used the dog as an easy excuse to start up her nosy conversations.

"Taking the dog out to do her business, are you Barb?" As if Barbara really thought Grace gave a damn about anything but the black person who just left our house. Barbara went up to the window Grace was talking out of, a somewhat subtle air of confidence about her. Rare, given how damned concerned with perception she always was; as if somehow this was her last conversation with Grace Bergen. Turns out, it was.

"Yeah, well," Barbara said to Grace. "I don't care if the dog ruins this lawn anymore, she's not going to ruin the new one. We just sold our house." I turned away from them, really beginning to think Barbara was serious about getting rid of Christy. I would not let that happen. After all the faint mumbling between those soon to be former neighbors, I could hear Grace say clearly, "Well, Barbara, now I have them living on both sides of me. That Elektra and now this new one in your house. I don't know where or when I'm going to go from here or what to do. I thought I'd retire here permanently, but now I know that's not happening."

Even the old nosy Grace would be flying soon enough. Would everyone go? Could I ever come back here? My parents were oddly happy for a change, at least they appeared to be so. They still thought they were saints for selling this house and moving to a new town. I would often overhear them talking. I may not have realized it then but sometimes; I think they knew I was listening and either they simply didn't care, or they took the opportunity of my attentive ears to enjoy reveling in that audience. Yes, my door was always closed, but sound does travel through wooden planks.

"Everything is ready to go," old Joe said to his wife who loved hearing it despite drifting away from him all the while. "Joey's furniture in his room is too old, we can sell his bed and dresser at the second-hand store and get whatever money we can for it. We can keep the stuff in Jack's room for another year at least."

"Well, that's good," said Barbara. "I'll ask Tina if she wants to go furniture shopping with me, she probably has a good eye for taste. I really like her. They might get married; I hope."

Compulsory. I admit I tuned out a bit from listening in at that point, enjoying what little was left of the solitary kingdom of my room. I did hear something else though.

"Well, Joey is out of school now, it looks like he's not going to go to college," old Joe said. "Jack's going to have to go through a big adjustment in Moorestown. A lot of those kids come from money. They are really competitive and smart students, and it's not going to be like Pennsauken with all the niggers around."

"I think Jack's going to be fine, and he'll be grateful," Barbara replied quickly. "And yeah, he might get mad at us for moving him in the middle of high school. I hope he makes new friends; he's going to have to, at least they will be nice friends. Moorestown has nice kids. He should appreciate what we are doing for him anyway, he's damn lucky. He'll probably still be ungrateful."

I could hear old Joe say, as if deliberately louder, "If he doesn't like it, tough shit."

That was the end of that subject, never to be spoken again

except in enraged exchanges to come later, as if the issue was a religion. Unbreakable, however self-serving, and clearly questionable. I wish I could say I was surprised to hear it all, despite wishing that I hadn't.

A couple days later, our last week in Pennsauken as a matter of fact, Joey's furniture was sold. Barbara told me that they would be breaking down the furniture in my room, and that I would have to spend the night before the move at my grandmother's house, and take Christy with me. Joey would be sleeping at friends' houses. Well, his one friend, or his girlfriend's if her parents would allow it. Right then, Joey started bounding up the stairs, asking if they sold the things from his room yet.

"Yeah," Barbara said. "We were able to sell them at the second-hand store, they are sending people over later to pick them up."

Joey looked at Barbara with visibly offended and arrogant eyes. Shocked even, at the indignity of not being told what he expected to hear. He put his hand out to Barbara and snapped his fingers twice in rapid succession; that sinister visage shining darkly in the gloom of the hallway. Fear works. The consequences of appeasing a bully be damned.

"Let's go here," he said. "That was my stuff, I want the money for it, whatever they paid you. Give it here, come on."

It was hardly rare for Barbara to use the staring tactic to treat any problem, but it was even more rare for me to be on her side on the matter, albeit momentarily. Why should he be paid? The nerve to demand it. The silence in the hallway wasn't going to work for him. Barbara looked away and went to her dresser to get her purse, and hand that asshole his money.

I suppose she figured that would be easier than crossing him. She didn't want any fights; she didn't want any problems. Not only that, Barbara had me box up old toys that I didn't want any longer so we could maybe sell those. She put my brother in charge of that job, as he said Tina's younger brothers would like them. He pocketed that transaction too.

That house, that entire town, was on its last leg if I wanted it to be or not. We were packing up boxes again, this time I kind of enjoyed that at least it kept all my books and junk organized. Strange that I was getting into order as times were anything but, I spent a lot of time at Michael's before moving day. I desperately wanted to keep visiting him and the other guys when I could, all of it literally priority one despite the fact my parents saw a bright future in Moorestown and me holding on to Pennsauken, well, that rather undercut the entire facade. That summer was only getting hotter.

Sadly, really shamefacedly, I only hung out with Damon one last time before we moved and even then, it was sort of by accident. Despite all the constant time spent with whatever girlfriend he had, Damon still liked to read comics and walk to the 7-11 despite the extra distance for him. Not to mention he just happened to be single again, however briefly, when we took that final comic book run. So with his new availability, we caught up.

Old times. No girls, no ride, just our own feet and purpose. It was sad this would be the last time I saw Damon. We didn't keep in touch after I moved. I didn't know why that was, which is probably why I felt even more like crap. Was it because he was black? Did my family and neighbors' eternal racism rub off on me? I didn't believe that. It was probably the girls; I just wasn't ready for dating quite yet and my tendency to hold on to the past in so many ways might have led me to a "who let the girl in the clubhouse" mentality. More likely I was jealous, at least a bit. I liked girls probably just as much as any of us, I just wasn't there yet.

So moving, as well as the lure of the opposite sex, led to Damon and I drifting apart. Girls often have that effect. We don't talk about it much. I still hated losing friends. We still had the comic books, at least for that brief moment. Damon thought it was cool that I would be living down the street from Comic World in Moorestown. He thought we might even bump into each other there at some point. That never happened.

After we started walking back home from the 7-11, I remember telling Damon that it was good for kids to read, even if only comic books and that these characters have been around on shelves for thirty or more years by that point in time. And it was like we were reliving those old days even as we were fifteen and approaching the millennium.

Damon gave me one of his "too cool for you" looks. I conceded at least to myself he actually was.

"You are far too nostalgic, Jack," he told me. "I like history as much as you do, I guess; but it's time to move forward. It's always that time. You keep harping on the past, you will lose sight of where you are going. Even though you clearly don't want to leave. Don't get me wrong, I wish you weren't. But we all have to go. I hope those Moorestown rich chicks are hotter than the girls here; you might enjoy that."

With that, he shook my hand and left. I watched him go for a minute until turned his head and looked back at me with a clear "what the fuck, Jack?" look on his face so I turned about and left. So he thought I was too nostalgic. He was probably right. In fact, he was dead on precise.

I didn't walk right back home after Damon left. I had not been there in a few years; I used to walk to Longfellow Elementary School every day, so that is where I went, for one last time. It was a more than painful trip, a disgustingly muggy day and I had already walked blocks out and back with Damon. But I kept going anyway, sweating, though less so by the heat, getting sunburned and oddly walking faster than I would normally have, to the point where my shins started to hurt. Near frightened, as if in peril. From what, I wasn't sure.

I walked to Longfellow countless times when I was a student, but it felt wrong right then and there. It was never an issue before, but this time, I got all kinds of weird looks from people outside their homes, some driving by. They seemed for some reason to wonder what I was doing there. Was I the outsider now? It was not a white kid's neighborhood so much any longer; even though I still didn't see the problem. I grew up here. This was mine too.

Finally getting there, I noticed how old Longfellow really was. It was built in the twenties, back when my grandfather was a toddler, long before my parents moved here, well before the Coyles, and far long before I even existed. Things have certainly changed in this town. Maybe the eighties really was the best time in history to be a kid. Maybe it was time to go even though I still didn't want to. It was all over too quickly. I would be moving in less than two days from that moment. All because a bunch of black kids played tag football in the middle of our street. That, and our ladder was stolen. Nothing there was "ours," I supposed. Who really cared that the ladder was stolen to begin with, and subsequently stolen again by the same criminal? I was supposed to care how much that embarrassed my parents. I didn't.

This was all part of this town's history, and I was right within that history. I didn't understand then why my family was becoming more and more fucked up. I didn't entirely understand why there was all this racist hysteria. Pennsauken still shared a border with Camden, New Jersey, it always had; and they chose to live here, to raise me in what was for better or for worse; my own hometown.

It always would be my town, though I was leaving at the worst time in life that I could have. Between my freshman and sophomore year of high school, starting all over when "new" was ending for everyone else. I knew a lot of things were wrong; despite not really comprehending all the what and why of it. They thought this farewell was all for the better and quickly all to be forgotten. It wouldn't be. The cake was never good enough without the crumbs, and they would have those too. But they could not take my memories away. That I would never allow.

Chapter Ten

WHITE FLIGHT

My door was always closed. Not locked, because the old man who owned that place before us never put locks on the bedroom doors and my parents were too cheap to bother to replace them. I tried to recreate my old room in the new house but faced facts it was never going to be the same. I did remove my old T.V., I just had to make room for more comics and other books. Among the new problems I was causing was refusing to accept the new normal. Even still, there was a new, yet somehow unmistakably familiar scenario going on with the living situation in the new house. I still considered it an overvalued trailer and I still couldn't say that aloud. Yet they sure as hell could read all of it right on my face.

It was darker there, not only because of the cheap lighting all throughout the little house, yet the trees and brush outside always managed to shut out a good deal of light that could have crept through the tiny slide windows with no real view of anything worth looking at. I even kept a flashlight by me as I read, which was nearly all the time. Music tapes helped drown out the noise factor, otherwise I was diving into the world that comic books lent their portal to. Always an escape but they were never enough.

It was an older, smaller house. A rancher, noticeably tiny sitting upon the large front yard engulfed with far too many trees. White vinyl siding, in desperate need of a paint job which was taken care of fairly on, along with replacing floors and some windows. Any amount of money sunk into that trailer was a waste. I knew it then even with my growing disinterest in money. Surroundings matter, and they take their toll.

That was the set-up of the new house, or at least of its new occupants. Old Joe was always watching T.V. in the little living room next to the old, damp, and in the winter, freezing garage. That is of course if he was home at all. He was out drinking with his friends at least twice a week. I'm not sure if the claustrophobic feel of the little house got to him or if he simply did not want to be around any of us. The mutual sentiment about the house made it that much more easy for him than it should have been.

Yes, my door was always closed, and I was also sleeping much more often, which is something else that pissed everyone off a lot. As if they knew it was one of my methods to block everyone out, or that it was at least half effective. Joey was always in his room with Tina. They often referred to it as "their room."

Joey still sheltered his little hot chick from the times, but I found that by then, there had been another issue introduced into their ridiculous relationship, in that they were officially living in different towns. Sure, Pennsauken was only about twenty minutes away, even less considering the way that screwball drove, but this was a small step aside for his obsession. Not to mention the fact that Joey was out of high school, and he just had to consolidate that grip he had on Tina all the more. Barbara and old Joe stopped objecting to any of it, not as if they resisted that much to begin with. So they stayed in "their" room, where the door actually locked. One could guess what they were up to.

Christy wandered around the house to get whatever attention she could. The kitchen was a lot smaller and that was her favorite room in any house. The family more often ate separately; all the more meals for Christy to sniff out. Barbara would constantly complain the dog was always underfoot, or shedding on the carpets too much, the dog's nails ruining the floors by simply walking around. Though interestingly enough, it was the pet basset hound that visited Barbara in her particular quarters the most.

With the then established scenario of old Joe perched in front of the living room T.V. if he wasn't out drinking, Joey and Tina locked away in "their" room. Myself in my little room reading comics and books, that left Christy to often wander into my parent's bedroom. Where Barbara would be, either reading or on the phone. The reason the dog would more often visit was that her bedroom door was always open.

A closed door for Barbara would be an implication that she could never stomach. A closed door would mean she does not want to talk to anyone. Barbara loved talking to Tina every chance she got but Joey monitored the time his girlfriend spent with others and he was not to be challenged. At least Barbara could sometimes attempt to appear happy.

Sometimes no one but Christy and I were home. Then the doors would be open. I didn't forget who my one friend inside the house was. I would feed her doggie treats and run around the small house with her just to see her wag her tail. She could sleep on my bed and sometimes sit on my lap while I petted her at my desk. That never lasted long, she was only getting heavier with time. All part of the basset's charm. Something else to love about her.

Closed doors aside, it didn't matter where we lived, even with less talking and more walking on razor sharp eggshells. Bleeding. Even Barbara was probably sick of everyone, watching it all fall apart within the noticeably small four walls. To close her door would be to admit just that, and her only visitor for conversation was a fat little dog with gigantic ears.

My brother and old Joe could not be questioned. I was not so privileged. Besides my closed door and reading, everyone disparaged the comic books in general and would never explain why, but since I was "living" in Moorestown by then, I had to also like it and I made no secret that I didn't. Such insolence lent its own reprisal.

Any single undesirable comment about the house, the town, the yard, or the neighborhood in general was met with curt comebacks, talking over me as if I never had anything to say in the first place; as if it mattered at all. It did matter, just not to them. If everyone was not on board with this new living situation, then it wouldn't work at all, and they knew it. Some of this new brand of vitriol even came from grandmother Marie, essentially cheerleading for Barbara to make sure that this inane move was undeniably the solution to all her daughter's problems.

Moorestown. Maybe it wasn't right blaming the town itself so soon, yet they hated that I hated it. Dissent was unacceptable. A working religion. Though on the subject of worship, the worst was and remained my inability to accept Joey's girlfriend being there every night. That sentiment at least remained consistent from Pennsauken.

Tina had been "in" the family for a few years by that point and the fact that I still did not accept her, and still questioned why the hell she was dating the egotistical lout that she was, albeit silently, was probably the worst sin I could possibly commit. It was bad enough that I would never speak a word to her. In turn, Barbara and even Marie would ask, "Why don't you say 'hi' to Tina once in a while, Jack?"

Aghast at the absurdity of my indifference to that girl. Ignoring the outright disdain on my part, but accepting that would require them to actually ask why. Rinse and repeat. I never gave in. It's not as if Tina ever made any effort to accept me. She didn't have to. One simply had to look at her to know why. That relationship was wrong. I owed not an ounce of indulgence. Even less so after that move. I couldn't take a piss without being reminded of it.

One of my favorite reels of that grim comedy show that was the first month in Moorestown, was the moving boxes themselves. All the boxes I was given for my things had green stickers to indicate that these belonged to Jack. Since my room was smaller and I liked keeping things organized, I left a lot of the boxes intact, with some old toys and games being stored in the basement. These were also unacceptable. Barbara demanded I "get rid of these boxes." She never really explained why it was such an issue but didn't have to. The boxes meant we were not done moving yet.

Remnants of Pennsauken. That town they evidently never lived in. I never removed the boxes, but Marie actually went out to get replacements so at least the sight of their old town of choice would lose all remnants or reminders. Think it, and be it, apparently. Marie often made the point to me how this move was evidently done all for me, and I should have considered that, ideally with more uniformity. The respect meter for my elders was digging a grave well into China.

I soon began going to Comic World down the street even more, easily three times a week, even if I didn't have money. Most comic book stores are as good and nerdy as any other. Somehow that particular store was becoming like a refuge. That's probably because it was. I took my time and the selection there was nicely organized. They separated everything by comic book publishers, which is how I organized my own books at home. I kept track of all the different universes that way.

Damon himself had been in this store. More than once. Would he be there right then? I know we never exchanged phone numbers, and blamed myself for it forever. Yet for a chance to have some Pennsauken here in this new town, even if briefly to collect my own bearings, is something I needed then more than ever. It would have been nice if Damon had shown up, but he never did. Hell, he was probably too busy with the next girl in his pipeline and even I knew I was far off from dating any girl, and that path wasn't clearing in the local comic book store either. They often call comics "escapism." No joke there.

Even still, this place was better than what had become "home" by that point. The comic book store down the street from the trailer felt like home or as close as I could ever get to it. That would have to be enough. There were only three employees at Comic World, an older owner not there too often, a mustached Freddie Mercury clone manager guy, and one kid my age with very long, black, and snaggly hair. He had a cigarette in his mouth but it wasn't lit, as if he was about to take a smoke break, or at least wanted everyone to know that he could.

Too cool for me, obviously. He had a bit of an eighties metal vibe to him; Slayer T-shirt, ripped blue jeans, Converse "Chucks" shoes on his feet (also torn and dirty) and a bent silver fork around his left wrist that he wore as a bracelet. I'm not sure if he bent it that way or melted it in shop class or something but it was there and he had a look about him as if he liked shocking people, or deliberately offending others. Nice. I wasn't scared of him, but he did look a lot like one of Kenny Del's friends; driving their old, beat up, cars while blasting metal music. Fork- bracelet kid was cut from that same cloth, apparently.

The kid glared at me through his thick eyeglasses, I was not sure if he was going to ask me if I needed help, or was only wondering what I was doing there and where the hell I came from. He didn't say a word until I selected a couple of books and checked out. Maybe he was too cool, but then again, he was working in a comic book store. Whatever he was, I knew I wasn't from his world, not his universe, and I couldn't be.

Barbara hated the fact that I spent so much time at Comic World throughout my entire stay in that town. If those books were escapism, then what was I escaping from? Maybe there was at least a smidgen of sympathy for me having to actually move, when all they did was simply live in a nicer neighborhood, or at least a whiter one. Right from the first day in Moorestown, all I cared about was calling

Michael and some of the other guys, and begging Barbara for rides to see him on weekends whenever possible. It was not as if I could ask old Joe or my brother for a ride. That was unthinkable.

I knew Barbara felt Pennsauken and everything to do with it had to go, but hell, she was still friends with all those girls she went to school with way back in her Philadelphia salad days so there was something to be said for that. Or so I believed then. It seemed she was happier chauffeuring me to the mall or movie theatres to meet the guys, much more than if we actually had to go to Michael's house on Browning Road. Barbara always had this half disgusted, half terrified look about her whenever I had to be picked up at my friend's house. I was only fifteen then and could not drive myself. This placed me in her debt as well; in addition to all the meals I ate as a child. Barbara often managed to cover up her derision with more convenient looks of disappointment. That did wonders for everyone.

Some complaints were directed at me as my friends seldom visited me in the new town. I understood the concern but then again, I left their town, not vice versa. I was holding on to what I lost and would be damned before letting go. It was not as easy as they wanted this to be. That yearning I had for my former town was a rather large coal on the fire, and it wasn't burning away.

Tina still lived in Pennsauken, and they loved the ground she spit on; could that town really be that bad? My brother still worked in our former hometown; we didn't have a shed at the new house for him to stock all his stolen goods in but it's not like that would ever really stop him. He had since crashed the SPEED DEMON car and went in for something larger. The trunk of his car served a new purpose.

All the same, I was so desperate to get back to Pennsauken whenever I could that even he took notice, anything to ensure he was still ahead. Joey had one of the best girlfriends he would ever have, in more ways than only one; hence keeping her locked inside all the time. He had the larger of the two extra bedrooms besides the master, obviously. The requisite ageism that dictated this could never be otherwise, and certainly could not warrant discussion. One day, soon after the move he banged on my door, rare that he would ever give me much direct attention by then. He likely knew how I felt. Another feather in his cap.

"Open up the goddamn door, Jack! What are you doing, jerking off in that little room of yours all the time? Jesus!"

Perhaps he supposed I should be grateful he was sharing any of his valuable time with me. Perhaps I was not as cynical as people often thought of me to be. I opened the near broken door to see him smirking at me; he was in his work boots so he must have just come home from the hardware store. He was holding something in his hand, a black tube thing attached to a small chain, a keychain it looked like. All encased in plastic like it was right off the shelf, but that's because it was. He stuck it in my face, the label read "Pepper Spray" on it.

"This is mace. I took it from Rickles, I keep one in my car and I gave one to Tina even though her fucking parents won't let her drive or have a car. You should be happy I decided to give you one. Since you like to go back to Pennsauken to hang out with all your nigger friends, you might be better off if you can defend yourself when they try to rob you. You'll probably get shot if you keep going back to Browning Road. You know it was niggers that stole the ladder; and they will hit the Del's house sooner or later."

I looked at him. The ladder again. True that I despised dead silence as an answer, but it was better than indulging in this imbecile even in the slightest manner. Slight was too good for him.

Not enjoying the lack of reciprocation, Joey shook his head in complete disgust and threw the plastic package at me, enjoying the fact that I picked it up off the floor. I closed the door, wishing it had a lock and a ten-inch steel barricade to block out that entire little house which may as well have been a gateway to hell. I was never even that religious. My family would say they were. Joey could never have cared less.

I held that pepper spray in my hands, not having any idea what exactly to do with it. It was advertised as a self-defense tool to be placed on a keychain or in a purse. There was a silhouette of a mugger with a trench coat and fedora, with white devilish eyes. I just looked at it for a little while, near laughing but I couldn't. I was never going to use this thing. Why did Joey steal it from his store? Probably because he could. It's any wonder why the idiot was never caught. He'd been working at Rickles for years by then, I think he was an assistant manager by the time we moved to Moorestown. I had no idea what his future plans were, but it was not college. Maybe he would continue his crime studies. Didn't matter. As long as he had the girl. Charming fellow.

I did unpackage the pepper spray and kept it in my lower desk drawer; not really knowing what to do with it. I was not going to test it. What if it exploded in my hands, or got in my eyes? I was never really fascinated by guns or weapons anyway and never given a reason to. Yet new ideas were always on the horizon in that town.

Christy had a love/hate relationship with the mailman, even back at the Browning Road house. It was either something about a man consistently coming to the house each day, but not to pet and fawn attention over the dog, which is what she wanted, nay insisted. Or the dog's aversion to hats and people in uniforms in general. That basset hound would freak out and bark like crazy on Halloween. But the mailman was a daily trick-or-treater.

In Pennsauken, the dog had fun running down the long hallway that led to the front door; slamming her fat little body into the screen door and often scaring the shit out of the mailman who eventually got used to the dog's shenanigans, and often laughed on each occasion. At the Moorestown house, there was a huge window that stretched across the living room from the far wall to the front door, which had a convenient window sill just high enough for Christy to jump up with her front paws and harass the new mailman every day. Her scratch marks remained on that window sill for all time, that home's most charming decoration, if not the only one.

Yet that was the issue. Funny as it was, and even old Joe laughed at her mailman "attacks," the dog was apparently ruining the house by scratching the hell out of the window sill every day. Barbara would often react with heavy sighs, and even tears for some reason, at the dog's cute level of destruction. It was true I overheard everything from my room, yet one conversation on this issue was recited right in front of me.

"This damn dog is ruining my house," Barbara remarked to her husband, who happened to be home and not out drinking in Philly at the time for a change. Oftentimes, the dog would know when they were talking about her and Christy slinked off into a corner to lie down. Barbara frowning at the adorable little basset all the while. For someone apparently so happy to move, there was not a whole lot of contentment to be shared. Not sure if it was because of the increasing weight, the denial of the house size, or that none of this was hiding how steadily her marriage was deteriorating, but those were some unhappy people.

"Well get rid of her then!" old Joe said while not looking at anyone directly. As always working that fake yet potent sense of self-assurance on anything he spewed out of his mouth. He didn't bring up the word "nigger" then, rare as that was, but it was probably on his mind. There was a reason for that. I couldn't question it, hating myself for the silence, and even more so for his transparent victory.

They wanted to get rid of Christy, my only friend here and the only family member who could love anyone unconditionally. My heart sank into my already sick-filled stomach; it would have been a lot worse had he not said awful shit like that before. What was sad is that old Joe really loved Christy, and had grown up with dogs all his life. He even made Christy bacon and eggs with toast to be gobbled from her food bowl every Sunday morning. But it was more important to be cold, and hard-assed; or at least appear so. No road for tears in this world. That was because it was their world, and appearances mattered more than anything. How better to keep it that way?

I was standing right in front of them. I supposed that was the whole idea. Not only was this house their escape from Browning Road, and all the black people they hated for the audacity of existing. But everyone, particularly their youngest son, should worship the ground they walked on for the heroism of moving away from what they hated. Why should they have to explain a thing? I may not have missed certain charmers from Pennsauken like Coletta on the bus; yet all I wanted was to go back, impossible though it was. The trailer was not my home. It wouldn't be.

Maybe that's why they wanted to get rid of the dog, not because she was "ruining" the new house with her dog nails and shedding hair and poop on the lawn. No, it was because it would be the perfect punishment for the slap in their face that was my dissent on the move overall, however quiet that may have been. Who would they be showing off that ridiculous trailer too? Barbara's friends? They were not blind and probably not idiots. The house's size is the first thing literally everyone noticed. They would know it was small, embarrassing even. They would simply never say it, and not realize they were causing such dreadful harm as a consequence.

They could see it all. I was essentially saying they were wrong with my revulsion, no matter how silent. They read the body language. That was enough and if I didn't like their decisions, if I thought they were the "bad guys," well, there was and is always the importance of being an asshole. I needed to follow suit, to become them. I was fifteen years old by that point, and it wasn't happening. That was unacceptable.

Not too much else was said, old Joe collapsed his fat ass and beer gut on the couch to worship the T.V. and Barbara walked away to her bedroom, quipping out loud, "Well Christy, you better clean up your act or you're out of here." He might not have, but I could almost see old Joe smirk. He adored that dog. But not more than himself. The dog was no contest. Neither was I. What would they be willing to do to make their example?

Silence was no excuse, only the refuge of a pathetic coward. I just stood there in the living room for well over ten minutes. Old Joe came back, and asked with a legitimately confused face.

"What's your problem?" I didn't answer him. I walked away, wishing my asshole brother gave me a gun instead of a bottle of pepper spray. I had found my line. I wondered if they knew it. I didn't wonder if they really cared.

The mace wasn't enough. But there were ways. I hate admitting it, but I was always scared of old Joe Pszcynack. That constant about to blow up in a rage look he had about him, overweight and out of shape, yet more than willing to beat anyone into a pulp on the strength of his rage and arrogant immaturity alone. He was half or full drunk all the time by then, but he established himself in fear, like a drill instructor; to respect a man you are also afraid of. To never defy him, even if he was wrong. No, especially if he was wrong. This didn't command respect. I didn't love him. None of them. No accountability. "Just forget it." No move to whiter Moorestown would ever make me forget the day Barbara broke her arm. Or as they would have it, I broke it. Delicious liability. Perhaps I could break her other arm; and this time it would be my fault. That was their favorite "F" word, after all. If they were not mature enough to take any responsibility for anything, maybe I could.

All over the dog, the other pet scapegoat. I didn't sleep much that night. All for fear of having nightmares of them getting rid of the dog and looking at me as if I was wrong to even think of challenging them. Not this time.

However full they were of exotic and colorful shit; they were malcontents all the same. Racist ignorami who thought they were saints for their clumsy white flight from the last town they chose to live in. Now here we were in Moorestown, I had not even started the new school year yet but no matter; this illusion needed reinforcement, it needed tons of support. They would not get it from me. She would not take my dog away. Never. If they did, what would have happened next would have ruined my life for sure. I would no doubt be jailed for a long time, possibly forever. And worse yet, what would all her friends think about her? Even still, none of that would matter. Not to me. Unspeakable dread yet no illusions, I would do it.

I knew old Joe did not actually want to see the dog go. He loved how Christy leaped for joy every time he came home. No one else would. He supported Barbara's suggestion to get rid of the dog only to save face; to prove yet again that he was a hard-nosed asshole and proud of it. He would get rid of the dog and think he was a saint for this reason. He may have been sad, yet he was never going to be soft in front of his inferiors. What he didn't know.

Barbara was the source of this egotistical, ignorant, and all-around childish notion of getting rid of the dog because Christy was a threat to her home's newfound perfection. She knew what I thought, which made the Christy exile all the more possible. Never. I would kill her if she did.

Murder. I was more than willing, terrifying to me as though it was then and for all my years after. I was entirely willing to kill my own mother for getting rid of that dog. This would never go unpunished. I was actually shaking. Barely breathing. I never told her. No threats, only action. Indeed, why would I have bothered? There would be nothing left to say.

If the dog was to go, I would not speak a word. The stolen bottle of mace in my desk would not be enough. We had no guns, and I didn't want them. There were some carving knives in the kitchen. That would work. I would slit her fat, greasy, fake, racist throat while she slept. I could see the blood everywhere as I thought of her smug, ignorant face when she told me Christy was gone while not looking me in the eye or feeling any need to. There would be no stopping it. It would make me a murderer; and I was entirely fine with it. I cried more than one night thinking of it. Knowing it.

Imagine that. You died not of old age, not of cancer, a car accident, nothing of the sort. But death claimed you because you could not love a cute little basset hound who loved you all of her life without condition. The idea was sadly becoming less absurd each day. Let that be your epitaph.

As it turned out, they never got rid of the dog, and she never knew how incredibly close she was to her own demise. Sometimes I wake up in a cold sweat at the crime I didn't commit, yet certainly would have. Sometimes I still have nightmares. This was no way to grow up. I didn't know what was right, but I did know what was wrong.

People are so ridiculously sensitive to their precious bullshit; they will protect it at all costs. It took forever to learn, and longer still, for me to really accept, but most people detest honesty. Most are not interested in the truth at all, really. Honesty fucks up everyone's game. I simply didn't understand it well enough then. It would not have mattered anyway. At least the dog was alright. They didn't cross that line. They were still watching me. All of them. I wasn't playing along with that game; I wasn't accommodating anyone, or anything. Whatever they wanted to happen with me wasn't. There are worse crimes than murder, and there is even far worse punishment. A miniature house, a trailer, on a huge, dark, tree tangled lot. The prison yard.

Chapter Eleven

TOUGH GUY

"I swear, it's like he's a single man," said Marie, loud enough for me to hear from my room. Trailer house, the new normal. No one cared about the noise any longer, if they ever did to begin with. "He goes off to the city every weekend," she continued. "He doesn't even ask, does he? He just goes off to drink and have it up with his friends like he was never married in the first place. It's not fair to you, Barb, and he should know that."

I tried to tune both of them out. It's not as if they will do anything about old Joe's weekly or daily trips to hang out with his friends at his favorite bar he's been drinking at since he was eighteen years old. They would never complain about it to his face. I don't know if he liked stepping back into his past or just could not stand this small house any more than I did. At least he was gone. Old Joe never talked much but when he did it's all capitalism and N-words, so to be spared his particular brand of charm was most welcome.

Even as I was trying to ignore my grandmother defending Barbara's valor, there was no stopping the clock. We had been here since the middle of that summer and the school year would start in only two days. I still spent a lot of time on the phone talking to Michael. We had hung out at the mall the night before, talking to him was the highlight of my Saturday except for another obligatory visit to the comic book store as soon as it opened. Fork-bracelet guy still would look at me weird, but it was getting less awkward. Comic book stores always needed regular customers anyway. We didn't know such establishments would eventually become a dying breed. Burned away over time.

None of that mattered that day; Michael called earlier and mentioned he had some classes with some of the Longfellow school guys, saying it was weird watching kids we played with in the schoolyard now smoking or sporting bad teenaged mustaches. He didn't know the beginning of weird. I tried not to let on how flat out envious I was that he was starting a new year in high school where he was no longer "new." That's what sophomore year is, essentially. I had to start all over again, and just me. No friends in school, and nothing was good at home. I could never slow down the time. I just wasn't going to degrade myself by not at least thinking about it.

Michael did ask if I was able to visit the new high school before I actually started, which didn't help my own pathetic denial game by that very question. Earlier in the week, Barbara drove me down to meet with the guidance counselors and welcome wagon people for new students. I hardly even looked at the building. There, but not there. I smiled a lot less than was expected of me. In fact, some minutes after we left I had all but forgotten what anyone had to say.

Most of them didn't seem to like bothering with me anyway. I wasn't a freshman; I wasn't from their town. The odd man out before I even walked through the door.

There was one counselor who was nice to me, or at the very least, honest. Mr. Palmer. They let me speak with him privately in his office. He barely fit through his own office door, quite tall, pushing seven feet it seemed, pressed suit and slicked back hair that made him look less like a high school counselor and more of a rich finance executive. Maybe he was both.

He told me besides working at the school as a counselor, he was also the basketball coach. Another reason I kind of liked him was that he wasn't really disappointed when I told him I was not interested in sports. I would not be getting involved in anything there. Nevertheless, he told me something I needed to hear but would never understand until maybe ten years later in life.

"Well, Jack, you are from Pennsauken. You are going to find that the students here are rather different than what you are used to," he said in a not at all condescending, yet almost warning tone.

"The kids here behave almost as if this is a private school, which it's not. That's why you are here. You see, a lot of the kids in town come from well off families, some even go back and forth from here to the private schools. They are all very competitive, not just in sports, but also academically, you should prepare for that. You may not be used to what you are getting into, but that is how it is here. A different world, for sure. You more than moved from just one town to the other."

He was right but I ignored him, just happy to leave. I thanked him for his candid nature, but I didn't realize then that Mr. Palmer probably knew I was altogether fucked there. What could he do? I was surprised he indulged me as much as he did. I simply didn't understand wealth inequality when I was fifteen as much as I would know it later in life. I would know it a little too well. The only thing that never changed was how almost everyone never talks about that subject, most notably, not the haves.

Barbara and Marie were still deliberating everything about old Joe and the weekend situation. It was practically every day, but the weekends hurt more, that was more deliberate.

"I'm sick of him and those damn friends of his," Barbara said, even louder than normal. "Goddamn polack. He gets to go out every weekend since we moved here and today he's going to a picnic or something near where he grew up in Philly. More polack shit. Then after that he'll probably go to that bar all night and won't be home until after two in the morning. I swear, I don't deserve this. Cathy Decker and Jean's husbands don't go out every single weekend, they stay home with their families like normal people. I don't know how much longer I can deal with this Sellers Street crap."

There was some silence after that. "He should appreciate what he has more." Is the only response I caught from Marie. I wished I couldn't hear everything.

Sellers Street was not spoken of in front of old Joe much, and as a subject, had lapsed long ago into ill repute. I always found it interesting for how little I knew about it in general. Browning Road was not the only street in this goofy, racist universe that my family forged for itself. Old Joe Pszcynack did grow up in a Polish neighborhood in Philadelphia, specifically on a block called Sellers Street. I have vague memories of visiting my other grandmother when we were very young. Old Joe didn't really get along with most of his brothers and his mother died estranged from him; we had never been back there since. I really knew nothing of it other than Barbara was not proud of the family she married into, and apparently considered everyone from Sellers Street to be "polack white trash," her words.

I think I asked Barbara about the Pszcynack side of the family once or twice when I was little, she only got quiet and said my father grew up in a rough neighborhood and that I should appreciate that he worked hard to raise Joey and I in better circumstances. Conversations like the one she had with my grandmother in the Moorestown house were becoming all the more common, though I knew, and everyone else did too, as to if my parents were to ever divorce or not. That would never happen. There was failure, then there was admitting to it and there were entirely different levels of courage required there.

Marie would never tolerate it. It would be too honest for anyone to handle, sadly. It didn't help how much she was coddling Barbara in the aftermath of the white flight. This was a multilayered denial cake and everyone had to take a bite. The narrative was that old Joe wasn't out drinking more because of anything wrong with Barbara, or the house. Certainly not any of those. Impossible. Indeed, unacceptable. No cake for me, thank you. That was a problem too, everyone had to play their part.

Old Joe was in fact gone all day and night that particular Saturday. Marie left before the sun went down; she was getting older and hated driving in the dark. I was sympathetic to that but didn't like being expected to be so. All this left four dejected souls in the house, only one ever admitting it. That and Christy wandering about. I didn't miss old Joe, but the dynamics didn't get any better in his absence. The second they knew the older Joe was out for the night, Joey and Tina would leave "their" room and watch T.V. in the small den. The T.V. room, where old Joe would refuge if he was not out in Philly. Barbara would not object to this either. At least she could actually see Tina in the house this way, and maybe talk to her a bit if her boyfriend allowed it.

Even so, I would stay in my own little room hoping to tune them out in my own way, wishing I could not hear the laughing, that exasperating twang which somehow increased in volume when Joey and his girl had the run of the house. Nails on a chalkboard. Music to their ears.

Joey liked being older, I could tell. Why wouldn't he? It's a permanent advantage, and one that was held in high esteem in a house without any. Joey could never have cared less that I was always in my room. Still, the fact that I was deliberately shutting everyone away meant there was or may be something wrong with him too, or worse yet, his prized girlfriend. There was. Implication is often more than only implication.

I still always remembered that night (and it was actually more than once) in Pennsauken when he wouldn't let me out of my room, even if just to pee. In my own efforts to not be anything like him, I always wondered if Joey's evident hatred of me extended from me being that different from what he always was, and thus, being ahead of him in confidence; to somehow surpass him, even if indirectly. Was I too self-indulgent to think this? Somehow, I knew I was not that off the mark. His antics almost always worked. Hell, his own mother, some twenty-eight years older than him (thus all the more superior), was terrified of my brother when I dared to take the front seat in the car before he did. That meant something. Barbara's defense was far too often "I don't want any fights," but for certain, that was the point of the whole game. Give Joey what he wants, or suffer.

Bullies. Why do we indulge in them? Is it fear? I always doubted it was so simple. We like bullies. Well, I don't. That's more of a problem in and of itself; and another reason I didn't belong there. Another reason Joey hardly ever acknowledged me, while still loathing my existence all the same. Another reason I didn't feel bad about that. Another reason Tina Columbus liked him. No, she loved him. This wasn't just wrong. It was sick, and I was wrong for even bringing it up, even if within fairly consistent silence.

Joey and his girl were still in front of the T.V. Barbara was in the kitchen, not sure why but probably trying to hang out with them, at least by proxy. The kitchen was Christy's favorite room in the house, in any house for that matter. That dog knew where the food was. But she wasn't there. Christy had her nose to the living room window and even though it began rather faint, I could hear all the growling.

"What's she growling at?" Barbara asked in that high-pitched tone of hers from the kitchen. Always so piercing, how could she never know? She probably did, that was the point. Be that as it may, the dog was growling at something. There could have been anything in the pitch dark of night. A cat, maybe a fox, or likely she thought it was the mailman who was always fun to growl and bark at. No such luck, Christy.

"Stop it," Barbara said to the dog.

From my room, I could hear Joey laugh and say, "Maybe it's those niggers following us back from Pennsauken. They don't like their new house." Tina laughed. Probably looking at him with long-ing eyes and shining teeth. Her man was not only charming, but also funny. This told everyone nothing about her.

Barbara quickly replied with a predictable "that's not true," and went back to the kitchen. I sat in my room and could not help but to remind myself how much Pennsauken really was an off-limits trigger word to my parents, particularly Barbara. They lived there for over fifteen years, not to mention it's still where your precious Tina lives. Why such vitriol and denial at the very mention of that town's name?

A few minutes went by and the growling began again. Now I was looking at my door, even closed. The dog could be a hilarious jester of an animal but why all the growling? Had to be a rabbit, I thought. She hated those, too.

"Why the hell is she still growling?" Barbara asked no one in particular. I heard Joey's narcissistic laugh again and listened as he got up from the T.V. room. "She's probably growling at nothing," Barbara said as my jackass brother barged into the living room. This would not turn out well. Not the dog.

"Let's see what she does when I put her outside, then we'll know." By then I was outside of my room, watching. Barbara knew it too.

"Oh, stop it, Joseph." Yet she didn't stop him. He smirked some more as he carried the fat basset hound out the door, into the drive-way to see what was the matter. No leash. Just him. Not for long. Christy was no longer growling.

"No," Joey said. "Let's see what she's growling at." I didn't see her as she was still on the couch, but Tina was probably smiling. Enter-tained. No consequences for her. Least of all for that.

I trailed after him. If that dog saw a rabbit or cat, or even someone who looked like the mailman, she would run off after it. Christy always had to be on a leash or a chain. Her basset hound nose would pick up any faint smell of food, and she would wander off and essentially run away. That concerned me even in the Pennsauken house, even more so by the time we moved to the Moorestown trailer. Barbara wanted that dog gone. Christy running or sniffing herself away, well, that would be just too convenient. The dog would be lost, probably gone, and more importantly, no one could ever blame Barbara for it. Perfection.

"No, we're not having any of that!" I said as I followed him outside.

I could faintly hear Barbara say as she trailed behind us, "Jack, he's just kidding."

Well, I wasn't kidding. I headed outside, the timid little dog now oblivious while sitting between my brother's feet, no longer concerned at whatever she was growling at. I lightly hockey checked Joey and grabbed the dog to take her back inside. Not the dog.

"You are such an asshole," I said as I brought Christy back in the house. Barbara just stared at him, as if another employee at the toxic office just insulted the boss. How could I? They will not be challenged. Fear. I placed the dog back down in the kitchen. Christy was safe. It didn't matter. Time for payment.

"Come here, tough guy!" Joey said, repeatedly as he marched behind me. Barbara asked him to "Stop it," almost as often. No such travesty would be allowed. Time to show me my place. I interrupted Joey, I interrupted him while he was showing off in front of his girlfriend; who could never be criticized, especially when she was wrong. She was. Worse yet, I showed confidence. I was not going to let my dog run away. He knew I cared that much. This was worse than leaving my room to pee in Pennsauken.

He kept repeating those words over and over again in the half minute it took me to reach my bedroom door. "Come here, tough guy! No, come here, tough guy!" All the denials from Barbara continued. She was telling him to stop this behavior. That didn't help his ego either. No. He didn't want me "tough." Never confident, and certainly not at his expense. He was going to show me.

Joey grabbed me by the shoulder when I got to my door. I shoved him right off and he flew a few inches, landing on his feet, hating that even though younger, I was actually a little bigger than him, broader shoulders from old Joe's side of the family. Another reason Barbara would refer to me as polack. Joey's frame came from the Bearens' side, taller and thin, like my Dracula loving grandfather. Another reason he detested me all the more. No reason that was never kept in check.

"Get the fuck over here!" he screamed as we made it down the short hallway, this time going for my neck. He landed a lame punch to the side of my head as I pushed him away again. Barbara now demanding we stop. Not him. "We." Weight off his shoulders. She didn't, and couldn't, know what else to do.

"That's enough, Joey. It's over," I said to him. I didn't know why, but after we reentered the trailer, I just didn't want to fight him. I protected the dog, and that was enough for me. But if we didn't fight, that meant I won, or at least got ahead. Not fighting meant he was wrong, or at least had his egotistical jets cooled, and that in front of his obsession. Or at least that was all implied, and that was bad enough.

He leaped his skinny body on top of me, placing me in a head-lock, ramming his fist into my forehead at least three times, grunting a loud, "Ugh! Ugh! Ugh!" every time he landed a blow. His teeth then gritting in a steel trap. I could feel my blood getting hotter, sweating in fear and anticipation of how much this maniac was set off over a dog. No, over himself and the prettiest girl in school loved him. No Justice. That distressed me more, even as he was striking and screaming at me. To the matter at hand, I threw him off me, sending him sailing over the living room couch; I didn't even realize we made it back to that room somehow. I faintly remembered Christy letting out a high-pitched whine while running away. She spent that entire night in a corner, shaking.

A lamp fell from an end table, good enough for Joey to notice it, grab it, pull it from the wall with a loud spark and come at me with it. I stopped him short of hitting me with the lamp, holding him back; he was still stronger than he looked, all that given to his rage and my reluctance to fight him. Barbara kept demanding for us to stop it. She knew better than to blame him specifically for anything. She thought she was the adult in charge that night. She was neither. Tina was nowhere to be seen, probably hiding in the T.V. room, I didn't know. I doubted she was rethinking her relationship choices.

Joey kept leaning down on me with the now broken lamp, try-ing to stick me with the cracked light bulb at the end of it, getting angrier even more at his inability to do so. I kept telling him that this was enough. It had the opposite effect. He lost some energy pressing down on me and I pushed back, the light bulb cutting his hand in the process. Joey grasped his hand in pain, muffled scream-ing through gritted teeth, angrier all the more at any given slight, at any point lost, any inch in anyone's favor but him. He worshiped himself, and he would kill in his god's name. Just like most people. I heard Barbara scream from behind us.

"Now you did it! Are you bleeding, Joseph? You broke my goddamn lamp, Jack. That's enough!"

Joey went to the kitchen, I thought to clean his hand off, but he grabbed a drinking glass from the dish drainer, scowled, and threw it right at me. I turned and somehow it shattered right on my hip, at the belt. No pain, just shattered glass. He gritted his teeth again, this time hardly in agony, likely disappointment that I was not bleeding and he was. He wouldn't have done any of this if his polack father were not out enjoying a few glasses of his own. Barbara kept demanding we stop. "Authority" long gone, if it was ever there to begin with.

I wanted to get back to my room, but he was not having it. Joey leapt on me again, throwing punches and getting more aggravated each time I shoved him off. He kept repeating the "tough guy" phrase. The blows didn't hurt that much but fights always made me tense up to the point of nearly freezing. As if paralyzed. Odd sensation considering how angrier I was getting by the second.

Fighting, pain, trouble, blame, fear. This was my family, and we never have a second run of our youth. This was my history. He was such an absolute asshole, a bully in every sense of the word, and I hated my entire life up to that point for being his brother. For being in that racist, dishonest, and altogether ignorant family. It would never be spoken, even if he had killed me.

In all his flailing arms and fists at me, Joey somehow landed a chop right at my neck which made me choke for a second. He liked that. This behavior was acceptable from him somehow, yet not for me. We want what we expect from others. To not do so, one could end up in my particular predicament that night. Interesting lessons in that blurry line between right and wrong. Whichever serves us best.

I grabbed the monster by the neck, and he squirmed in rare fear that my hands were big enough to wrap around his throat. I punched him a few times in the side of his head, but it was more of a slap. I didn't want to fight, so my "fists" were not entirely closed. This was mostly due to the guilt. That damn Catholic guilt, and I didn't believe in the god delusion. I figured it out long before then. I didn't value bullshit. The result was pain.

I was always wrong, and fighting was wrong; no matter what, throughout all my fifteen-year history at that point, even when Joey instigated the fights, on the rare instance I fought at school. Or when I should have slapped that bully Coletta in her slack-jawed obnoxious face, it was my fault. She had it coming. If you stand up for yourself, you will be punished. Especially when standing up to the boss; to the bully. So often the same.

I slapped him once more and Barbara demanded I stop. I could faintly see Tina looking at me in fear. I never knew what she thought of me. I just always presumed I didn't matter. That was always the case. They hated that I didn't talk to her, and now what she might perceive of us. Just like the cop knocking on the door that night. I was wrong for not covering everyone's reputation. I was not theirs. It didn't make me feel any better knowing that was good.

Maybe due to him being out of shape, Joey stopped charging at me, only for a second. He might appear weak, after all. I looked right at him and said, "That's enough, Joey. It's over!" True to form, he started shaking his head at me. I could not be right. He dove for me again, this time tackling me at the gut, and we flew backwards onto a glass-topped end table and it shattered. Barbara screamed at the top of her lungs in horror of her worshiped trailer suffering more than just scratch marks from Christy's nails. Then more.

"Stop it! Stop it! Stop it!" Barbara deliriously screamed, her tone piercing my ears even as Joey continued pummeling me with his weakening fists. As I felt broken glass sting my legs and backside, I wondered if the hysteria was due to the broken furniture, or the fact that Tina Columbus saw what this family and this criminal really were. Or that the neighbors might hear. The fact that none of that mattered helped me get up faster than Joey, slamming his face into the ugly and uncomfortable hardwood floors, and he began squealing like a little pig. He would not have it. It was my turn.

"Jack, stop it! You're hurting him, and you're scaring Tina! Stop it!"

"I'm scaring Tina?" I asked, not to the aging sensitive racist, not to Tina herself (which I should have done), but to Joey, still screeching into the floor, hating that he could never get up, unless I let him.

"Your goddamn girlfriend is the sickest thing about you!" I said, Joey still struggling to get his face away from the floor. I wouldn't let him move.

"Why the hell does she have to be here every night? You are afraid because you know you'll never do better than that immature fucking idiot! What's worse is that she's the pretty and evidently smart girl in school, yet here she is, in the worthless new town, still dating the biggest asshole from Pennsauken High School. Why the hell can't she date a nice guy? There's a reason for it. There's something wrong with her. No accountability! None of you fat, racist assholes care, and that's because of her appearance. That's all there is. She makes you look good. But it's only appearances, nothing more. How's that for the truth for once?"

I finished my little monologue, knowing that no one was listening yet knowing how much it pissed this monster off, so that would have to be good enough. He treated me like shit all my life, and here we were, in the apparent paradise of Moorestown, away from all the black people who did so much to us, and it was never enough. No more words, I picked the worthless bully off the floor and punched him square in the face and down he went again. As I went back to my room, my crappy little room with no lock, I could hear my mother say "Jack, what's wrong with you?"

I heard my brother scream "He's fucking dead!"

As soon as I shut my door, I pressed my back up against it to brace the incoming. I could see blood all over my white t-shirt. I hoped that most of it was his. He banged on the other side of my door screaming as if he was possessed by demons, which I also never believed in. Though I knew it was actually all unadulterated ego; people really do get this sensitive. Self-worship, not a god, though no one is supposed to question that. No limits. No compromise. Only fear, and a lot of dishonesty. The latter hardly matters to anyone.

At first, he banged on the door with his fists, then slamming his little shoulders against the wood, sometimes getting the door ajar despite his size. He cared that much. Barbara would not stop demanding that he stop. I wondered if she was more horrified by his rage or the fact that her words just did not matter.

"You're shit, Jack! You're nothing!" he taunted me as I kept my back pressed up against the unlocked door. Again, Barbara told him to stop. She might as well have not even been there. Neither would ever give up. So they kept going.

"I'm getting through that door!" Joey screamed. I heard a loud clanging against the opposite wall, then my door got even more difficult to hold. He was striking the door with a metal picture frame from the wall outside my room. I could hear the door cracking and could even see some splinters coming from underneath my feet. He wanted to murder me, and he would not give up. I'd rather be jumped by Coletta and her sycophant "friends" every day on the bus than have to deal with this. A man with no friends at all, an adoring girlfriend, even with his bottomless pit of hate. Though there I was, only fifteen years old and my own brother was desperately trying to kill me. All for interrupting him while he was showing off; for standing up to him even in the slightest. For winning.

"Open the fucking door now!" He kept banging, over and over again as more splinters fell to the floor, Barbara screaming at him to stop and he kept going. The door actually did slightly open a couple of times, but I held it back. He kept this up for nearly an hour. Banging, cursing, Barbara screaming, my dog shaking, splinters, my heart racing, and the blood on my shirt washing out with sweat. I didn't know how long I could hold that line.

"I'll get a chair!" he screamed while the pounding on the door finally stopped for a minute, enough for me to catch my breath. He didn't come back with a chair, there were no chairs in the house small enough to use, let alone any for his scrawny out of shape ass to pick up. He ran back to my door, again picking up the metal picture frame, the one that used to hold a picture of our grandparents, and resumed the pounding on the door, probably inserting at least fifty dents into the wood. It was never repaired. This went on for at least another ten minutes, then he stopped. Barbara stopped yelling too. Then almost complete silence.

"Joe, stop it!" I heard her voice say. That's why he stopped. Tina. She actually thought this was wrong.

Predictably, I heard through my now ailing door. "Go back in the other room."

"Joe, I want you to stop," she said again.

"Go into the other room," her boyfriend replied immediately. Silence. Certainly nothing from Barbara on that. I couldn't see her, yet upon the second command, Tina went back to the T.V. room. More banging, more screaming. More Barbara demanding that he stop while being ignored entirely. Still not giving up; I hardly wondered if that was for me or her.

Joey took a running charge at my door; he would break it down even if it meant breaking his own shoulder. The door came loose, and I lost my balance. Luckily, so did he, and I was able to brace the door with better footing. Again, I heard Barbara's squealing voice.

"Joseph, stop it right now!" The bombardment stopped. I then heard his voice fading down the short hallway of the little house, that damned trailer.

"I'll go through the window!" he screamed, and I could hear him parading through the living room, slamming the screen door as he made it to the front yard of the house, where my windows faced.

I could also hear Barbara's high pitched "Stop it, Joseph, or I am going to call the police!" Mostly an empty threat that it was, there were the neighbors to be concerned with. What would they think of police officers at the little house?

He really thought he could get through my window with all the trees and bushes out there, cutting his way through the brush, and then smashing open the small window with his bare hands only then to crawl through more broken glass, he was not going to get to me that way. I only had that much time. It was still in my desk drawer.

Joey was on his way back to pound on my door for probably another hour. I could hear Barbara following him back inside the house, more empty demands. I didn't brace the door this time. I waited. My finger was on the trigger of the pepper spray bottle, pointing right to where that monster was coming. The door opened with a violent thunder that broke three thick splinters of wood at the knob. I saw him, his face was snarling, spit flying from his mouth like a rabid animal, raising his fist and cursing all the while. He didn't quite realize what was happening as he got into my room. It took him just a few seconds to see why I let him in this time, and what was pointed directly at his face.

"I'm going to kick your mother fu…!" He stopped himself short of that "fuh" word, immediately turning to run away from what I was holding.

"Why are you running away?" Barbara shouted in horror. It didn't matter, I got hold of his shoulder as he ran, turned him around with one hand and blasted a generous amount of pepper spray right into his arrogant face. If only it would have burned it all away. Yet down he went, collapsing to his knees, crying and screaming at the top of his lungs. Then coughing, desperately trying to wipe the burning from his nose and eyes, only taking more in with every single breath.

I watched him run back into the kitchen, Tina then consoling him with her hands over his shoulders, a woefully concerned look on her face, turning on the kitchen sink for her love, that victim hurt by the horrible little shit with the pepper spray. I walked back into my room and closed the door.

It only took a few minutes, I could hear Barbara screaming through the splintered door, somehow herself afraid to face me directly.

"Jack, I can't believe you did that," she said, all focus entirely on me by then. "What the hell is wrong with you? You want to go to jail now? No, Joseph, don't!"

Tina must have finished wiping her boyfriend's burning face, at least long enough for him to take care of the real problem here. Joey charged into my room and leapt on top of me, nothing I could do to stop the immeasurable, rage-induced strength that he had at that point. I sprayed him with mace. I would have shot him if I could have. I would have had every reason to and then some.

He got me to my knees screaming over and over, "Spray mace in my face, huh? Spray mace in my face, huh?" I could not get him off, for a skinny eighteen-year-old kid, he was like a thousand pounds of solid bricks on top of me. Trapped, almost suffocating, strangled. The fear. I could hear Barbara say she was calling the police; I didn't believe her, but I faintly heard her telling someone in a panic that her sons were trying to kill each other. Joey would not let up.

Still pressing down on me, his hands had turned into steel vices, he bit down into my skull, through the hair and deep into the skin like biting into a tough, hairy apple. His teeth were digging into me like a set of knives, the shock almost instantly turned into excruciating pain, and I let out a scream. He would not stop, at least not until Barbara announced that the police had arrived. Christy was barking.

Joey immediately released his bite, got up and ran to the kitchen, whining and crying like a little bitch that his brother had hit him with a bottle of mace. I got up, head throbbing and near bleeding, the bump on the back of my head excruciating to the touch. When I got out to the living room, four policemen were standing in the living room, two with mustaches and all standing with their hands on their hips. Joey was screaming even more from the kitchen, keeping his head under the flow of the faucet, demanding they take me off to jail. Christy kept barking at the cops, she likely thought they were mailmen with the uniforms and hats.

"Don't worry about her," I said to them. "She doesn't bite."

They didn't seem scared of the dog. Didn't blame them for that but why are they always overconfident pricks? It's nothing to respect. One of the cops, an older looking man with glasses, walked into the kitchen to check on Joey. Maybe because he seemed injured, maybe because he was older, I don't know why. The cop asked him if he needed medical attention and Joey lashed out at him.

"Why the fuck aren't you taking him to jail, can't you see what he did to me? What the hell is wrong with you cops?" I never liked cops, but Joey was one true fucking idiot. Tina still had her hand on his shoulder.

"Listen you, I'm not some fifteen-year-old kid, got it?" the old cop said to him with his aging finger. "Now I can tell you are hamming up whatever happened here! You calm down because you look old enough to be taken to jail yourself."

As if Joey's ego could be tamed by an old, agist cop. Another run in with the police. The proverbial strike three had come, this time in Moorestown, where we had only lived up to that point for less than two months. The cops took both of our stories and looked at my bedroom door. I think they got the idea.

Eventually, all of them left. One of the cops with a mustache stopped himself on the way out. That was for him. There's more than one bully in this dishonest world. Barbara despised all of it, cops have perceptions too.

Mustache cop pointed his overconfident finger at my brother. "You like fighting and beating up little kids, you just remember, you are over eighteen and you will wind up in jail." Joey just nodded. Tina still had her hand on his shoulder, still concerned for his injuries; such a nice girl. Then the cop turned to me. Superior in more than just age, though not nearly mature enough to ever be above it.

"And if you like spraying people with mace, you'll end up in juvenile hall, so you better watch it, got it?"

I nodded too, with no pretty girl to console me. I hated myself for it and wanted to tell this strutting jerk to go fuck himself and get a shave. I was only fifteen, true, but the worst of it was, that's exactly what I was expecting. Ego. Fear. Despots. It does not work. Not for me. That cop probably disliked me the most for that reason. He could read my body language just as much as any other bully, and he was looking for it.

Bizarrely, Joey told Tina to get ready to leave, and even packed a small bag for himself. I went back to my room, nowhere else to go. Things became shockingly calm, more fear for what was coming. I could hear Barbara from Joey's room.

"Pack what you can and get out," she said to him. "You know your father is going to throw you out of the house, so just leave now." He didn't argue. Tina did not say a word. Then they were gone. Barbara knocked on my door. Christy was there and marched in to say hello to me, no longer shaking.

"This goddamn dog," Barbara said. "If it were not for her, this wouldn't have happened in the first place. I'm very disappointed in you, Jack. If you just left well enough alone and didn't start a fight, the police would never have had to come here. What the hell are the neighbors going to think about us now? We just moved here. They are going to think we're trashy people, none of them have the damn police in their driveway! Your father is going to be so furious when he gets home. This isn't what I wanted."

They loved the blame game. Joey was now officially out of the house, where he belonged, and they would have to accept that. Worse yet, who would know what had happened here? The cops at the very least filled out an incident report. Whenever they drove past that house, they would remember. Priorities. Barbara told me to go to bed.

"Where the hell was he then?" I asked.

"What?" was her only response, frowning at my challenge to her, as if simultaneously disappointed and confused I could even have any questions. How could I forget my place after any of that night's festivities?

"Dad wasn't here tonight, where the hell was he? Out drinking, and I know it. Just because you don't talk about it, doesn't mean it's not there. I have to sit here all night and be afraid of him. Well, I don't love him. I can't love someone I fear. No one can, they just tell themselves they can; and I don't love that piece of shit bully or his idiot girlfriend. She is accountable for her actions. Denial is wrong. You don't want to hear any of that, and I'm younger so it just doesn't matter anyway!"

Barbara just stared.

"This house is terrible," I said. "and I hate it here! You are not getting rid of my dog! Your drunken husband doesn't want that anyway. He just likes to prove he's an asshole at every chance he gets, just like Joey. Though I'm not allowed to ask why that is, and you still don't give a shit what I think. It's okay, I don't want you to like me. If you don't, and none of you do, then I'm doing something right. Fuck that idiot girl who's here every night, fuck this town, and fuck this trailer!"

More staring. Gawking. I didn't actually want to hurt her. But this was beyond unacceptable. We would never talk about what we would never talk about. That's effective too. Barbara went to her bedroom and closed the door.

I couldn't sleep most of the night. A few hours after Joey left, I heard old Joe pull into the driveway, and I was afraid. I should not have had to be. The next morning, he was screaming his head off at what happened. That's what I woke up to. But when he pulled in his car and parked in front of the trailer that night, he didn't notice a thing. He just stumbled past the broken end table, past all the dents in the walls and the missing picture frame, and right past my lacerated door probably drunk over the limit but he was never wrong anyway because he's a boomer and white. The drama was coming. He went drinking again the following weekend, the one after that too. That trailer could have burned to the ground that night, my brother could have killed me and wanted to. None of the above, had any of that happened, would have stopped the denial train even an inch in momentum, in fact it had to push it forward. This is who we were.

Chapter Twelve

THAT'S MY ROOM

I walked to the bus stop on my first day at the new high school with cuts on my arm, pain in my back and a still throbbing skull. I tried to comb my hair over the bump and hoped no one would notice. It worked, but that may have been because no one was looking at me. If they did, they could probably tell that I was new. Very new, I didn't know one single person there and had never spent more than maybe an hour at that school. Part of me wondered why I was even there. But I found my home room and went through the routine. Right then Michael Del, all the guys; and yes, even Damon, were beginning their sophomore year in Pennsauken, I wasn't. I felt like running through the doors and hitchhiking back to my real school. All for my own good, apparently. Incidentally, there were some black kids in the new school, certainly not as much as the school I wanted to be in. My parents demanded to know how many.

Obviously, that was still way high up on their priority list, even with the half destroyed little house and that maniac out on his own where he belonged. I did wake up the next morning after the fight to old Joe yelling his head off over how disre-spectful Joey had been to him. I stayed in bed until he left for Rickles to collect Joey's house keys; old Joe almost salivating over the opportunity to scream at him in public. It was not as if I couldn't listen to old Joe's morning tirade. He would never admit it, but he knew and liked that I was listening.

"That motherfucker!" he screamed to Barbara's silences. "We raised him, we fed him, we got him away from all those niggers in Pennsauken, and he has the nerve to keep acting up like that! We paid for this house, we paid for that door and picture frame! If he comes back here, I'm going to make him look at it. I should get at least half his salary for the damages. He's over eighteen! Doesn't he realize he can't piss me off like this? I own this fucking house! I should kick his scrawny ass for what he did, but then it'll be me who ends up in jail with all the niggers and not him. The fucking police were right here in this house? How many cops were here last night?"

That incredibly important question. He asked Barbara that specific inquiry at least three times. The hopeless racist. What did black people in Pennsauken or anywhere have to do with any of the crap that went down in the Moorestown trailer? Nothing, and that was a problem to address accordingly. The fact that there were four cops in the house meant there were four human beings who saw us for what we really were. They saw and knew what dirty laundry was there.

Barbara repeated over and over that morning, "What will the neighbors think?" Neither of them met any of the neighbors by that point, as far as I knew. I was less concerned with that, yet this racist and abusive family had been in town less than two months and cops were visiting the house. The neighbors could see the police cars in the driveway. What would they think? Perception is everything; problem solving wasn't.

If it wasn't black people somehow causing all the problems, it was money. More so, the apparent lack of proper respect for it. The house costs money. My door costs money, the end table costs money, the cleaning costs money, and the dog food costs money. Not to mention, my own meals. I was in their debt. Joey was in their debt. How dare the younger children defy them even one iota based on that monetary reason alone? That could not be challenged and the capitalism cup was filled to the brim with ego, rather overflowing by that point.

That was their way. Tough guys. When in doubt, whenever challenged, pull out the "ledger." That invisible booklet that keeps a record of everything they paid for back to my first bottle of baby formula and diaper change to the food I ate right before the fight I evidently started. It's effective. Money cannot be challenged. It's their real "god." The Pszcynacks were Catholics, after all. Catholic guilt is still guilt. I wondered how being raised religious results in incessant racism, flamboyant capitalism, and domestic violence with no real action other than strutting superiority. My parents went to church about once a year. They had to check in with the boss after all, or at least convince themselves they did.

Never once was there a mention or even whisper about the fact that old Joe was out drinking when that fight broke out. After bragging like a professional wrestler about how he was going to confront Joey for his house keys, old Joe tore apart Joey's room. All of it.

Barbara helped him; just as determined to find what they wanted to find. Two aging racists with laughably stern expressions tore apart his room, searching. They looked everywhere for it. Even going through his underwear drawer and tossing everything aside in the hopes, yes, the hopes, of finding drugs; or at least drug paraphernalia.

They really believed that Joey Pszcynack was on drugs. How could he not have been? He went completely berserk the night before, and right in front of his incontestably smart and delightful girlfriend. There would be no other possible explanation for his behavior, for his rage, the ceaseless banging on the door, all the violence, the screaming, the biting; all of it. He had to be on drugs. They found no such thing.

From my bedroom, I did hear old Joe say, "Why does he have beer in his room? He's not twenty-one yet!" Apparently, Joey liked to emulate his father, even despite all the recent defiance. However, the beers he kept in a little mini-fridge in his closet were not going to cut it then. The real problem was: no drugs. That was a major disappointment. The notion that he was on drugs was not an absurd idea, though quite simply not the case. His behavior the night before, that was pure rage, it was pure ego; that was the real Joey Pszcynack that night. No influences whatsoever, at least not of a recreational value.

Not giving up, Barbara even suggested that maybe he keeps needles or something in his car, or perhaps with his friends. Grasping for straws. Joey was not on drugs. If they could not blame his behavior on the drugs, then it was something else, something they would have to take responsibility for. Drugs would have been rather convenient. It could not be on them.

After that, old Joe stormed out of the house, the tires on his car unsurprisingly peeling hard on the pavement as he drove off. Barbara knocked on my door and told me to wake up. I came out.

"Your father is really upset with you, Jack," she said with a confidently disapproving look, slightly shaking her head at me in a vain effort to bring it home. "You shouldn't have started that fight with your brother; he's being kicked out of the house because of the way he acted. But you should be ashamed of yourself for starting it. Don't tell your grandmother this happened. She's probably going to cry, I know it."

So I started the fight. I was responsible for the tears. I supposed someone had to be. They had to take at least some weight of responsibility off of that asshole; or more specifically, themselves. Marie was kept in the dark about the whole thing for about a week, until she noticed the dents in the walls one day and that was that. She cried, and she agreed with Barbara that I instigated everything. That and the whole Tina thing. She was still great.

The fact that Joey was exiled was a rare smart move on my parents' part, even if I found the execution wrought with failings and questions. I may have "only" been fifteen, but I got it. Good thing for them I was younger and that didn't matter. But those people, those people "out there" where Joey was, they mattered. Or what they perceived mattered, at least.

Every time old Joe came through the door, at least when it wasn't late at night, Christy would go crazy in greeting him, even if he was only gone for ten minutes. He loved when she gave him that attention. He loved the dog. I didn't see her standing in the kitchen, but I knew Barbara frowned at Christy's jubilation. Also, blaming the dog for that outrageous fight served her needs rather well. The dog was not going anywhere. I was half surprised. If there was ever a time to really flaunt the ego and regain any face they had lost, getting rid of the dog was a suitable way to do that. The deal I had made with myself if they did was still on.

That aging married couple were heading in two very distinct directions, more after moving to that town. Yet still united in "authority" and capitalism. How could those ever fail? After chewing me out for fighting and therefore defying him, I just stared at old Joe. Anything I could say in my defense was talked over anyway. Inferior. Fighting was fighting. Pepper spray was pepper spray. No requirement. No respect even given a thought in my direction. Never. After all, I was still quite firmly in his debt.

"Did you know he had beer in his room?" old Joe demanded. Barbara only cowered before him. How can anyone love someone they also fear?

"No," I replied. "But I know he steals from Rickles." That didn't matter either. Old Joe only shook his head and waved his hand at me in derision to the consistent theft thing. That was not the issue. At least until the cops found out. In which case they could not believe such a thing would ever happen.

"Well, I have his keys now, he's out of here. Let him go live back in Pennsauken with the all the niggers! You should have seen his face when he saw me standing there waiting for him at that goddamn store he works at. He turned white and almost shit himself. I bet the people around the store wanted to call the cops on me for yelling at him. I could give a flying fuck! Now let's see how he acts when there is no roof over his head. He thinks he can keep beer in his room behind my back? You think I can't go in there whenever I want? That's not his room. That's my room! You don't like that, tough shit! You know it! Money talks and bullshit walks! Now he's walked. Go live in Camden or Pennsauken with the niggers!"

Naturally, no mention of old Joe's drinking. I suppose Joey did act like he owned the house while his father was out every single weekend before and after that night without exception. But his parents, specifically his father actually paid for the house, paid for the roof over his head (as we were so often reminded), and Joey clearly should have had more respect (respect defined as a lack of criticism to his superiors), and his behavior was the antithesis of that entire production.

She was not nearly as wonderful as they thought, but Tina being locked away in the house every night, and old Joe dropping the N-word everyday even after the flight from Pennsauken was not questionable, evidently. It still all came down to money. Inarguable leverage. It's easy when you make your own rules. Problem is no one really follows them but one person.

What got to me more than anything was the lack of professional help; not even the very suggestion of it. We needed it. Joey really needed it. It wasn't that necessary, but they didn't even take me to a "regular" doctor to look at my head or any other injuries. It was okay, I didn't want to see a physician over bruises that would heal, but there was a perfectly good reason not to visit one even if it was worse. Same premise for the question of how many cops were there at the trailer. What would that doctor think? He had to at least ask where the bump on my head came from. Impossible.

This was the drama, for the months that followed, it was all "we paid for this, we paid for that, he's eighteen, he's only fifteen,

Moorestown white and good, Pennsauken black and bad, money, and 'respect' your elders." Constant music in the background. No accountability. Never once did anyone mention the elephant in the room.

There was a greater problem here. For as far back as I could remember, the notion of psychological counseling or therapy was absolutely off limits to my family. In fact, it was generally off limits to my parents' and grandmother Marie's entire generations. Seeing a shrink or a counselor meant one can't handle their own problems. You can't take care of it yourself. If you fall and break your wrist, fine, see a doctor. Though not if you have to explain where it came from in this instance. You have itchy skin, see a dermatologist. A toothache, see a dentist. Bad vision, see the optometrist. However, if you are depressed, despondent, or prone to rage induced fits after being interrupted while showing off in front of your questionable girlfriend, you do not see a doctor for any of that. That would be admitting you are wrong. Not happening.

That's the problem with psychology. Barbara and old Joe, they simply took it one level higher by not visiting or even suggesting the possibility of counseling. It wasn't happening. What if Barbara had taken any or both of her children to a shrink? That means she is a bad mother. She would be admitting it simply by going to such a doctor, or even suggesting it.

Hell, what would the doctor think of my parents? He is human, just like the four cops, and he can make judgments. He might think Barbara is a bad mother. What if neighbors or friends saw her taking her offspring to a counseling office? They might think she is a bad mother. The damned receptionist who checks patients in and collects the revered money for the doctor visit; she may very well think Barbara is a bad mother. Never.

My parents still felt Moorestown was a paradise in comparison to Pennsauken. That particular pigment of a town was the real cure; may the white flyers be praised. My people were still all back in Pennsauken. I did tell Michael every single detail about the fight with my brother and his subsequent exile, he said he saw it coming, as even back when we all played together on Browning Road as kids. Joey and I would get in a fight just about every day. Why would Michael be surprised? I was always less concerned with my own "reputation" in the neighborhood, but good thing no one knew me in my new town. Didn't stop my yearning for the old one.

I pondered all this even as I went about my first day at the new school. Not many people talked to me, some asked if I was from out of town. But I kept to myself almost entirely. I did see one person I knew. That was fork-bracelet guy from the comic book store. He did look at me in the hallways in recognition. He didn't say anything to me though. Still all the same with him; long hair, glasses, heavy metal t-shirt, and tattered jeans. Fashion was obviously not his thing but then again, I was never Mr. Popular in Pennsauken and I knew there was not a chance in hell at anything for me in Moorestown. Beyond that, I continued to swim in the sea of strangers. At least I figured out where my classes were for at least the first day.

None of these strangers knew what had happened shortly before the first day of the new school year. No one knew who I was or where I came from; or that I was happier with at least part of my mind still in Pennsauken. I hated thinking about her, she was a senior in Pennsauken High School by this time. I wondered if Tina told any of her friends about the brawl, or if any of them would even care or disparage her ridiculous relationship with Joey if they knew. Doubtful.

Again, at least she was gone, and I didn't have to have their goofy relationship shoved right in my nose every night. Barbara missed her. No one really knew where Joey was staying those weeks and months following his exile. Most everyone presumed it was maybe at Tina's house for a change but that was unlikely. One of the reasons they never spent any time over there in Pennsauken at the Columbus house was because her parents wouldn't let them hang out in her room with the door closed all night.

I doubt they would take to Joey's newfound homelessness too well, but it was too much to expect they would break up over this. Apparently, Joey spent time sleeping in his car, at least that's what he told everyone for a shot at some sympathy points. Poor guy had nowhere to live. However, we did know where he spent that first night away.

The drama and back and forth over what they paid for kept going on and on between Barbara and old Joe for the whole day and night after the fight and Moorestown police arrival. They were presuming he was staying with Tina, or perhaps with Carl. That was actually more likely and indeed, true. Yet it was only for one night. Apparently, after the fight, Joey drove Tina home and then fell asleep in his car somewhere. Barbara kept lamenting about how unsafe that was and how she felt bad for him now that he was essentially homeless. Old Joe said it was a lesson to be learned. I rather enjoyed them not being around, farce that it all was.

But Joey had nowhere to stay, Tina's parents were not having any of it. It didn't stop them from dating. Not good enough. The very night after the fight, the phone rang. Both my parents and even myself for some reason became flat out silent when it started ringing. They may have been more concerned it was the police, but it was actually worse.

"Hello," Barbara answered with the fake apprehensive confidence. "Yes, this is Mrs. Pszcynack," she continued. Her face told it all, like a terrified deer in headlights at whatever the other person was saying on the phone. How could she ever cover this up?

"Yes, I'm afraid we had some trouble with him last night. He got into a fight with his brother and this was after a string of incidents, unfortunately. His father visited him at work today and confiscated his keys."

I had never seen anyone so uncomfortable to tell the truth verbatim like that. No room for lying then. The call went on, Barbara just listened, doing her best to come off as a competent adult. She was becoming famous, hardly in any good way. On top of that, she was on the phone with someone from Pennsauken. Heresy. She listened on.

"Well, thank you for letting him stay there." Barbara replied. "If you told him it was only for one night, I'm sure he will understand. We did teach him to respect his elders. I appreciate you calling me and telling me. Have a good night."

Before she even placed the phone back down on the receiver Barbara cried, "She probably thinks I'm a terrible mother. God damn it!"

"That was Carl Schimer's mom," Barbara said to old Joe. I just sat on the couch. "He's staying there, but they said it's only for one night. Joseph and Carl are out at the movies right now, and she said she wanted to call me to tell me." A noticeably long silence came through those two while I sat there.

"Now she probably thinks I'm a terrible mother," Barbara said. "Who the hell else is going to find out? Damn her." Barbara marched away to the other side of her small house. There was no one else to discuss this with, and even less to say. This was going so well.

Mrs. Schimer was right to call our house and speak to Joey's parents. It's obvious what happened. Joey could not stay at his damned girlfriend's house and he had little to no friends as a result of his corrosive relationship with her. As if friends are a threat somehow. So, he goes to his one friend and asks to spend the night. Mrs. Schimer was nice enough to let him, but also sensible enough to make it clear it was only briefly. It's obvious the bully was in trouble with his family and even though he is eighteen and therefore an "adult." Mrs. Schimer did the right thing in calling his parents to let them know that he had a place to stay, albeit only for that one night. Mrs. Schimer was responsible, and mature. Give credit where it's due.

Back to square one if we had even left it. Life is all about how you are appraised. Not what you did right or did wrong but how others perceive you to be. We are simply just not supposed to admit that. Mrs. Schimer all but ruined that façade rather quickly and she should have. I doubted even then that this was her intent. Carl's mother did what she felt was right and she was. It was hardly about perception. But that's all we had to offer. The Moorestown house was shaping up to have a character all of its own. That town was denial. I was coming up in it. I wanted to leave. There was only one path to take, unfortunately, and I wasn't sad the way everyone else was. Since day one at that "house," it was still raining inside.

Chapter Thirteen

TOO MUCH HORROR BUSINESS

A few days went by after I started school. Barbara unfortunately ran into Joey and Tina at the mall one night. Apparently, Tina didn't speak, and looked at her strutting boyfriend in fear after Barbara said hello to her. Joey was still copping his ego, pretending to be right in everything he had done, never apologizing, and no therapy. Unheard of. That may have changed him, and change would be an admission of fault. Where did he learn that trick? Sometimes he would come by the little house to get some of his clothes. I was always asked to stay in my room, and he would never come by if old Joe was there. Barbara was always asking if Tina was doing well. Often, she would ask if Joey was ready to come home, usually following up with the lame excuse that the maniac had nowhere to live. She didn't say "maniac." That would not work. This was theatre, not home.

Barbara's main argument was that none of this behavior was 'family' like. No kidding. Her and old Joe developed the daily hobby of deliberating all this back and forth, loving all the drama yet never admitting it. The problem was still black people, old Joe constantly dropping his favorite word, and Joey's consistent defiance. They still believed I started that fight. That was in the books.

"He needs to come home," Barbara said once. Old Joe was

petting the dog and shaking his head at his wife.

"He wanted to play hardball, so we are playing hardball." This was met with over a minute of silence.

"Joe, we are a family," Barbara pleaded. "This is not how we should live. He's only going to listen to you, and I want you to ask him to come home. It's awful. Cathy, Jean and all the other girls are not going through this. Their husbands don't fight with their sons. I don't deserve this shit! My mother is worried sick all the time. It's not fair to Tina, either. I don't even know what she is thinking of us. We can't live like this!"

"That's not going to happen," old Joe said after an all-too-common pause. "I paid for his food and clothes all his life. All those goddamned toys they got for Christmas, who do you think paid for those? I put a roof over his head, moved to a nice house away from all the fucking niggers, and he decided he didn't want to appreciate any of that. This is what he gets. He blew it. You want me to beg him? Kiss his ass? Tell him it will all be all right and to come home? Fuck you!"

More silence. I was attending a poorly acted play every night in that trailer since Joey was kicked out where he belonged and it was still all about Tina, and Barbara's friends from Nineteen-Fifty something. It was always about how she's perceived, as if happiness is only achieved by the comparison to or assessment of another. I always tried to resist the erroneous notion that so many people behaved like that then and forever after. That didn't make it less wrong.

None of this mattered to old Joe. Joey had done something worse than flipping out to the point that cops had to arrive at "his" house. Joey had done something worse that having beer in his room and even worse than not having any drugs in his room. It was not his room anyway. Apparently, we were only tenants, renters living there at the landlord's grace and discretion. Joey slapped all that in the face. No opposition, that's how it works. For them, anyway. Fine deal. He was over eighteen, after all. I never met too many adults in life even decades later. I didn't know any then.

This was a stare down. A game to see who would admit wrong-doing first. I had no leg to stand on, no respect granted due to entering the world after all of them, but Joey had something. He also had that hot girlfriend. None of this would stand up to pride. Unwritten rules. Never admit you are wrong, or even imply it. Never apologize. Never show love. It builds character, though it would never be mine.

While all this continued on and on, I was reminded that not only was I entirely incongruous within my own family, but I also hated my own name. Physical Education classes, or simply "gym" as we called it, began on the last day of my first week at the new high school. Mr. Donahue, one of the few teachers in this school that I would ever actually half respect, did a roll call for each of our names while we sat on the gymnasium bleachers, still in plain clothes, a big giant M on the wall leering down at me. So much history in that gym, and I missed it all. Not so much of a loss. That school was for them, not me. I supposed I would feel even worse had I really cared about them at all. On paper, I was still a student.

"Where is…" Mr. Donahue paused, and I knew what was coming. "Jack Puh…Puh…Puh…Pushin-u-iah-kah." For shit's sake, is the name really that bad?

"Right here," I said while raising my hand and slightly rolling my eyes. He gave me a short thanks and moved on to the rest of his roster. It turned out fork-bracelet guy was in my gym class with me. His real name was Rob Sippen. The first day of gym class was nothing but role calls and threats that if we do not change into school issued gym shorts for the two class periods, that counts as a cut class. Rob would later almost fail out of school his senior year for hardly ever changing his clothes. For the first day after Donahue's name humiliation, of which I could do absolutely nothing, the students had to just hang around until final class period. Rob came by and sat next to me.

He looked like he never changed clothes at all. Still in ripped jeans, tattered shoes, long black hair with the thick glasses and of course, the Metallica shirt and accompanying fork bracelet. His own fashion statement, I supposed. At least it was something unique.

"Hi, I'm Rob," he said while offering his hand. I shook it and told him my name. "I see you at the comic book store a lot. You're new here right? From where?" I told him I was from Pennsauken, and my parents moved me there a month or so ago. It seemed though Rob himself had been in that town a long time, but was actually not there, almost as I was not. Just not quite.

"That sucks you moved before your sophomore year. At least there is a comic store near you for you to go to. I do not read comics much anymore. I used to all the time, and I thought working at the comic book store would be fun. Now I can't stand them. Sensory overload. I'm like a vampire working as a lifeguard most of the time now."

I still loved my at least bi-weekly visits to Comic World. Even with Joey nicely gone, I still didn't want to spend any more time at home than absolutely necessary. But that wasn't Rob's problem. I was surprised how friendly he turned out to be. I wanted to ask him what the hell the fork bracelet thing was for but held back, only commenting to him that I used to be scared of Metallica, as my best friend's older brother and his pals were into that band a few years back. I don't know why it was so then, but I just didn't get into heavy metal music; probably because of Kenny Del and his cooler and scarier friends. I still missed that town.

"I've listened to them forever," Rob said. "I never saw them live but they were always a thing, and it was my twin brothers that turned me on to rock music in the first place. I play the guitar too, even have my own band. It's a garage band, sure, we never played live before, but they are having a Battle of the Bands show right here at the school next month and we are probably going to be in it."

"That's cool," I tell him. "I actually used to be a drummer back in middle school."

Rob's face lit up. "We've been looking for a drummer! You want to try out?"

I didn't have any idea what to say to him. "Well, I don't really have much experience with it," I said.

"That's fine! Most of us have only been doing this for a little while. You should try out! Our old drummer left his drum set at Ian's house. That's out bassist. The set hasn't been picked up yet, so sometimes we use it."

"Well, the thing is, I'm not very good at it. I suck, actually."

"That's okay! We suck too!"

I just laughed out loud at him, and he was laughing with me. I was actually enjoying him. Somehow in the midst of our mutual clowning, I agreed to try out for this band. Were they a Metallica rip off? Would I have to learn a bunch of rock songs? I never sat on a drum set in my life, it was all school orchestra or marching band music with Damon and I in the back on drums, and doing it badly. That was the extent of my entire musical experience. Now I was about to play in a local rock band in a town I could not have cared less about.

I ran into Rob again later that day, near the school buses. He was talking to someone I didn't know (which was still everyone), I never even learned his name. Bald kid with a badly growing beard. He didn't seem to mind who I was but probably didn't want me to be there. New is scary. Rob beckoned me over.

"This is our new drummer," he said to the other kid without introducing us. I told both of them I didn't know if I would join yet and I was not very good as a drummer.

"You'll be fine," Rob said, shaking his head with a smile. "You want a smoke, Jack?"

I just looked at him. I never smoked a cigarette in my life, and I didn't want to, let alone right outside school. Was he crazy? I told him no thanks, and Rob just shrugged, lighting up his cigarette and smoking quickly, keeping his eyes alert for what I could presume were teachers or a principal or the like. They were looking. Rob's clothes reeked of smoke, I noticed that even in my visits to Comic World. The smell alone occasionally gave me headaches.

While he and his friend smoked in front of me, I actually figured out some follow up questions.

"Rob, what is the band's name anyway?"

He didn't remove the cigarette from his mouth and said "Xonxe." I just looked at him.

"What?"

"Xonxe," he said again. It sounded like "Zon-ey" or some such. It seemed such a ridiculous name for a band. I learned rather quickly that ridiculous was the point.

"We're a punk rock band," Rob said. "A cheesy punk rock band, yes, but still punk rock."

"What does the name mean?" I asked him.

"You can ask Craig when you meet him. He's our lead singer and the band and name were all his ideas."

Craig. I didn't know who he was either. Could never have imagined what he looked like considering Rob's appearance, and these were all kids from a rich town. What the hell was all this? Because Craig was evidently mysterious, and Ian the bass player didn't go to our high school (turns out he attended a private school all the way out in Pennsylvania every day, even though he lived in Moorestown), we could not find the time to meet until after school the following week. I didn't mention to Michael or my parents that there was a band thing in the works; or even that I sort of made new friends in the process. It was simply better to keep it all quiet, and most of the time I didn't want to talk to my family anyway. My life was mine, not ours.

It was one of Rob's brothers that gave him and I a ride to the practice place house for my "try out." This brother looked much more strait-laced than Rob, even wearing a tie when he drove us, like he had some kind of business meeting to attend that day. He actually seemed to get along with his younger brother. I was simply jealous over something so natural to them. No, I was admittedly hurt by comparison. There was something outside the trailer, and it was all happening, yet not for me.

Rob and I were dropped off in the far side of town, out in the "boonies" as Rob put it; at a house that was almost the size of the mansions I had only seen in movies up to that point. I was never one then or ever to really be impressed by real estate, yet this place was huge and somehow barely visible from the street for all the trees and the long driveway going up to the gigantic house. It didn't seem like a real house or neighborhood to me.

Too rich, and way too quiet. No one was around, as if the neighborhood was deserted, however magnificent. It was as if these rich people owned these enormous houses in backwoods neighborhoods away from the peasants and proud of it, yet somehow, no one was ever home. None of the neighbors seemed to really occupy the houses they owned. Where were they? Nothing was lived in, all immaculate and abandoned. All to ourselves. That was Ian Teasdale's house.

Rob simply opened the front door and walked in as if he did that all the time. "His parents are never home," Rob explained to my confused expression. We walked through the large hallways, past a library room, then a study, and into a kitchen with a counter island that looked bigger than the Pszcynack house in Moorestown. A tall hippie-like character with long blonde dreadlocks and a black leather jacket with a creepy skull stenciled on the back was sitting at the island shoving French toast into his mouth. He took notice of us and wiped his hands on his shirt then walked over to me.

"Hi, I'm Ian. It's nice to meet you," he said with his mouth still full of food. Up close I could see Ian had a large goatee disconnected from long sideburns in addition to the dreadlocks. He had thick earrings through both ears. Like Rob, he reeked of cigarette smoke. He did not give off the impression of a rich kid to me at all. Well, that was two of the guys. For the first time in my life, I felt weird for having short hair, and smelling a lot better than anyone around me. It didn't really bother me so much on its own, but I was not smoking.

Then I met him. Craig Doyle was by far and beyond the most imposing and bizarre individual I had ever met in my entire life at that point, and he was actually younger than me; he just didn't look it. He was something I was not ready for at all the day I joined Xonxe. I could try, but never expect the unexpected like him. No different then or any other day though. Still a stranger in a strange land. Yet somehow even among those freaks, I started to feel welcome, at least for a short while.

The even taller teenager opened the glass doors from the back porch to the kitchen. Craig stamped a fresh cigarette out in an ashtray next to the door and he came in. I could barely see his face. He had a thinly grown beard of red hair, and had freckles all about his arms, even amidst the zombies, strippers, and skulls tattooed all over him. He was a ginger, but the hair on top of his head was dyed pitch black and it ran down in front of his face in a single lock that made it hard to see his face at all. I didn't know how the guy could even see.

Craig shook my hand. He was strong, intense like he was hopped up on coffee all the time. I was slowly getting used to the cigarette reek, which was even worse on Craig. Whenever he talked or smiled, I could see yellowish slime across his teeth from all the smoking. Even with the cigarettes, the freckles and the tattoos, he looked like he had not showered in a week. He hadn't, truth be told. Craig was wearing a tattered old white t-shirt with an image of a terrified cop with a gun in his mouth. The shirt was slightly torn as well as his jeans which were draped with a rather long metal chain to his wallet.

"So, you are our new drummer," Craig said to me through the hair. That was harder to get used to. "We are glad to have you."

Again, the presumption that I was their drummer already. I had not played in years. This was going to be embarrassing. We walked downstairs into the basement where they had band practice. We had to go through a room filled with pottery and dried clay strown about the tables. Ian explained his father was into pottery and fashioned handmade pots and vases. Ian seemed so artsy, as if he belonged at a museum himself. They all did in a way. Not me, not yet anyway.

"Ian's dad made me this," Rob said, holding up his wrist. One mystery solved. I asked him why he wanted a bent fork as a bracelet.

"Because nobody else would ever have one," he replied. Fair point.

Rob and Ian strapped on their guitars. Ian's was a white bass that looked almost brand new. Rob's guitar was red with green knobs at the strings, and had a sticker of the same skull that was on the back of Ian's jacket. Craig picked up his microphone and pointed to the drum set in the middle of the practice room.

"This kit used to belong to our last drummer," Craig explained. "He was older than us, in college actually. He left because we were not good enough, I wanted to kick him out because he was too good, not to mention an asshole. So, we can use this until whenever he decides to pick up his own drum set."

I sat down at the kit, picked up the withered drumsticks from the floor. This was a first. I didn't even know what they wanted to play. Metallica songs? Those were going to be hard, even for garage rock standards.

"Craig, why is the band called Xonxe?" I asked him. Rob and Ian laughed. Again, Craig just looked at me through the hair in his face.

"Xonxe is the Latin term for honkey, or at least the closest to that word in Latin you can get."

"Honkey?" I asked him.

"Yeah, honkey is a funny word," said Craig. "I've never been called that, mostly because none of us were alive yet in the early seventies. The racist slur never really took off, and it takes a lot more to offend me. Still funny though. I came up with the name when Ian and I first started playing, then it was more or less a real band when Rob joined. We've all known each other since kindergarten, though Ian goes to that Friends school in Pennsy."

I stifled my laughter. I didn't even know why their band name was funny, but it was. I could almost hear music in the background just being in a room with those guys. Clown music at a carnival perhaps, but welcome all the same. We had not even started playing yet. Completely ridiculous, and I liked it. They've known each other a long time and I've been in town for less than two months, in school only a few days, and there I was among them. Apparently, they really wanted me there. All the same, I didn't know how to play.

"I'm not that good, you know. I'm not sure if I'm going to work out here," I said.

"Rob told us," Craig said while shrugging his shoulders. "We all suck at this. That's why you are good for us. It's punk rock anyway, no one here is in the Beatles." Craig looked at me, really noticing that I was nervous, and that even in this lackluster punk band, I had no idea what I was doing.

"Hold on a second, guys," Craig said as he put down his microphone and began to sift through a bunch of records and cassette tapes lying about the amplifiers. I didn't recognize any of the band names, yet Craig was going about them as if they were all his close friends. That was another issue I saw. These guys were "cool" when it came to music. They listened to artists and bands no one has ever heard of, and had certainly never been on T.V. or the radio. Nothing mainstream. Exclusive. It was like I was dropped into another world through hardcore punk rock music, and I wanted to know everything.

"We have a lot of original songs that I wrote and I can teach you everything," Craig explained. "We still like to do a lot of covers though. We have a hell of a lot of influence from all the old school punk bands. I can start you off with something you can catch on to easily enough. You know the Ramones?"

That band I had heard off. The rest was all a mystery. Craig played a few songs for me and then suggested we play along. It was all disorganized incoherent noise for a while, not to mention the guys had to stop for cigarette breaks every twenty minutes or so. Avoiding creative burnout, that's how Rob put it. Still, I was able to get the hang of the fast and heavy music, riding the hi-hat and snare drum along with kicking the bass drum pedal mostly correctly as I went. It all sounded awful. But it was fun. The music was insane. Loud, angry, and intense, and that was being nice. Livid sound and lyrics. Pissed off. Furious. This was something for me.

"We're going with you." is all Craig said after we were finished. Somehow I caught on. I was a punk rocker. We could only practice so often because of Ian's erratic schedule of going back and forth out of state to school. Craig himself was even more inconsistent. He was around at home more often, he lived not far from me, in the poor people's section of Moorestown. His dad was a plumber or something. Craig went to my high school, but he took the little bus to school. I didn't ask him why. I didn't really have to.

The previous Xonxe drummer picked up his drum set shortly after that first practice I had, apparently upset that the band had a new drummer, even one with days experience. He left us with no drums. That was a new problem. To my complete shock, Barbara and old Joe actually bought me a set of my own. It was used, posted by someone in the newspaper, but it would do just fine. I didn't understand why at first, but was glad to have it.

It more or less hit me soon after. I told Barbara that I was offered to join a local garage band with guys I met at school and she immediately said, "do it." I supposed they wanted me involved with something. They knew I was not into sports and I told them point blank I was not interested in anything Moorestown had to offer. I was only into moping in my room and reading comic books. They hated that; for themselves, but they hated it. So the band was welcome, at least at first. Jack Pszcynack had been thrown a bone.

Despite the Joey situation, they were enjoying that town. No distasteful colors, no Grace Bergen, and they had more or less the same commute to wherever they went. Even with Joey out of the house, nothing changed for him. He had graduated already, and of course nothing changed with the girlfriend. All of them just enjoyed not being around black people, hell, they still thought they were heroes for getting me away from that and my hometown. I could not imagine what I was going to tell Michael about Xonxe. I would have given up the punk rock thing in a heartbeat to be in my hometown with him again. But I supposed I didn't have to.

I needed more of that music. We still had that gig coming up in less than two months. The practices went on, with Craig and Ian actually devoting more time to it now that they had a full band they were happy with. Craig let me listen and practice to more of the punk rock music. Incredible names like Black Flag, the Circle Jerks, Fear, Minor Threat, and so many others. Most if not all of these bands had long since broken up by the early to middle eighties. We were all in kindergarten or first grade around then. Denied by happenstance of time. It's like we were somehow reviving that past. We were happier there.

Punk rock was by some means both angry and exciting all at the same time, speaking to that pissed off person I had been for so long, and was becoming even more since moving to that damned town. The guys had been here all their lives and they hated it too. This was our escape, our own way out of it, however tortuously we were still imprisoned there. Rejects. My kind of people, though I had always wished it otherwise.

It was new to me and I could not get enough. Craig had written songs we worked on but playing a cover of any of those old bands was too much fun. We had to perform some live, and show everyone else the past we were never a part of, yet somehow were. I had to know everything about those bands, or those legends. Reliving a past I never had. Music in the background, indeed.

Then there was the Misfits. Everything I had heard up to that point was elevator music compared to how they affected me and my perception of what music was and could be. This was the punk band that Xonxe quite simply worshiped. It was

Craig who introduced me to the Misfits, this phenomenon that once existed in the past, in our very own state in fact. Craig and the other guys insisted that we were going to play a Misfits song at the upcoming show. Craig collected vinyl records in addition to the cassette tapes that were available in stores at the time. He played some songs for me and showed me the record covers. For all my nerdiness and pop culture persona, never once before could I have been mesmerized by anything else.

The Misfits were not just an old punk rock band, they were horror punk. The album covers were adorned with creepy photos and monsters; which immediately reminded me of watching Dracula movies with my grandfather so many years ago. Fear. The good kind. The Misfits band members themselves wore their hair in their faces like Craig, which I was told was called a "devilock," and the band's logo was the very skull that Ian had on his jacket and Rob on his guitar, not to mention one of Craig's many tattoos. Horror movies and punk rock, the perfect mix of attitude and image. This was more than music. This was everything.

Not only the horror motif, but this band was from New Jersey, long since passed away as a group themselves. Legends. Something from the distant past. Mystique. Apparently, Metallica themselves would often say the Misfits were one of their favorite bands and influences. If the best of the metal world thought these guys were legends, then this band was on a whole new level I had never imagined possible, and I wanted to know everything about it. Craig made copies of what he had and gave them to me, even though I kept my drum set mostly at Ian's,

I had to learn all the songs, and I could not wait for Xonxe's first show.

I was going to invite Michael. Both him and the Pennsauken visits themselves remained my priority. I thought he might like the punk rock guys but didn't know how they could ever possibly mix. It was all so different in every way, shape, and form. Pennsauken was where I was from, what I identified as my home. Yet I wasn't there, and life was moving on for Michael and everyone in my old life too. Nothing but drama at home every day, old Joe never backing down or letting Joey back home. Joey would still say he didn't want to return. All fine with me.

On top of all that, my friend Michael was a normal guy from a town twenty minutes away, but it may as well have been in China for all anyone knew. How could he ever get into punk rock and mesh with these goofballs that I linked up with? They were all insane, and not to mention rich, apart from Craig. I didn't quite get it then. I saw teenagers. Crazy, yes, but how much difference could there be? I didn't want there to be as much as there actually was. I wanted to fit in. I loved the music, not the cigarettes, which was a fixation for all of them. We practiced as much as we could, and I never saw Ian's parents there once.

One day when we were finishing up practice, I saw Ian packing up a second bass guitar, a brown one, and on the guitar case itself was the word "Sugar." I wondered why that particular label. As it turned out, he named his guitars.

"Why is it called Sugar?" I asked him.

"Because it's sweet!" he said in that goofy court jester voice of his. I just had to know.

"What about the white bass you used on my first day in the band? What's that called?"

"Anorexic Bitch!"

This just kept getting better. Who were these guys? "Why do you call it that?" Ian just looked at me half confused, as if I should have known.

"Because it's white and it's thin, and I can't get it to do what I want it to do," he explained.

Then he reached for a cigarette that looked like he rolled himself, not from the store. How the hell did these guys get so many smokes if they were under eighteen? Ian did look a lot older, and apparently Rob's brother bought them cigarettes if they had the money. Though sometimes I did see Rob's mother pick him up for rides. Craig and I sometimes walked home together. It always took forever but the long walk through town wasn't the Pszcynack house, so good enough. More punk rock education from the professor.

After practicing that day, Craig wanted to head to the roof. There was a walkable path from one of the bedrooms in Ian's house, also abandoned except for old books and records. We walked outside and sat on top of the house, looking over the rich neighborhood and forests of backyards, many of which had inground pools and even tennis courts. No one was swimming or playing. Quite a view from on top of Ian's home. I thought they wanted to smoke more. They did.

"I know you don't smoke, Jack," said Craig. "But we go up

here for something else."

Ian lit up one of his homemade cigarettes and I realized it wasn't tobacco. They passed it around between them, inhaling heavily and giving me that look that said "try." I didn't know what to say. I didn't say anything. I never smoked cigarettes. Not for me. I was a straightlaced kid for the most part. No drinking. That was for louts like Joey and his father. Not happening. Not for me. Then again, the Pszcynacks were never into smoking weed. That was not for them. Then it became interesting. I reached out to Craig and he passed me the joint. That nervous fear was there yet remarkably soon, relaxed. We were up high on that enormous house, and soon thereafter even higher than that.

Chapter Fourteen

STARS IN HEAVEN

That first season in Moorestown passed by in a blink. The Xonxe show was an absolute blast, even though probably everyone but us absolutely hated it. We were the second band of the night, and soon forgotten. That is, except for all the other bands and their ilk telling us how terrible we were, how much punk rock was awful, and that our band would never go anywhere. I admit it was a bit of a calamity, so much fun as it was. Rob's amplifier shorted out at least twice in the middle of our set, we were never admitting we were "great" and on top of that, it was punk rock, which was always an acquired taste, that being an understatement there. Hardy befitting any existing trends, but that was the point. I wondered if the audience didn't like the abrasive music or that they simply didn't like that we were so pissed off and deliberately something they were not prepared for. Craig welcomed all the indignation we received; all of us did. If we turned off all those trendy, unoriginal, snobbish rich kids; then clearly, we were doing something right.

Punk rock, even our own particular brand of punk rock,

was intentionally offensive. People needed that more than they would ever admit. We were saying "fuck you" through lurid and pulsating music, even if it was only that to us. Maybe they didn't like the unexpected; or even being indirectly told there was something wrong with their world we lived in. We offended everyone, and we were still waiting to hear their point. If everything is offensive, then nothing is. We had more fun than any one of them ever could have by tossing the entirety of their misgivings to the wind.

Our homage cover of the Misfits was probably our best song, working very well live even if played by a bunch of teenagers with minimal talent even for punk rock. It was more fun than only listening to them at home, and even though few and far between in our band's career, I wanted more live shows to perform at, and more people to horrify. Michael and some of the guys from Pennsauken showed up to watch the show. They said they liked it except for the fact that it was so loud they couldn't hear themselves think. It was nice to see my home life meld with the new world, even if only for one night.

None of our parents showed up for the show which was fine with all of us. Band practices continued with the erratic schedule we always had with cigarette and weed breaks in between and after. Xonxe was a hobby at best. The band was disorganized, and we accepted it for whatever it was. Any Pennsauken visits I could garner were still priority one for me any day. Rob would sometimes miss practice due to working, Ian because of Pennsylvania school, and Craig because he was Craig.

In essence, Pennsauken became my excuse for missing band

practices, if they were even planned at all. I couldn't lose my friends from home. It was Michael, Alfie, Johnny, and Adam (often referred to as Shag), who all came from Pennsauken in one variation or the other, Alfie and Johnny were actually Longfellow Elementary alumni like Michael and I, but it was a different world, a completely different time by high school. I had friends to hang out with on weekends in my hometown. I wasn't missing out on any of it, even if I was by then the guy from the other school.

Xonxe did hang out together in Moorestown all the same. Old Joe was never around to meet them, and it took Barbara some getting used to that she never really got used to after meeting those guys, especially Craig. Joey was still out of the house; Barbara had asked me not to mention it but I did anyway. Denial wasn't for me. The band guys didn't judge that scenario anyway. I managed to get my hands on an old V. H. S. tape that had a broken, half-garbled, grainy video recording of an ancient Misfits show and invited the guys over to my house to watch it. Even Christy thought they were weird, but it was just more people to pet her and play with. Basset hounds have naturally bloodshot eyes, Craig would pet the dog and said she was smoking too many blunts. Christy's tail never stopped wagging.

After we watched the show on T.V., Craig and Ian decided to walk back to Craig's place, perhaps for a bit more autonomy. I wasn't letting on that we smoked special cigarettes even though I doubt Barbara had any idea what that would even smell like. Rob had to call his mom for a ride, so we let him use the phone. Rob had to explain that my house was down the street from the comic book store, asking me for the address and landmarks so Mrs. Sippen could find it.

"Tell her the house is on the corner," I said while Rob was still on the phone. "It's a really big yard, and a really small house."

"It's not a small house!" Barbara shrieked as she barged into the T.V. room, clenching both her fists and gritting her teeth to the point I thought she might crack them; quite adequate ferocity to make any Xonxe member pause. "It's a big house, just because it's on a big lot doesn't mean that it's small. The house is perfectly fine! Stop saying it's a small house, dammit!"

That went down well. The guys gazed at the walls in fear. No one challenged her point, ignorant that it was. Bullies. This is where life had come in the so short a time since moving from Browning Road. Joey was out of the house after trying to kill me, old Joe was almost always out drinking, yet the priority here was defending the perception of the size of a little house that was somehow not little. I remember Craig once telling me he could always feel the tension in my house, except for the dog of course. Every single time he was there he thought it was probably better we were somewhere else. Coming from him, that was not at all encouraging.

Rob's mother eventually found the house. Craig and Ian had already left. Barbara went out of her way to introduce herself to Mrs. Sippen and she did get a hello in return, however distant. Mrs. Sippen, rather heavy set with a three hundred dollar haircut, seemed nice enough but something was off that I just didn't get at the time. Barbara did. She simply denied what it was. It could not be true, or at least not acknowledged. After the subtly awkward pleasantries, Rob and his mom drove off in their luxurious SUV.

A little over a month later, New Year's Eve rolled around and Joey was still not living with us. No one knew where he was living all this time and he wouldn't speak of it. He just had that arrogant smirk on his face every time he happened to come by. He fought with old Joe too much and deliberately would not visit or get anything he wanted if the older bully was around.

Barbara and Marie announced (while old Joe was gone) that Joey and Tina would be visiting us for part of that New Year's Eve, all but making me want to throw up. I wasn't afraid of him and didn't expect any more fighting. Yet the questions. What the hell was the purpose of this visit other than theatre? When we were kids, Marie and my grandfather would always visit on New Year's Eve, that day was another holiday among the many at year's end. Old Joe used to be there back then, noticeably less so as time went on.

That year he was well away and gone for the night. It was New Year's Eve, after all. I knew that this is why they invited Joey and his girl. Running some more interference and damage control, Barbara told me that night that old Joe had gotten a second job. She said the bar he always went to needed his help and he would be bartending that night. No other nights, evidently, just that one.

Barbara never looked me in the eye when lying, which was becoming even more frequent. That was bad enough on its own, and even in my young punk rock mind, the premise of that particular lie is what still vexed me to the point of nearly breaking out in a sweat thinking about it, and think, I did. It's the tried, albeit tired, and true manipulator of all of them: money. I knew old Joe wasn't actually bartending, but drinking his ass off and dangerously driving home later; but the lie was clever, and that was good enough. I didn't miss him, becoming ever more allergic to dishonesty, that difference itself probably brought the deceit out of them even more. The jerk in knee-jerk.

As it always was, money could not be challenged. So old Joe was "sacrificing" for all of us. For me. Therefore, I cannot question why he was not home on New Year's Eve, just as he was not home the night Joey tried to kill me. Not allowed to mention that point either. It was a lame excuse so I asked anyway.

"He's never bartended before, where did this come from?" I asked.

Barbara's face turned beat red, just like it did when I told Rob we had a small house in a big yard.

"This house and your food cost money, Jack!" Barbara snapped. "I swear, I don't know what's wrong with you anymore. Joseph is still out of the house and Christmas has already passed. This is so hard on me. You don't know, and you don't seem to fucking care. Your father and I deserve stars in heaven." She sighed louder than Craig's screamed at band practice, and longer at that.

By then, I did not believe in heaven. For the lack of any evidence, it seemed more like a made-up theme park invented to comfort the fear of dying, not to mention the arrogance of being upset at only living once. The party is over at some point. Too important to be mortal. Be that as it may, I didn't see money was any justifiable pretext for abuse, or a shield from any questions. That all said, the fact that old Joe was out having it up again didn't upset me as much as being informed that Joey and Tina were by then engaged.

Yes, engaged. He was still out of the house, with apparently no home to live in. His girlfriend was still in high school, not even eighteen herself at that point and he got her a ring. She witnessed him go berserk and nearly kill his brother, and continued dating him nonetheless and then it was somehow completely unquestionable she would want to marry him. Bad comedy. It didn't make sense to me then, but as time went on, and with later firsthand experience, I began to realize that placing a ring on a girl's finger was dropping an anchor to a drifting, turbulent, or otherwise sinking ship. So in that light, it all made perfect sense.

Those four months or so that Joey was out of the little house, those were uncertain times. What better occasion to then put a ring on a girlfriend's finger? Call it an insurance policy, something to make sure she would not drift away. After all, she was still in high school and Joey was not. There were other guys at that school who could have their eyes on Tina. The notion that she did not have other options was beyond absurd, and Joey knew it. Not so absurd as her decision to accept that ring from him but then again, engagements were somehow both cute and incontrovertible. Being engaged. Perhaps it made her feel like an adult even if she never would be.

Barbara and Marie were ecstatic to learn they were engaged. Joey and Tina had not even arrived yet, yet still they were going on and on about how wonderful it was, and that this farce was somehow the beginning of a cure for the epidemic after the fight and police visit. All the subsequent drama since was by then healing, thanks to this new turn of events. Old Joe was still out drinking. Though there was a larger problem.

"Jack," Marie told me. "I want you to shake hands with your brother when he arrives. It's all getting better starting tonight. Say 'welcome to the family' to Tina. Okay?"

"Not happening," I replied. Then Marie's jaw hit the floor. Unthinkable.

"I don't understand you, Jack. Now what is the problem?" Marie asked. I started to wonder if she was drinking too. This was real, and that disappointment was far too akin to the failed search for drugs in Joey's room. Nothing else to blame.

"This is ridiculous!" I explained, by then wanting nothing more than to get back to my comic books and punk albums. I started moving. "He hasn't changed at all, and you know it. You think those two getting engaged is a good thing? It's a joke, at best. Why the hell is that girl even dating that monster in the first place? This is wrong."

"Stop it, Jack! Now things have been bad here. Think of your mother. This is the first step in the healing process. Tina is a sweet girl; you should be proud to have her as a sister-in-law."

"No. It's wrong."

Marie walked away and I shut my door. No accommodations. Alone again. Thankfully the punk rock was louder than the comics. I stayed in my room most of the night, though I did eventually come out. Joey and I ignored each other, as did Tina. She didn't give me any acknowledgement, not that I wanted one. No doubt I was the villain in her eyes. What that girl refused to know. No fighting occurred even if that was entirely possible. Barbara and Marie beckoned to me to say hello to them, Barbara even snapping her fingers and frowning at me. I got some food that they paid for from the kitchen and tossed some down to Christy.

Marie was holding Tina's outstretched hand, studying the rock on her finger up close. For some reason, she had to look at it several times, and that was not due to poor vision. I stayed in the kitchen to keep it all out of sight, but Marie marched in after me while Barbara and Tina were discussing wedding plans. Marie placed her hands on her hips and was shaking her head at me. The wretched.

Still younger, and still accountable for that fight breaking out. Now dressed always in black; the black jeans, black t-shirt with the skull on it, all of it and the attitude to match. I never changed my hair or got any piercings or tattoos, but the punk rock was clear and present more than anything then. Always reminded how offended they were. Being "offended" is hardly an argument on its own, though for some reason, we so often like to treat it as such.

"Jack," Marie insisted. "Go out there and talk to your brother, damn it. They are talking about wedding plans, you will likely be in the wedding party, maybe even the best man. Won't that be wonderful? Go out into the living room and tell him it would be your honor."

I knew I was a terrible liar, and didn't see why that was wrong. She did.

"Grandma, I'm not indulging in this nonsense. This isn't good. He's a criminal, abusive, and in dire need of counseling; and he has not answered for what he's done. Denial is not going to make any of that go away."

"Oh, shut the hell up, Jack!" With that, Marie barged back into the living room to ogle over Tina's ring. I walked past all of them and stayed in my room to read and listen to more obnoxious rock n' roll. I stayed inside there long after Joey and Tina left, ignoring Barbara's knock on my door to tell me they were leaving.

Maybe it was the music that was causing all these apparent problems within me. Perhaps it had nothing to do with what was going on behind those doors, in either house. Clearly, everyone had the opposite opinion to me, so I must have been wrong. Truth was, the music that was telling me that it was okay, and making me feel better about not accommodating ridiculous denial. It was okay to disagree. It was okay to call a spade a spade.

The rifts were widening, sure. I just didn't see any reason to indulge in any of it. I still didn't want to be there, I'd rather have been in Pennsauken, or failing that, at band practice with Xonxe. Anywhere but there. It was too dishonest. Bullshiters were always worse than liars. They didn't know they were lying because the truth was completely irrelevant. All far more dangerous than punk rock, horror movies, or skulls. I felt more comfortable among the dead.

Old Joe found out later that Joey and Tina were at the house he owned that night, and that they were engaged. He seemed to like the outrageous marriage idea, but the ego train didn't stop for another couple of weeks into January. It was getting harder for Joey to stay at friends' houses, or sleep in his car, wherever he was. He was running out of time, as well as space. With little fanfare, he asked to come home. Barbara insisted the fighting between him and old Joe cease and he came home after some four months of living away. Of course, the prevailing theme after that was "forget about it." No resolution. Repudiation, that was easier. Be it all immature was of no consequence. Convenient.

There was at least some pathetic drama that night he returned. That, and a hell of a lot of false confidence. When Joey walked through the door, now back at the little house again, old Joe was sitting in the kitchen, and Barbara demanded the two of them shake hands. Neither of them said a word, yet nevertheless buckled under Barbara's apparent sense of superiority on the matter, and then loosely shook hands as if they were each on an interview they didn't want to be on. Joey went back to his room. As he walked Barbara didn't look at the still damaged walls and door, and then demanded Joey and I shake hands as well. Joey kept walking. I simply stated, "Hell no."

Old Joe shook his head with the usual disregard. He said he would talk to me the next day on this issue. What I had to say or think was below even the slightest consideration. Barbara walked away in disgust. No one said a word to each other the entire night, and the fight, the drama, the mania, the police, the neighbors, the lack of any psychological counseling whatsoever, or even any mention of it; all of that was persona non grata. Unmentionable. Sacrilege. Only to be met with the worst and therefore most effective reaction imaginable: silence.

Old Joe never 'talked to me'. In fact, we spoke a hell of a lot less from then on, and that was saying something. What mattered was that it was all coming back. Nothing changed and all the tensions brought on by Tina being there every night under the cloak of Joey's ego had then returned full force. Old Joe drinking (that never stopped), Barbara (and her mother) still demanding I say hello to the trophy girlfriend and looking at me as if I was from Mars if I would not. As if they could not understand even for a moment why I would have any problem with any of it. None of this did well for the collective self-esteem; and I was not capable of denial. An outcast in my own home for that particular disability. It was "their" home, not mine. How could I forget?

A couple of days passed after Joey's return. It was only Barbara, Christy, and myself at home that day, Barbara was watching something on T.V. She didn't look up when I came into the room.

"How long is he going to be here?" I asked.

"What do you mean?" Barbara answered, then looking at me as if I had bonsai trees growing out of my ears. Creative defense.

"I mean how long is he going to be living here?"

"What do you mean? This is Joseph's home, it always was. What do you mean 'how long?'" Again, looking at the T.V.

"Is his leashed girlfriend still going to be here every night?"

More squinting, staring, and shaking of her head. What the hell was I talking about? Clever. Then more silence, as if I had never asked any questions in the first place.

"You didn't do a damn thing about any of this," I said to her as she gawked even harder. "That maniac tried to kill me. All for being interrupted in front of that inane girlfriend of his. He was out of the house where he belongs, yet only for four months, and that idiot gets engaged to him. She's not even out of high school. If you really believe that their sick relationship is ever going to last, it is obvious. It won't, and you know it. But that doesn't matter. She's pretty and therefore makes you look good. It makes it all appear as if Joey is not an abusive monster, and that you haven't made any mistakes by moving us to this gilded town and fucking little house. It's all a joke, and a bad one at that."

This is the result of speaking down to "authority," which is often where they are.

"You don't like it here?" Barbara all but screamed that question at me. Christy slinked away to her dog bed. "You should be praying to heaven above that we moved you from Pennsauken! Away from all those niggers and crooks breaking into homes and ruining the neighborhood when they should have stayed in fucking Camden where they belonged. You don't like it here? Then leave! Then you would not be able to be in that band with all those freaks you made friends with. What the hell is wrong with you, Jack? We moved here so you could have nice friends. Not longhairs with tattoos who reek of smoke. Why can't you meet nice friends in Moorestown?"

"They are not bad guys," I said, sadly knowing I could never win.

"Not the way they dress. What about that one kid's mother? Ronnie or whatever the hell his name is? I saw her at your high school last week for that parents' night, I said hello to her and she just ignored me and kept walking! How is that for nice? She's got fucking nerve!"

I didn't know that happened, though I could see it as it did. I just did not understand it well enough then. As I got older, I was more able to comprehend. Mrs. Sippen picked up Rob (and Barbara deliberately could not even remember his name) from the Pszcynacks' little house. She faked being nice because she had to. Then she sees Barbara at the school for that parents' night thing and ignored her when Barbara struggled to be friends. Consequently, the responsibility for that disregard falls to me. I made bad friends as their mothers will not say hello to mine. That was on me. No one else, or that's how the narrative was then.

I realized later that Mrs. Sippen ignored Barbara not because Rob or any of the other guys were "freaks." Barbara was ignored because she was clearly not wealthy. Rob and Ian's families were rich. The rich Moorestown people, hell, generally most wealthy people, did not want to associate with lower classes. Part of the whole game. Mrs. Sippen drove her rich, fat ass up the driveway to our Moorestown house and probably shook her head in derision at how small it was. We were not a rich family. It was blatantly obvious, and that was enough. I didn't get it then. I didn't understand the wealth inequality for what it was, and all its various charms, until maybe ten years later in life. Too late, but it didn't make it right. Even still, I was paying for it and then some.

"This is wrong," I said to her. Barbara continued to stare at the T.V.

"You want this family to be miserable," she said, again without looking at me.

"I know it's wrong. He shouldn't be here, nothing was resolved, you are just ignoring it and hoping it will go away. Denial. That's wrong."

"You just want this family to be miserable." She turned away, looking at anything but me. Again, more staring.

That's how that particular saga was settled. Staring. Ignoring. Accusing. Silence. Denial. People in denial do not like being told they are in denial. The accuser is always wrong. There never was any psychological or family counseling, nor would there be any mention of it. Compulsory. Nothing happened and nothing better, just more steam inside the pressure cooker getting hotter. Denial works. Denial is attractive, kind of like Tina. Just as cute, and just as fake. Certainly just as questionable.

Narrative matters. The narrative is Jack won't get over anything. It was not a problem that Tina was there every night locked up in a bedroom, the problem is Jack points out that this is wrong; and her being with him to begin with, was wrong. The problem isn't that Joey exploded into a murderous nightmare and it got so violent that police had to break up the fight; the problem is Jack won't get over it. Stars in heaven. Jack should be kissing his divorcing but never actually divorcing parents' asses for getting him away from all the black people in Pennsauken. For shame that he constantly wants to go back to that very town, and on top of that he made new friends with rich kids (exception Craig), who look and act like they are anything but. Freaks indeed. But friends, and friends were mattering more with every passing day.

I also didn't understand, at least right then, the need for all the racism given the fact that they were no longer living in Pennsauken. You "won," right? You got what you wanted. You got away. What's the problem? Why did it continue? Was racism itself denial? Damon and every other black kid, including the still very white Michael Del and crew were still living and breathing in my hometown. Yet here were the Pszcynacks in Moorestown, little more than a shack their new home was. Maybe I was wrong. Maybe they really knew things were bad even under that comfortable blanket of renunciation. Ceaseless spewing about how much they hate black people, even after the Pennsauken white flight. Forget that town even existed save for the lesser people living there now. After all, someone else being worse off, invariably makes another better. I supposed that was rich too.

Chapter Fifteen

THE SHAKES

As soon as I got my driver's license almost a year after Joey's return, I started heading back to Browning Road every weekend I could. This was not too different from any time before yet by then I had the independence; the means along with the will. We would always start our nights at Michael's house. Alfie and Johnny only lived a few blocks away and would often walk. Shag would get a ride any time, his dad owned a taxicab service. Not too bad a scenario, always having a ride for himself.

While Alf and Johnny more or less melded into our little group from their days at Longfellow, Shag was new to Pennsauken, or rather new to Pennsauken High. He had always lived right in town like us, but went to Catholic school until he was fifteen, and that's where Michael made friends with him. His real name was Adam, we liked calling him Shag, based on a certain seventies cartoon that had a tall, thin, and all around goofy looking figure and presence like Adam; though the cartoon Shag hung out and went on adventures with a talking dog. Most of us forgot his real name altogether. Nicknames do not always stick, but he enjoyed it.

Even with the taxi service, I would always drive. Barbara hated me borrowing her car, in fact she hated me driving, period. All due to Joey's track record of speeding tickets and police knocking on the door. Even with all that, I usually got away with driving her car to Pennsauken nearly every single weekend. Maybe she knew it made me happy, or maybe she enjoyed the time alone. My utter loathing of Moorestown and everything to do with it was still proudly worn on my visage, if anything me going away for a little while gave her a welcomed break from the vitriol.

Nonetheless, I was never going to tell her I kind of agreed with her, but Barbara would always complain that while guys like Michael and Johnny had their driver's licenses by then too, they never came to the Moorestown house to pick me up for a ride. Never once. I didn't really mind, but admitted at least to myself it would have been nice once in a while for them to come to me. I suppose it was the price I had to pay for moving. I was not in their school, regardless of how close it was. I wasn't a student at their school, and kind of hung around them by a vigorous yet altogether singular thread. I tried as I could not to admit it, but these things mattered. Young ideals.

We normally would not even stay out too late, be it out at the mall or the movies or wherever. Since I had the car, I would never go straight home. Surreal as it was being "back" in Pennsauken, I would drive around town, blasting the Ramones or Misfits while touring my old neighborhood; almost as if on a tram at a theme park. I would always drive by my old house. Sometimes I would see Rosie outside, she never noticed me. Sometimes I would keep it up for hours, driving around Browning Road, or on other streets past old friends' houses from a decade earlier, even past Longfellow Elementary itself.

Home yet homeless, at the very least lost within all the familiarity. I was the stranger there, even though it was my town. The town was definitely getting "browner," much more black people in houses I used to walk past at a time when that was unheard of. Back when polite mobs came by to any home audacious enough to erect a sales sign upon its lawn. Some of the new residents looked at me with curious, even offended eyes from time to time. Home is where you hang your hat. They had no idea who I was, let alone why.

It didn't stop me. I loved taking my nighttime tours around town, blasting punk rock and just killing time. It's not as if I was in any rush to get back to Moorestown where my actual bed was. I would even do these punk rock old town tours in the pouring rain, driving around with the windshield wipers at full speed, the dashboard vibrating with that loud, heavy, gorgeous noise while I would cruise past old haunts yet never go in. Why go home when there wasn't one?

I still hung out with Craig and the Xonxe guys whenever we did but the two towns with the two sets of friends never really melded together. Michael and the other guys never knew I was smoking marijuana in Moorestown, and I kept that activity exclusive to the punk rock band. Often, by that junior year, it was just myself and Craig smoking the funny cigarettes and even then, only on rare occasions. Xonxe as a band was practicing less; no gigs came along after that first one. For nearly that entire year, the band was all but dormant, even to the point I moved my drum set from Ian's huge house to my parent's musty basement. Practicing when I could and scaring the hell out of my dog.

Ian was spending much more time in Pennsylvania with his private school friends, and becoming more "hippyish" according to Craig and thus spending much more time smoking whacky tobacco with kids who had far more autonomy and access to it. Yes, it turns out the rich kids were into drugs. They had all the time, privacy, and money in the world to spare. True privilege at its best. This is what the offspring of the wealthy were up to. It went where it could go. For the kids at least, drugs were all the rage in my new town of Moorestown, New Jersey. Not all the kids, obviously, but rampant enough. That was the "in" thing there. Welcome home.

Rob met a girl in school, and suddenly, we were not seeing him too much as any time he could have spent with the band was time away from the girl. A threat to his newfound relationship, perhaps. I can't recall one good reason for him to presume that exclusivity was necessary at all, especially with us. We were a bunch of weirdos, sure, but so was he. So much insecurity when a guy finds a girlfriend. Why couldn't anyone handle their fucking relationships?

So it was only Craig and I, smoking and watching a lot of horror movies. And above all wishing we were seventeen at maybe seventeen years prior, when our favorite band was active. Unfortunately, that year, Craig's family pulled him out of our high school and placed him in the "Alternative School" which was for troubled kids such as himself. Still taking the little bus albeit to a different school, Craig said he liked it as the classes were far less demanding, and gym class now consisted of walking around the building and smoking cigarettes. The high school wasn't the same without him, made less fun for his absence. That counter-culture just hanging around in his goofy wake. No more. Thus, Xonxe had unofficially broken up that year, and I retreated back to the comic books and Pennsauken visits; that which took precedence to begin with.

I also started a job that year. That was at the Video Stop in Moorestown. It was a hike every day on foot, but I didn't mind walking to the store and Barbara liked that even more since apparently Joey got pulled over again while speeding around with Tina. Charmer. That was swept under the rug like everything else. Why break precedent? The end result was they didn't want me driving at all by proxy. They were not too strict with him, and there were consequences, even if they never spoke of them. They would correct their mistakes with me; though again, never actually saying so.

I did hear old Joe mention that he was sick of hearing (he was never around when it actually happened) about Joey's numerous speeding tickets, but that police should not be pulling him over because he's white, and they should "know better." Pull over the right kind of people? How could he ever be wrong? Self-worship. Nothing to brag about.

It was good that I had a job, just something else to keep me away from the little house. Video stores were remarkable. People used to have to go to a store and see what was new or what was available in video format to rent and take home for a night or two. Sometimes this was treated as an evening. People would go out to dinner and then see what was available at the video store, and on weekend nights those stores would be packed. An entire business genre completely extinct within about ten or fifteen years. I wondered what all the yelling at screaming was really for. Ghosts of the past. We probably should have known it then.

Much to my manager's and store owner's consternation, I would often suggest we should hire bouncers for the video store or call the police as it was a nearly daily occurrence for a customer to scream and humiliate clerks like me over three-dollar late fees. That was a long-ago gimmick. Movies would cost two to three dollars to rent, but if they were brought back late, additional fees would apply, and compiling that every day it was late thereafter. There were even one-dollar non-rewinding fees for tapes. That charge was not often enforced. We simply did not want to listen to them complain. That's how bullying works.

That's where the screaming came in. Customers didn't like having a balance on their account, and would far more often than not lash out at me for even saying there was such a fee, and this was a rich town. Not everyone in town and at the store was rich, sure, but even the upper echelon would complain. Three dollars. How dare anyone beneath them tell them they needed to send their money in another direction? Blasphemy.

The narcissistic customers would often argue everything down, saying things like they dropped it in the night box on the day it was due, and even though the store was closed, then the movie was not late. Some would say the movie was terrible and blame us for that. Some would say they were not informed of the late fee policy before they rented the movies. Some simply did not give a shit, and would not "lose" for the sake of saving face, and they took that rather seriously. So many demands. After all, there was that old school fallacy that the "customer was always right." Who indeed could argue with them? That was blasphemy, and treated as such. Dishonest though it was.

Pure ego. That was the real issue. If they were late or didn't rewind, that meant the younger, therefore inferior, wage slave working behind the counter was telling the eminent customers that they were wrong. Intolerable. They would often ask for our name. For what reason, it was easy to know why. I suppose it was so they could complain to a "superior" which I also never really defined too well. Fear does not command respect, they just thought it did, which was good enough for them, and they would not be questioned.

The guys at the store and I enjoyed making up names for ourselves to tell the complaining customer. My favorites were "Phil" and "Ruettiger." Then the customer would complain and the reaction was infallibly: "Who's Phil?"

That was always hilarious when those egotistical bastards tried to tattle on me, being so enraged with my indifference to money itself. They took themselves way too seriously. They really did worship themselves. Looking back, they probably knew exactly what I was thinking. But that was only because they were looking for it well before they walked into that store, and after they left.

The sad truth of that job, and probably every other retail store, is that nearly one hundred percent of the time, the customers would win. Wrong as it was, it was damn near compulsory. More often than not, their late fees would be removed. This was not so much due to the "customer is always right" nonsense, no, that was for ego. If they "lost" their argument with the clerk, or the manager, or sometimes all the way up to the store owner; they would not come back to that video store. They would have to "punish" the Video Stop by no longer shopping there. No maturity was even to be found, let alone expected. I learned that quickly enough, though never respected it.

The so-called management knew it too for all the good that did. Same story. Rigged game, and those businesses are long dead.

I found it all so very awful that, as in my childhood, money became the excuse for everything, especially dishonesty. Compared to money, dishonesty was never a thing. I often referred to this openly at the store as the "customer pandemic." That made me more than a few enemies. No one liked it when I analyzed ego, even rich asshole ego. The wage slaves wanted to be rich too, at least yearned for it, and they were not getting there by criticizing them.

Despite that monetary fallacy that everyone seemed to ignore except me, the owner did let us take movies out for free as long as they were not new off the shelf. I watched just about every horror movie in that store, especially zombie movies back then. The older movies were bringing me back to that time when the Misfits were around, some even years and decades before. Better times.

There were those movies, yes, but the free movie rentals also included porn tapes. That was something else in those days. A significant portion of any video store's revenue came from porn rentals. It wasn't talked about much, but silence was a flimsy veil for the truth. Some of the more "moral" stores would not carry porn, and would go belly up and close as a consequence. The Video Stop was perfectly comfortable with the bellies and everything else going up considering how much money it made them. It was mostly men who would rent these things, though occasionally I would see the married couple enter the back room marked "adults only."

Kevin Ruskin was a fellow clerk I made friends with at the store. The short and pony-tailed dirty blond that he was, Kevin was into punk rock and smoking weed with me behind the store. Sometimes, he and I would go to the back office and turn up the volume on the security cameras if a couple was in the porn section together. It was just somehow hilarious listening to them review each porn movie box, pictures and everything, and say things like "We haven't tried this one yet. That looks like it might hurt. Well, let's try it anyway!" We had to fight back all the laughter. Those couples were not too often the rich people. For my own part, I did feel weird at first, taking that genre of film home did come with additional stigma. But eventually I realized they were free and just too tempting not too. I learned a lot from watching them.

Any cash I made from working, which wasn't much, was spent on comics, the occasional marijuana delivery with the punk rock guys, and hanging out in Pennsauken. Even with Craig and most of the Xonxe guys gone that year, I did hang out and sometimes play in another punk band with Kevin. Those guys were freshmen, and for whatever reason looked up to the members of Xonxe as if we were mentors, or even cool. What they didn't know.

Much like Ian, Kevin lived in a big house across town. His parents were divorced and never around so that marital distress hardly seemed to matter there. His punk band was called Ruptured, which I would occasionally hang around with to smoke green tobacco and play in their band. No live shows which was disappointing, though having plenty of fun.

Cratch was their guitar player and he was constantly strung out on drugs; looking like a young Homer Simpson with long hair and a stringy beard. Paul Eagen, or Paul-E was their bassist. He was the most "normal" of those guys yet constantly would wear blue jeans with a white collared shirt that he never ironed or even washed, apparently.

Paul-E didn't seem to like me much and would often never speak to me, sometimes not even look at me. Kevin told me not to worry about it, and that I should continue to fill in on the drums when I could. It was explained to me that Paul-E just didn't like new people, especially from other schools. He was too concerned that new people (therefore I) would ruin friendships, so anything new was bad. I couldn't fit in anywhere.

Given all that, it made me tighten my grip on what I had in Pennsauken even more. They were all good guys, just not into the punk rock and weed thing, which I could switch on and off no problem then. Alfie Buchman was from my childhood days, by then an overweight nerd who was really into comics, Star Trek, Mystery Science Theatre, and all kinds of nerdy delights. He was smart. Johnny Eastman lived in town and was always working with his dad's tree surgeon business, but he always made time to meet with us. Sometimes he would even drive, just never to Moorestown to collect me. Adam McDevitt, or Shag, was the "new" guy in that he only started Pennsauken schools in ninth grade, but that was our group. New friends all around. It was so much easier to make friends in those times. Maybe that is why our elders looked down upon us so much. Youth, it doesn't come back again.

One night, it was only Michael (whose parents had completely divorced by this time on account of his father's drinking) and myself hanging out at his house. Michael said Wendy would be joining us. Odd that I never heard the name Wendy. Odder still a girl was joining us. Wendy was actually Johnny's sister, and then a freshman at Pennsauken High School. Wendy was something different, and not just because she was the only female who hung out with us. She was a somewhat "punky" girl in that she had a number of earrings through her ears and nose, even a small tattoo of a dragonfly above her wrist. She wasn't into the punk rock music like me but said it was cool that I was in a band.

Interestingly, before she joined us at Michael's house, she mentioned she was on a date right before and it didn't go too well. While Johnny was the quiet, hardworking guy always wondering when his next shift would be, his sister was just the opposite. Perhaps too young yet to work; but certainly involved in the social world coming around her, she spoke as if she hung out around town more than me two years her senior, and she probably was more experienced. I loved her smile. She was quite gorgeous with long, curly black hair, along with an attractive slender figure, almost dancing as she walked across a room. She was everything. Younger than us, yet almost too cool to hang out with us.

Neither Michael nor myself asked her, but she explained why her date didn't go so well. I had to admit, I found her bad date situation all the more intriguing.

"He wasn't ready to be dating, honestly," Wendy explained while rolling her eyes in slight disgust, yet still maintaining that friendly and irresistible smile. "I'm not interested in being with a guy whose mom drops him off at the restaurant and he has to go to a payphone periodically to check in with her. I felt like I was being spied on somehow. So that one was going nowhere; and he was only so cute, now that I think about it. All done now, so here I am with you guys, probably better off for it."

"So that's how you ended up hanging out with us tonight?" I

asked her.

"Well, yeah. I am close with Johnny and I have hung out with these guys before, mostly at school. Are you the guy who used to live down the street and then moved away? I heard you are in a punk rock band. You look normal, I would have never guessed you were into that."

"Punk rock is in the heart, I guess," is all I could say to her, or anyone who asked me that question. Yes, I looked and dressed "normal" but that was mostly because conservative old Joe would kill me if I got a piercing or tattoo. I was never really that committed to punk rock, at least in that way, and didn't see it lasting for the rest of my life. I didn't want or need a punk rock girl. The music still fascinated me, but right then not half as much as Wendy Eastman.

"Well, now you have two guys," Michael said to her. "It's only me and Jack tonight, so you can go out with us both." Sometimes if you are relaxed enough around a girl, or simply not interested, you can talk about anything with her, even the sexual innuendos. Not the case for me. I liked Wendy, sure, but accepted I wasn't cool enough for her and that was it. I spent most of the night trying to hide the irresistible discomfort. That said, I actually liked it.

"Too bad you could not invite one of your friends out," I said to Wendy. "Then we could double date." I was only hoping not to sound like an idiot by that point, yet finding myself alert enough to think upon her answer.

"I don't have any girlfriends," Wendy replied, still smiling but apparently dead serious. I could not help myself but to delve.

"Why not?"

Wendy shook her head in derision. Not so much in disdain of

me, yet all the more confident in her own meaning.

"Girls are a pain in the ass," she explained. "All of my friends are guys. Guys are much more laid back, they are not petty and catty, and aren't stabbing each other in the back all the time and making me feel like crap. They can't be friends. On top of all that, they don't want to be held accountable for anything. I just get along better with guys, that's all. That's why I always hang out with them."

That wasn't good. It was sad enough that Wendy did not have any girlfriends, yet even worse that the girls of our time could have been so bad in attitude and emotional irresponsibility that they would not even hang out with each other. How bad could they have really been? Did they all feel that way? No girlfriends? It didn't seem right. They should have such friends. If girls like Wendy (or apparently all girls) were only hanging around guys, that is a lot of competition. That made the landscape more than a bit lopsided. As I thought of it, Tina didn't have any female friends either, and spent all her time with Joey, who had next to no friends. Wendy was beautiful and outgoing, definitely, but it was hard to trust anyone who had no friends at all. I still couldn't keep my eyes off her.

Wendy, Michael, and I went out for pizza that night, then to a bowling alley with a billiard room and played there. Old Joe used to take Joey and I to his bar when we were kids, and we would shoot pool. Joey didn't like losing but I did get rather good at it. Wendy joked with me that she would have her revenge for the defeat. Sometimes she would high five me when I pocketed a ball, and she didn't let my hand go right away each time. Then the looks. Those kind of looks that I could feel in my jeans pocket.

I still didn't think anything was going to happen between her and I, maybe that made it easier for us to get along. Eventually I dropped her and Michael off at home, and after a brief Pennsauken tour past my old house, made it back to Moorestown.

Michael called me a couple of days later and asked me if I liked Wendy. I played it cool on the phone, however besieged in trying to hide my excitement. Wendy liked me, and deliberately asked Michael to call me and tell me that. I said I was interested and then Wendy called me herself to talk about it. I didn't ask her, but later checked with Michael if Johnny was okay with me dating his sister. I didn't ask him directly. It turned out, that was all fine with Johnny, that was great, but again I found myself jealous and near depressed that someone else had a nicer sibling. Even amidst the elation of the new girlfriend. We don't grow up twice.

Maybe Joey and I would have gotten along better if one of us was female. I doubted it. Wendy would soon become my official girlfriend and a mainstay in our little group. She got along with everyone fine, yet constantly corrected us to stop calling Adam "Shag" and address him by his real name. Shag never complained.

I never really had a girlfriend in my life up until that point. I was glad I could drive myself back and forth to Pennsauken. I kind of had a girlfriend in middle school, one Kyla Buchanan. We never went on a single date together and never touched each other outside an awkward hug at the end of the school year. Kyla got annoyed with me that I would never kiss her, and we broke up with no ceremony, just drifted away. I welcomed the exit. I wasn't ready for a relationship then. With Wendy, I couldn't wait.

Our first date was a rare stroke of good luck. I picked Wendy up at her house in Pennsauken and talked to her mother for a bit. Mrs.

Eastman was friendly and was always good to all the guys back then. Wendy and I went to see a movie and instinctively cuddled the entire time, no resistance in body or mind, entirely natural. I thought I would chicken out. She held my hand as we walked back to the car afterwards and she felt me trembling. When she asked if I was cold, did I ever jump at that excuse.

When we got back to her house, no one was there. Perfect. Wendy invited me in and I sat on the couch, she sat right in my lap. I only stopped shaking then because I had to. Still, the fear. I loved being with her and the touch of her skin, beyond comfortable in each other's arms. But I realized then I was getting a bit older, not old but long since gone were the kid days of Pennsauken. Truth was, I was afraid of sex. I liked the idea of it, but this was the first time in my life that sex was possible. It may have actually happened. That was enough to give me the shakes.

Wendy put her arms around me and asked if she was now my girlfriend. I said absolutely and we kissed. All the way, open mouth and everything. That was my first kiss; she may have been my first love. We made out there on the couch for a while, the fear and trembling easily melting away early in the process.

We didn't have sex that night and we didn't have to. I was kissing her. She was my girlfriend and she cared about me. I would not screw this up. I would not treat her like Joey did his girlfriend. Not all girlfriends had to be Tina. None of them should ever be. Pennsauken was my town all over again. Wendy was far more to me than she ever realized. She captivated me more than punk rock or anything else ever could. This was a chance for something right. Sometimes knowing what not to do makes all the difference.

Chapter Sixteen

A LONG TIME

Joey walked past me with his head hung low, annoyed that I was there, in that little house, though this time for entirely different reasons. He wasn't crying but looked like he wanted to. When he noticed I was there, he walked past me faster, still stroking what little ego he had left. He didn't say a word. He had his car keys in one hand, a bagged dozen roses in the other. Christy wagged her tail and whined at him as he left. Unusual though it was, he didn't peel his tires when he drove off. The trouble never seemed to end with him, the narcissistic disorder still not spoken of. This time he punched his girlfriend in the face.

"What's wrong with him?" I asked Barbara. Any other time she would have ignored me or changed the subject. Bizarrely, despite not really looking at me, she decided to be candid. I'll never really know why.

"Joseph got arrested for drunk driving," Barbara explained. "It was two nights ago and he's going to have to go to court and probably serve probation time along with all the fines. Tina was upset at him, and she gave him an earful over how disappointed she was. He didn't like that, and he punched her in the face, and now she has a black eye. A doctor had to look at it. Now they've broken up. He bought those flowers to apologize. He really misses her."

Unbelievable. He was an absolute megalomaniac, and he could never deal with half an ounce of criticism, especially when he was wrong, yet how could he and why would he punch the object of his life's obsession in the face? That, and how were flowers supposed to account for such a thing? What scared me more is that their repulsive relationship was not actually finished, and that Tina would stay with that bastard regardless. I still referred to Tina as Joey's "girlfriend" all that time, willfully forgetting that her title had that far more re-pulsive term "fiancé." Later on in life, I was never quite comfortable with that word in any situation or frame of mind. Quite a legacy.

"Why is he giving her flowers?" I asked.

"Well, he's sorry," Barbara enlightened. "When you apologize, especially to a girl, it's a good thing to buy flowers to let her know you mean it."

"Wait, so you are saying that she actually might get back with him?" I asked, still refusing to understand how any of my questions would be welcome by then, or before for that matter.

"They were together for a long time," she replied, again not look-ing directly at me.

"That's insanity! He hit her! The dumbass gets pulled over for drunk driving, he's barely twenty-one, he screws up yet again and she finally gets upset with him. He didn't like that, so he smacked her? She can't get back with him, that would be just plain sick at this point!"

"They were together for a long time," Barbara said again. That tone, it was ceaseless. As if I should have always realized that Joey and Tina were dating for years, and this somehow was every justification for them to stay together, and my own reaction to this abuse was somehow abhorrent. What I didn't know. The contrarian.

I had to understand this, at least for myself. Crazy was dominating the atmosphere yet again, if it ever once subsided. Joey got pulled over and subsequently arrested for drunk driving. He didn't end up in jail, though that offense and many others were grounds for him to be locked up to find a new "boyfriend" for himself. Normally whenever shit like this happened, Tina would defend her boyfriend, or in this case fiancé, and coddle him. She would pat his back and rub his shoulders to make sure he was okay, kind of like when that terrible person hit him with mace after he pounded dents into his door for over an hour. It was pepper spray, but mace sounded like it hurt more.

For whatever reasons, reasons that I still cannot explain to any given day in my life, Tina had a change of heart. This time, she didn't coddle him. This time, she tore him a new asshole for being so irresponsible for drinking and driving and she let him have it. Nice going. The charming boyfriend decided to respond to his girl's sudden change of heart by punching her in the face and giving her a black eye. This is what caused a breakup. Well, apparently.

Later that night, Joey had not come home yet but the phone rang, and I answered it. It was Tina, asking if Joey was there. I sighed loudly and paused. I told her that he was not home. She asked if I would let him know she called. I didn't really answer her, and she seemed annoyed with the blatant lack of cooperation. It didn't bother me so much. I hung up the phone.

"Who was that?" Barbara asked me. I couldn't help myself, or think of any one reason why I should have.

"That," I said with a pause to Barbara, with old Joe listening. "That was the precise reason I always have, and will probably continue to have, a healthy suspicion of the dating world, girls, and what to expect from all of it. I will always question it, and I should not have to. That so-called relationship was always wrong. From the first time she set foot into the house on Browning Road, and even until right now. All of it. Terrifyingly wrong, even on a 'good' day."

Ten seconds of silence followed. Blasphemy. Bad enough I had to openly admit that the entire relationship between Joey and Tina was wrong from the beginning. But worse yet, I mentioned Browning Road, which was always a place my parents refused to admit ever existed somehow.

"Well, Jack," Barbara said after looking directly at Old Joe with awkward reassurance. "They were together for a long time."

"That's all the more reason they shouldn't be together. Or either of them in a relationship at all. If they were together for a 'long time' as you put it, all that time was not spent well, and it was never good, not for anyone."

Old Joe started shaking his head at me. Barbara walked back to her bedroom. That little hallway was only one path of denial of the many. A long time. How could I not see it?

Again, on my own, to provide only myself with any such examination or conclusions. Usually when Joey screwed up like this, old Joe would be screaming bloody murder and inexplicably blaming black people for everything; yet this time, oddly quiet. I knew why.

They wanted Tina to remain, even every night couped up in his bedroom, at least they could still tell their friends and various family
members that the sick relationship was still going strong. The success
that it was.

Appearances. That's why they didn't stand in Joey's way. They
wanted her back maybe even more than he did. Judging by the tone
of Tina's voice on the phone, unquestionably, she had every intention
of getting back with him, even while her eye was still swollen and
black for daring to stand up to him, for even implying he was wrong
for what he is, and he was. Precedent. There was no end to that ridiculous parade they called a relationship.

There was, surprisingly. Tina Columbus was going to get back
together with Joey Pszcynack, even after he was arrested for drunk
driving, and having subsequently punched her in the face. Having
no recourse, he apologized, gave her flowers, and yes, Tina was entirely willing to return to him even given all that lack of accountability or explanation. She apparently had returned to him, his girlfriend
again. This was for a day maybe, if even that long.

It turned out, that incident was in fact the final end of them.
They stayed officially broken up for all time, and we never heard
another word from that girl ever again. Gone. Done. Old Joe was
disappointed. Barbara cried, and forever would heavily sigh at even
the slightest hint of the name "Tina." No one would ever compare to
her, never again. That was her legacy.

They told Marie and all of Barbara's many girlfriends that Joey
and Tina "drifted apart" as the reason for the split up. No kidding.
No one ever bothered to explain anything to me, I never knew what
really happened, if anyone did. I never knew what made her stay

away from him after that brief reconciliation. I never knew what made her balk at continuing that sick relationship she had with him. I just could never accept that she was smart enough or remotely strong enough herself to do so. The evidence to the contrary was simply overwhelming. No one liked the truth.

My best guess for the brief reconciliation then termination of their relationship was that her parents likely found out that she wanted to and was willing to go back to him; even after such abuse. They probably put their foot down, quite possibly threatening legal action if she did not permanently part ways with Joey Pszcynack. If they had half a brain, they could have and should have got a lawyer, brought the monster into court for damages, placed a restraining order on him, and thereby drag Tina's relationship with him through the mud and whatever other filth it came from. She relented, and that was how it ended. At the very least, it ended.

Amazing how one relationship, one that I was not even involved in affected me so much later in life. I suppose I was part of that relationship with Tina, she was under my nose at each house, worse yet in the little house, and every single night for years. Constantly being made to believe I was completely wrong for even questioning their relationship. I was nearly killed for interrupting and thus interfering with what she was. I was part of it. Forever after, my parents, extended family, and so many others would see that girl as the best thing that ever happened to the Pszcynacks. As if truly regrettable for its own demise. To be missed as if a loved one had passed away.

Accountability is a sensitive subject. It's not wrong that their relationship ended, but who are we to blame for that travesty even existing? My family, racist and ignorant as they all were, wanted Tina to be around for all time. After all, she made them look good. Appearances mattered, and Tina had that in spades. I realized that when I was not even fifteen years old, and unfortunately verified my young ideas in the years that followed. Tina was excellent public relations material. A beautiful shroud to conceal the truth.

If Joey was dating one of the prettiest girls in Pennsauken High School, that means Joey was not as bad as he actually was. The fact that Joey was dating her meant that Joey's parents were "good" too. Look at us, our son has the prettiest girl in school hanging on his arm, and that for years on end. We must be doing something right, to say the least. Utter nonsense. Though I never learned that most people really are more than comfortable living the lie. As long as it works. I suppose that was a major cause of all the vitriol and distrust. The violence and loathing. I didn't buy into the bullshit game. A victim of thought crime, or the perpetrator, all depending on where they were standing.

Tina, and her relationship with Joey, was perceived as a good thing; therefore, she was so. There would be no barricade for this farce to spread. Not even violence where an unaccommodating young kid was nearly killed, and apparently not even violence where the girl center to this production was herself attacked and injured. They were all more than willing to go along with the river of lies. The acceptable deception. The fact was that Tina terrified the living hell out of me. The very climate, where the wind was blowing, where I was in it. Could Tina be the norm, and not the exception? Dating, caring for another human being. What was I in for?

Tina should not have been punched in the face. Joey should not have hit her at all, that was unacceptable. All the same, when you lie down with dogs, do not be surprised if you rise with fleas. I have met more than a few people like Tina in this world who would never accept responsibility for their own actions. Why did any of this happen? Why did no one question her, or at least question it? If this evidently "smart" girl is attracted to and spending her time with an abusive lout like Joey, why then is there no blame or responsibility reflected on her for making the choices she did? No one pointed a single finger at her, and certainly seemed quite uncomfortable at even the very suggestion of such responsibility. There were reasons for that too.

Tina did not spend too much of her life single after that. That's where she was in the storm. She always had a boyfriend thereafter, always someone interested, vocally in pursuit even. Never single, though she should have been. Never held accountable for in life, and that apparently by design. No one admitted it, including her, but Tina hurt people, and not just me. She got away with it all by and large, if not entirely. The least anyone could do is point that out. Her own decisions held far more weight than anyone seemed willing to even speculate. Why do we not ever question the pretty girl for the power she has or had? I suppose I just answered my own question.

But that day came and went, and Tina's picture was removed from the mantle at the little house in Moorestown. Small victories can matter. As for girlfriends, I never introduced or even informed my family about the existence of Wendy Eastman. Those years of them obsessing over Tina led me away from any notion of it. I would do things differently, I would follow another path, hardly omniscient yet knowing at least what not to do.

Sex was new to me though that was becoming less of a problem every single day I spent with Wendy. It took us a few weeks for it to really happen. First I had her shirt off during a make out session but was afraid to remove her bra. Later she would do that for me, then I for her. Then it was incessant dry humping until we got to a point where both of us were entirely naked. A learning process, and a rather fun process at that.

All of this was only done when we had her house to ourselves which was not often enough. One night her whole family was gone on some kind of occasion. Wendy got out of it, so we stayed home and went at the faux sex for a good while. Yet something else I was not yet courageous enough to do was go into a drug store and purchase condoms. Perception, perhaps? More fear. Wendy also took care of that problem for us.

My mind could hardly compute a single thought save for where I was that night, lying in bed under the sheets with a naked girl accompanying me. We only kissed for a while until Wendy whispered how much she really wanted me. I told her I didn't have any condoms on me and had not yet bought any. I really thought it was rude to presume that we were really going to have sex. As if she would look down upon me for bringing a condom, for having the expectation of sex. Lame excuse in retrospect.

"Hold on," she said. Even then in the moonlit room, I could not keep my eyes off of her. The smooth, silver skin in the dark. There was a gorgeous naked girl in front of me. I was almost like a deer in headlights watching her prance across the room to her top dresser drawer, bending over in front of me while she fiddled beneath her folded clothes for what we needed. She came back to the bed with a condom in her hand. I still could not take my mind off the fact that

I was very well about to have sex with her though still realizing she had an open box of condoms in her bedroom. There were other guys before me, clearly. Not that any particular bit of knowledge of that or any kind was good enough to break those proceedings.

Again, first experience, but the condom was easy enough to put on. We had sex twice that night, the first time admittedly only lasting a couple of minutes, which is what will happen after years of anticipation. We laid in bed for a while before getting another condom from her dresser. Again. Then it was different.

We went at it for over an hour, trying every single different position we could come up with. What mattered to me the most was Wendy enjoying it as much as she was certainly not afraid to let on. She became wetter to the point that I could no longer feel the condom on my skin. Soon enough I took control of the evening, I could not help discerning later how much my years of watching porn videos actually came in handy, and wondering why so many girls I met over the years seemed to have an aversion to such entertainment and film; not realizing it was, in essence, training for the activities we were to enjoy.

Wendy suggested a shower afterwards, something else I had never done and was not expecting, and half terrified that Johnny or anyone in her family would return home to interrupt us. I couldn't get enough of it. Holding her with the warm water pouring over us, I realized this is what I wanted in life and nothing else. I still didn't drink but was thankfully getting drunk on her. This was life with Wendy over the next four months. It was as if it could never end. How could it? Though the winds change a lot more than we prepare for, greater still when we are so young.

As cute and friendly though Wendy was, I could never disregard her penchant for always being "busy." Even when spending her time with me, she always seemed to have something else going on. Her phone was always ringing, she even had a beeper. What sixteen-year-old girl needs a beeper? She could never miss any one of her so important calls. She reviled any such questions, even if asked indirectly.

That and it was still a fact she did not have any female friends. Was I to presume it was all guys calling her? That was so, and that was just one problem. Ever since I moved from Pennsauken to Moorestown, I had always at least somewhat wondered if being the odd man out would be of any kind of benefit for me. I was never once "cool," and that didn't change with the move and new school. I was either that invisible, non-rich, new kid, or one of the weirdos in the Xonxe punk rock band. No paths to popularity there, not as if any were desired anyway. But such indifference to the norm can often come with a price.

What exactly did Wendy see in me? Was I wrong to wonder? Was I cute? I never knew or understood where I ranked with the opposite sex in appearances, though by later wearing leather jackets with a large skull logo stenciled on my back would lead one to make their own judgements. Was I cool because I drove everyone around in Pennsauken? Was I mystique, and therefore more interesting to Wendy? She went to a school with plenty of guys, many of which were my own friends, I tried to never think of it, but similar to Joey locking Tina away in his room for a purpose, other guys were likely attracted to Wendy too. She could tell those guys she had a boyfriend who went to another school. That lent for some mystery and "coolness" of her own.

Michael was never too helpful if I asked about any of this. All of those guys were gearing up to enter their senior year by that point, and I didn't go to their school. Hard as it was to face facts, I was not really part of their "world," and it was getting worse. Something was happening that I did (but really didn't) get at that time. A clique was forming. This was a clique that I could not ever really be a part of for not going to Pennsauken High School. Hell, in any school, seniors are often considered the most important students in all class years. It's "their" time, at least as students. We had been waiting for that moment since elementary school. I was not really there for the ride, and it was showing.

"It's not a problem that I can see," Michael answered me once with some derision in his eyes. I knew what people were thinking when they didn't look right at me. "You are friends with everyone, and you are dating Wendy, she's the only girl in our group. If that doesn't make you 'in' then I don't know what does."

Wendy was the only girl in our group, and in time she was calling me less, and not returning my phone calls even more than that. When we actually were all together, Wendy gradually ceased holding my hand, and sex was way off the table by the end of it. She referred to Shag as her "buddy" and hung out with him frequently while constantly getting angry with us if we referred to him as "Shag." No, he was "Adam," she insisted. I had to remind myself again, she was the only girl in our group. Yes, even the prettiest girl. Shag lost his nickname across the board with the guys in quick time. I didn't need to ask why they surrendered.

Eventually, Wendy stopped talking to me altogether. I still called and left messages periodically, not willing to accept defeat until that officially happened. One night she called me at home while I was reading comics at my desk. I tried to keep it all boyfriend status cordial, but that was hopeless.

"Hi, Jack. You know I've been thinking of you all week and I realized we should probably not be dating any longer."

"Why?" I asked her, still inexplicably using the friendly boyfriend tone.

"I don't know, I'm just not ready to be in the whole relationship thing."

"Well, okay. If that's what you want."

"Thank you," she said. It was only two words, that was the last time I spoke to her. Wendy's squealing, high-pitched tone knifed my ears well into my reverberated skull, like a serrated blade. A foreign object I could never remove. Your first breakup is always the worst. More so when all but being branded a heretic for even the suggestion of any questions. Even more so that I could not stop. She broke my pathetic heart, and I was not allowed to ask questions or ponder why. Sounded fair.

I hung up the phone and had that very real and sadly alive feeling of being cast aside, being let down, being broken up, and being alone. Breakups happen and we can get over them but then again there is always that nagging feeling that someone you cared for, even loved, hell, at least had naked time with, could indeed be enjoying the same attention from someone else. Someone who is not you. As I sat at my desk, I let my heart sink down past my gut, through my feet and well into the floor. It stayed there for a long time.

She was dating Shag by then. That should have been obvious, I suppose denial can capture us all if we let it. What would happen to friends after all this? What would happen to "my" town? It was still my town, yet no one was there. How could I be indifferent to any of it? That would be lying. I could never do that too well, least of all to myself. I was becoming exactly what I didn't want to. It was me staring, me shaking my head. I stared at the wall for at least an hour after that call, and kept wondering what kind of a world I had entered, and that everything I had feared was finally coming to pass. There was not a single thing I could do to stop it, and for the first time ever, I realized there was only one direction to go. Profound, maybe. But it didn't make me feel in the least bit better. What was "better?" It was better to not have loved at all than having done so and lost.

Chapter Seventeen

1981

A couple of weeks had gone by since I had that breakup call with Wendy. We never spoke directly again. Another sad truth was that I had hardly talked to Michael that much either. It was all so cynical, yet all so real. Part of the reason we were talking and hanging out less was because Wendy was by then a core staple in his group, and he knew it would upset me with her there. Better the issue be avoided, if he cared at all. Michael never admitted to me that Wendy was dating Shag, and he would stare at the walls if I even mentioned it, annoyed with any questions. Word gets around. That and in one of my punk rock Pennsauken tours, I saw Shag (sorry, Adam), walk out of the Eastman's house with his arm around Wendy. Humiliating, but I just had to know. I was not of their new and so-lidified Pennsauken High School clique and I had no business there whatsoever. My town had passed me by, left me behind, whether I wanted to accept it or not.

So Michael and I were not really speaking, the friendship I had with him since life began was unceremoniously brushed aside. No.

I wasn't going to accept it so easily, not after everything. I needed to try at least one more time. One more "real" visit to my hometown. I drove to his house on Browning Road one afternoon uninvited. I remember I used to just walk up to his door and knock and ask his parents if he could come out and play. So long ago. There were a lot of unrecognizable faces on the block by then, yet Michael still lived in the same house. After his parents divorced, his mother lived somewhere across town and his dad stayed on Browning Road for the rest of his days; much later dying at home and thereby being the last of the "classic" neighbors to leave. I had one more visit in me.

I parked in front of Michael's house and heard someone raking leaves in the backyard, so I simply strolled around to the back fence to surprise him. He was much taller than me as he always was, and still maintained that lanky, somewhat overweight look he had always had. Always in glasses, still probably wearing a retainer even then. Long, thin legs supporting a large bowl of jelly he called a stomach. Such a friendly guy at one time. So unselfish in the past.

"Need some help?" I asked. Michael looked up at me, first astounded but then immediately with complete inconsequence if not disgust, but he allowed me to help him. Maybe he didn't want to be rude, or at the very least look like the bad guy. Reputation, again.

"Uh, yeah. I have to rake all these up, then we can go inside," he said. I grabbed a bag and started stuffing piles of leaves into it, remarking that with me there to help him, we would be done in no time. I could tell what his favor level was to the free help. The sooner we would finish, the more he would have to listen to me talk. So many gut punches. I knew that backyard always belonged to the Del family, but it was our backyard. This is where we played tag, kickball, played with eighties action figures; all of it, it was for us, and part of our history. The Del's yard, but our yard, our home. All of it by then meant nothing because of a clique and a girl.

After all the leaves were collected, we went inside and sat in the living room. Michael could not turn off that look of his, still not wanting to be rude to me, yet wishing I never showed up all the same. No regard. This was my friend and this was that house. As it all looked like it did for years, I realized I wished the eighties remained frozen in time, and hating him and even myself that it was never happening.

"Sorry for just coming by like this, Michael," I said. "It's just been a while since we hung out and hell, I used to drop by all the time, right? Anyway, how's the neighborhood recently? I admit, my parents moved me out of here at a bad time, they were freaked out by that break in at the Graff's that time; that and they are just flat out racist. Didn't change a thing really, they still think they are heroes for it. Silly of me to expect accountability or even an explanation, I know. I just don't bullshit too well. I miss the old days." I could feel the thousand straws in the air.

"It's fine," Michael said under his breath. That was enough.

"Look, I know I'm not in your school any longer, but that does not mean we can't be friends. I have the punk rock guys in Moorestown, sure. We only hang out so often, and frankly the punk rock thing was always there for me to vent my anger, and to piss everyone else off. That worked, but Pennsauken is home to me, that's how I always wanted it. I know it's awkward with the Wendy thing, but I thought I mattered a little more. Shag's an idiot, by the way. It won't last with him either."

Michael looked up at me with that remark. "Well, his name's Adam," he said. "He can do what he wants, it's fine with me."

I stood up to leave. Michael didn't stop me.

"Look, Michael. I'm sorry. I am. I'm not sure what the issue is here but let's hang out soon okay? Just you and me. That would be good, right?"

"There's no issue," he replied, refusing to answer my actual question. This was not working. Just more awkward stares. I didn't even know this guy any longer and it was clear to me that's how he wanted it. I didn't attempt to shake hands with him when I left and he didn't get up until I was in my car, and that was only so he could shut the door, all but forgetting everything we were before that moment. Asshole. I guessed I lost my purpose, my use to him, whatever that may have been. I expired, and the pretty girl (the only girl) in his group didn't want me around. That's all it took. Gone.

I still continued to tour the old Pennsauken town occasionally, just not nearly as often. The neighborhood was always changing. I could not have cared less if there were more black people around. There was actually a decent mix of Black, Hispanic, Asian, and even new white neighbors by then. It didn't look too threatening, just more run down, less like home for the first time since I left. I was not them. Whatever I missed there was long gone. Lost to history, and evidently only to my memory. That was the real loss. Browning Road didn't become a black neighborhood after the move, or even a terribly bad neighborhood. It had become a graveyard.

Doom and gloom didn't last as long in those days. By the time my senior year rolled around, I didn't think I would ever play a show or even practice with Craig or any of the guys in Xonxe. Yet that

September, Craig randomly showed up at the video store with Ian and asked me to start practicing again because they had several shows lined up at local South Jersey venues and even a couple in Philly. I never thought those two could look any crazier but that probably gave them all the more reason to up their game. Gone were Craig's devilock and Ian's long dreadlocks. Now they were both sporting multi-colored "liberty spiked" mohawks they dyed themselves and raised the spikes on their heads with baking gelatin they bought at the supermarket. I thought it was hilarious, but just as before, I wasn't adopting that look myself. Not the look, but the attitude was welcome.

Craig did give me one of his older black leather jackets, which Ian was able to stencil a large Misfits skull logo upon the back of. This at least made me look somewhat as menacing as the other guys. Craig always told me punk rock is in the heart, and I exhibited that more than any of them. Rob kept his usual metal shirt and ripped jeans look, along with the never removed fork bracelet. It turned out Rob was more available then, as he broke up with that girlfriend of his and I could only hope that none of us would meet another girl any time soon.

It turned out Craig's alternative school had some well-established and well-connected punk rockers. We would be "touring" the local scene with some of Craig's A-school friends, members of the locally popular band Media Pandemic. I was able to get Kevin and the guys from Ruptured to tag along for the shows, thus the three-band set got around for the entire Fall and Spring of my senior year, even into the summer thereafter. That was the year of hardcore punk; playing our own shows, delighting the audiences that showed and more scaring the hell out of everyone else. Besides playing and attending shows, there was a hell of a lot of band practice and weed smoking for the reactivated Xonxe. All of this new insanity was more than welcome.

Never was I into the punk rock culture any more than that final year in Moorestown, and more than half of these ridiculous looking punk rock guys were rich kids. Go figure. It never sat well with my parents, the mohawks, that is. Not the rich kids part, that was okay. What was not okay was how they looked; worse yet in the face of how they were evidently expected to look. It all meant failure to the Pszcynacks, even if indirectly. Perception was still everything. Punk rockers in a rich suburban Jersey town. Unacceptable. If anything, they probably belonged there more.

Even with Xonxe's mini-tour of small venues and house parties, the punk rock music scene was going through a bit of a comeback in this mid to late nineties era on its own. A lot of older bands from the seventies and eighties were getting more appreciation; some even re-uniting after well over a decade apart. Craig, myself, and many of the other guys were visiting the Trocadero in Philadelphia, or the "Troc" much more often. Never playing a show there ourselves, yet never wanting to miss the next reunion or current punk rock show going on at our favorite venue, one only a train ride in from South Jersey. If there was a "revival" of this music, we were going to do everything we could to keep it alive.

The entire Xonxe band did an at least ten-minute jumping up and down group hug when we found out the Misfits would be performing at the Troc. It was not the original lineup of the band, this time with an entirely new lead singer, but we did not care. Our favorite band had returned, and we were not going to miss a single show. It was all a blast, and while none of us admitted to this at the time, I realized later that we didn't just want to see our favorite band that once existed in the past live and in person, we wanted those old times that we literally missed by accident of birth to return; to overlap or extend into the present. We wanted it to be 1981 again.

We saw the Misfits that year at least four times, whenever they were in Philly, and we also took road trips to see them in New York and North Jersey. Making up for lost time perhaps. While we didn't get to see the actual Misfits from the past; we could lay claim to seeing a "real" old school punk band with the two local Ramones gigs. Granted, it was that legendary band's final year together, but we were not missing them. Not a chance. This was our own time machine, albeit bespattered with loud music, leather jackets, mohawks, and all the while, our wacky tobacky.

The Ramones garnered popularity even with non-hardcore punk fans, and at one of the Ramones shows, I actually saw Michael and his clique right there in the crowd. He was still giving me those off-hand looks like he wished this would not happen, maybe even half terrified considering the company I kept. Johnny, Alfie, and even Shag were with him. I would always refer to Shag by that name, but at least Wendy was nowhere to be found. I didn't even know if they were still dating by that point. Maybe she found another boyfriend. She was never the type to be single for too long. Reminded me of someone else.

Even still, I found Michael and company in a large, crowded, dank, and discernibly dark concert hall. A room only illuminated by stage lights and the occasional smoking implement, bringing a haze about the crowd that fixed onto my jacket for days on end. There we were jammed in like sheep amidst the volume we could hear through even our bones. The Ramones were best seen in such an environment.

Those legends were still up there in their leather jackets and blue jeans, playing the old classics as if we never missed a single year, even given it was their farewell tour. I tried, but could not ignore the fact that Michael was there, along with most of his clique. I was not going to lie to myself, and it was almost impossible to simply enjoy the show. Michael was there, right in front of me. Damn that all to hell. If he was going to be gone, be gone. Or at least account for casting his friend aside.

Petty, but I could not help it. I didn't focus on Shag, the guy who "stole" my girl. I suppose it was entirely possible he did not date her to hurt me specifically, but we were friends and friends do not do that to each other. Not real friends. I would not have done it to him. In any case, Michael needed his receipt. I was not above revenge, and hell, he was not above accountability. Much like Johnny's sister.

While everyone in the crowd was jumping around and going crazy before the Ramones on stage, I would periodically slam into Michael, and he knew what I was doing and why. That's why he didn't retaliate other than with the predictable confused looks. Art of the unaccountable. That and he was probably horrified at the site of Craig standing next to me. When I got tired of the random slams and bumps, I punched Michael in the back of the head, and he fell forward into the crowd. Looking back, that was wrong. That didn't stop me from enjoying it all the same.

I never had any solid respect for authority, not after all I had seen. A huge, bald headed bouncer was standing only ten feet away from me, clad in black jeans and a bright yellow security t-shirt, glaring at me like a principal in a middle school lunchroom. He saw what I did, pointed directly at me, and charged. Before I knew what the hell to do, I was in a headlock about to be dragged out of the arena and out into the streets, hopefully not to be arrested. Out of nowhere a loud thud impaled the music and some random punk rock kid hit the floor next to me, he was wearing a black Ramones t-shirt, huge, tattooed, and bald; a skinhead by the looks of him. When he hit the floor, the skinhead's chains flew everywhere, screaming and plainly ready for bloody murder and instantaneous vengeance. The bouncer let go of my head and went after the new perpetrator of this violence. Then two other bouncers joined in and before I knew it, Craig was being carried off to the fire emergency exit on the far side and they tossed him out of the building and slammed the doors. Ian grabbed me and we disappeared into the crowd and the show went on; the full Ramones set and around three encores. They were not dying easily.

I didn't see Michael or his clique anywhere after that. When we finally left the show, Craig was outside smoking a cigarette and smiling at us. I felt terrible that he had to bail me out that way, and that he missed part of the show. It's not as if the Ramones were coming back to town the next year. They eventually split up, and most of their original members had passed away in the ensuing years; and perhaps the entire punk rock era with them.

"It's all good," Craig explained to me. "That huge bouncer guy was going to throw you out, and I didn't want to deprive you of seeing the entire show. For me? It was actually a personal lifelong dream of mine to be thrown out of a Ramones gig, and here I am. Besides, I had my eye on that skinhead I punched all night. I hate skinheads. They give punk rock a bad name in general. I'm not even sure why they come to these shows. Just to start fights? They're a bunch of racist, Nazi assholes. They should not be allowed to breed, we don't need that kind of bigoted shit anywhere, let alone at a Ramones show. What is the point of it? The racism makes absolutely no sense, but then again, making sense is not what they do. They hate being asked questions, so they can have a taste of my fist. So he went down and I got kicked out. Who the hell else will be able to say they were thrown out of Ramones show in this day and age? That was punk rock!"

This is what we had become, and I was not complaining, at least not right then and there. It was not enough to be angry all the time, everyone else had to know it too. This was a real end to a bygone era, even with the apparent revival. We wanted to cling on to a past that we never ourselves experienced in any profound way. So much so that Craig was willing to get himself thrown out of a show just to say that it actually happened. One can't deny his dedication. For him at least, I knew it was worth it. Somehow, I even respected him for it. He was never afraid to speak his mind, and more often than not, act on it. Maybe that's why he really turned off so many people, it wasn't his looks alone.

We smoked joints on the ride home. That calmed things down. If anything, smoking weed was the compulsory cap off (or launching of) any night's activities. I never heard from Michael, nothing became of my vengeful rabbit punch, and his hilarious crowd dive. Friends matter. Learn it. Craig said he saw Michael "run off like cheap mascara." Wise move. It may not have been 1981, but damned if we were not having our fill of it.

Later in the year, Christmas rolled around. There were no Xonxe gigs at this time but hell if the antics were ever going to cease. We had a million ideas in those days, and were just getting started. Ian's mother actually owned an aging minivan as a backup car for whatever reason. He drove around a couple of nights before Christmas and picked up all the members of Xonxe for a new exploit, eventually coming to my little house to collect me.

Joey was not around much after the Tina fiasco finally ended, spending most of his time working or drinking with his friends, what few he still had anyway. Old Joe and Barbara did not take too well to the Xonxe guys at any time during this era, but the purple and red mohawks were positively a bridge too far. Disgusted beyond belief for no good reason other than feeling superior. Someone else has to be inferior, apparently.

Outside of the members of Xonxe looking as obnoxious as they admittedly did, I never understood all the vitriol they received in turn from "adults" like my parents. Or maybe I did. It would be easy, and also true, to say that my parents didn't like the mohawks, the tattoos, or in Rob's case the long hair, because they were uncomfortable with anyone expressing themselves in such a way; or that they feared such individualism. Having been raised themselves quite the opposite.

None of that would be untrue, yet what they really feared was time. In "their day," boys didn't grow long hair, smoke cigarettes (or special cigarettes), or have tattoos, or Misfits skulls on their jackets. If they did, they would not be tolerated or last very long. The fact that times had changed that much was a slap in the face. As it was on Browning Road, their time had come to an end.

For better or worse, Xonxe and other such punk rock attitudes showed how much time had passed, and how irrelevant the "old" really becomes. That, and they were also rich kids. That drove them crazy. Rich white kids in Moorestown were supposed to be anything but. Stop proving everyone wrong. Stop telling us what we do not want to hear. None of this was part of their half-assed white flight plan, hence the loathing, and all the more detachment from their youngest son.

Neither Barbara nor old Joe said hello to any of the guys when they picked me up that night. After we left, they probably had a nice and long conversation about how much they disliked the guys' appearances. United in their disdain, strange bedfellows considering where their marriage was by that point. Then again, talking about how much they disliked mohawks and skull jackets meant all the less talking about failed unions and incessant drinking. Not to mention Joey police drama, pretty girls being smacked, and arm-breaking denial charades. Talk about their hair styles instead. Sometimes even the rejects can provide viable services.

When we left the house, Craig was able to explain to me why we were using the minivan that evening.

"Here, look at this," Craig said as he threw a tiny plastic object across the van at me, which I barely caught. I was still horrible at sports, nice reminder. I almost dropped it again when I realized what I was holding. It was a plastic baby Jesus, one that's usually in the manger of a nativity scene on front lawns at Christmas.

"What the hell is with this?" I asked, threw the baby Jesus back at Craig who caught it perfectly even while laughing.

"Craig and I stole it from one of my neighbor's front yards last night," Ian explained while driving.

"These guys are crazy, but this is going to be funny as hell," said Rob from the passenger seat, though not actually laughing, and hardly smiling. I didn't quite get it. Rob seemed to be happy to be with us, but I wondered why as we got older, his indifferent if not aloof attitude increased with each passing day. Perhaps he really missed his girl? I missed mine, but I missed my friends even more.

"Think about it," Craig explained. "When Ian's neighbors came out the next morning, they probably said to each other 'someone stole our baby Jesus,' so we are going to hit the town tonight, drive the minivan up to people's houses and run out and grab as many baby Jesus figures we can. That reaction will be funny as hell the next morning, even if we can't actually see them freak out. That, and maybe word will get around town that there is an epidemic of baby Jesus thefts going on!"

Easy to look back on these shenanigans as completely obnoxious. Back then it was pure hilarity. Frivolous, yet brilliant. I mean, really, who goes around stealing baby Jesus figures from front lawns? Offense can be an art in and of itself, and we were artists in more than just loud punk music. The fact that we found it much more amusing than anyone else was all the proof we needed, not to mention offending people was and is a remarkably easy thing to do.

The theft plan didn't go as well as we had hoped. Not that we were caught or had any police trouble, only that we would often chicken out if the lights in any given neighborhood were too bright, or if we thought the people living in the houses could see us. Only so many homes were "ripe" enough for such a theft.

The other issue was that not all the coveted baby Jesus figures were "free," in that we could not make off with the baby Jesus as he was often connected to the overall plastic scene on the lawns and was not going to move, let alone fit in the van. One lawn Craig and I came upon had a baby Jesus that was literally plugged into an outlet, thus making the figure glow in the freezing dark of night. We simply just didn't know what to do with it. Our only lack of option was leaving it.

Rob was entirely high for most of this excursion, and Ian kept demanding we get back into the van lest we get spotted. I wondered how rich families dealt with cops knocking on their door. Craig, being disappointed with the lack of progress in the actual count of baby Jesus figures we removed, grabbed this one and pulled on it with all his strength, gripping it with both hands while I played lookout. Craig got the baby Jesus free but not without an unbelievably loud popping sound and fireworks level sparks coming from the torn cable leading to the Jesus.

"Shit!" Craig yelled. I could hear yelling and movement from inside the house we just robbed of their god. Craig and I ran off and literally dove into Ian's minivan while he peeled away from the house, the sliding door still open as the cold wind blew into the van, making it next to impossible to close it as Ian sped down the street.

"I killed baby Jesus!" Craig screamed as he held up a broken, burnt beneath the knees baby Jesus up in front of us. This one we threw away immediately, but the job was done. I don't know why we even kept the other two baby Jesus figures we made off with, but I suppose every great story needs a memento, some evidence that it actually all happened. We didn't hear about any baby Jesus crime wave in the local news the next day but that was one for the ages.

No, it wasn't 1981, but it was our time. That was my senior year. Working, reading comics even still, band practice, playing live gigs to local audiences who thought we were crazy (and they were right); and smoking weed in the freezing cold winter with the windows wide open. That was something else with those guys every single winter. They would drive around with the windows wide open and blasting the heat because it was beyond freezing; yet this was for all the smoking, cigarettes or otherwise. No point in closing them after all. Ridiculous, yet practical.

Still, as we drove around that night, outrageously cold in our leather jackets, listening to classic punk rock while smoking joints and passing them around to each other with the bitter air blowing; I knew that while certainly unplanned and maybe not even the desired turn of events, I had good and even hilarious friends, and whatever "my time" actually was in this era of life, it was indeed mine. We were at the very least original, and that was far more than many others could say of themselves; especially as they actively tried not to go down our road. The Misfits and Ramones and so many others blared out of the minivan speakers as we drove to nowhere in particular. We were high as hell, and had more than one baby Jesus lying on the van's floor. We couldn't stop laughing, and no one but us would ever know why.

Chapter Eighteen

PAY AT THE DOOR

Somehow, we all made it to graduation the following June. The entire Xonxe band graduated together. Well, almost. Ian showed up to our graduation, even though he had already finished almost a month prior at his private school, and would be attending some college all the way out near San Francisco come the fall. Good for him, despite the crazy punk rock look, he was his parents' son after all. Even punk rock doesn't take the rich out of rich kids. Craig was actually allowed to walk in cap and gown with Rob and myself. Craig's alternative school didn't have a graduation ceremony, but the township schools allowed students to walk if they finished. Craig freshly shaved most of his head and dyed the mohawk spikes again to prepare. The graduation cap dangling off his pointy hair was a site to behold, and everyone who was not us hated it.

Shocking that we all made it to the school for the ceremony on time. We had been up the whole night before, a road trip all the way up to Sussex County, New Jersey to see the Misfits play at an amusement park of all places. We would go anywhere. After the show was over, we drove all the way back to Moorestown and the sun was rising by the time I laid down to sleep. Christy jumped up on my bed soon enough and off I went to graduation with the guys. With the usual exception of the dog, the Pszcynacks were in yet another uproar. Partially because Barbara was furious at me for writing "away" as to where I was going after high school next to my name in the graduation program. That was where I was going so why write anything else? I'd rather not remember Moorestown, and it didn't need to remember me.

It would always be a point of contention between myself and Barbara as to if I even went to Moorestown High School at all. I often would say I barely remember the time, and wished the move and new school never happened. Such blasphemy. Moorestown had to work, even well after it failed. She needed that, and words matter. I would not accommodate. The other issue that day was a loudish disagreement between Joey and Barbara over his complete disinterest in attending my graduation. With that I found myself somehow less disappointed. Barbara had to act shocked about his absence as if there was no basis or reasoning for it whatsoever. Maybe it wasn't even an act, natural denial long before that point.

"Go to your brother's graduation, Joseph!" Barbara demanded. "What's wrong with you? Cathy and Jean, Peg, Joan, all my friends, all their children go to graduations and everything else for their siblings, you should too."

Joey didn't answer her, then just walked out and drove off. Dead silence. Shocking. However impressive to its longevity, Barbara really did have an unhealthy relationship with those friends of hers. I suppose "success" comes with a price. She and old Joe didn't push that issue much by the time Grandmother Marie arrived. Why tell anyone what they didn't want to hear?

Just like most of the families in the graduation audience, rich and not as rich alike, my parents didn't go for Craig's cap on the mohawk spike look. Plenty of frowns with that false sense of superiority, all to conceal an unnecessary embarrassment for him being one of my friends. He certainly did stand out on that football field, his multi-colored hair adorned against the giant yellow "M" on the ground. I supposed I looked normal enough, even if that was never good enough.

That graduation was the first-time Marie had even seen my Moorestown punk friends. I couldn't hear her as we walked past but Marie literally stood up and wagged her finger at Craig, apparently scolding him for his mohawk and whatever other issues she had with him. My parents slinked away, I gave a rare smirk of my own, and Craig didn't even notice.

It's not as if he didn't know he was infuriating everyone. For Craig, days he was irritating others and freaking them out without really trying were called weekdays. Weekends too, come to think of it. I suppose had this been 1981, he would not have even been allowed to graduate. We still would have given anything to be ourselves in that time. Why was the past always so much more appealing? I suppose we knew too much to disregard such an obvious fantasy. Flat out guilty of golden age thinking. For being born at the wrong time and worse yet, knowing it. I never got the impression we were entirely wrong.

After the ceremony, all of us, Xonxe, the visiting Media Pandemic guys, Ruptured, the very heart of punk rock in South Jersey, at least for that time, slipped out to where no one was; the front door of Moorestown High School. None of it planned yet somehow understood, we slunk down the front wall in a line, protected somewhat by the trees and various shrubbery, not to mention the general fact that no one wanted to look at us; and in unison, all peed on the front wall of the school; laughing hysterically at that last final farewell. I never went near that building again.

I suppose that was one of the most epic relief sessions of my entire life, all the more fortunate it was on the wall of a school I never wanted to be a part of before, during, or since. I remembered peeing on the floor of my room in Pennsauken, being afraid of my brother's unsleeping wrath and not one thing ever being done about the unbridled bullying. All the while being made to feel worse because of it, let alone to speak of it. I continued to pee on the wall with the guys and it was still there. Pennsauken. I would not be where I was, pissing on the wall of a school and town that I loathed, had I never moved or rather been moved. Displaced. Punk rock was far more than necessary than I had ever realized. Deliberately and unapologetically offensive. Even necessary. Fuck them.

We eventually finished and lit up what could be smoked, albeit quickly. We knew how to keep ourselves amused, but my heart sank thinking about Michael and all of my former friends who were then graduating from my hometown school, and I wasn't there. I didn't make it. They didn't even want me there by that point.

Perhaps I finally accepted it was gone, yet still missed it all the same. My only coping mechanism was the Xonxe guys, our upcoming summer shows, and then all of us besides Craig planning on going to college the following Fall. Time burns, and its scars do not often heal. Never entirely.

But Pennsauken was gone. I wondered then and even so many years after what point cliques actually served. Is it the exclusivity of it? We have something you don't? I am cooler than thou art? I want something you can't have? I never bought into it. Maybe that was the problem. I couldn't bullshit right, or at all most of the time. Thus, I was shown the door. Xonxe was never really a clique. I still always felt like the odd man out, not for my lack of wild appearance, but the fact that Craig, Rob, and Ian knew each other since they were five, and I came into their world at fifteen. That is more than just nothing. I was out of both cliques. That may likely be the reason that neither would last in time. So much ado. It seemed so much more important at the time.

Then there was the family. Despite her ageist outrage at her first sight of Craig, Marie was having a week of her own; more than just a little cranky, albeit with some level of justifiable reason. Not just because old people are not fans of change and they are not alone. For everyone, there is that one final change. That moment in time when the party ends, well at least for you it does.

About five days before my graduation, Marie lost Aunt May Bearens, Marie's aunt by marriage. She was very old, late eighties, apparently. I only faintly remembered her from Christmas days long past, or any other vague family gatherings Aunt May attended. She was a widow for a long time. Marie's uncle, May's husband passed away years before I was born, and they had no children. Aunt May almost entirely lived alone all her life. No kids, no vacations, just living.

Remarkable how life turns out for some people. This was part of my own family's history. Maybe Aunt May's death could explain something, even if no one but me wanted to know. Old Aunt May had no family whatsoever besides my grandmother. That was all that was left for her. My family never talked much about death, less so around me, as if that was somehow noble. Yet less than a year before I graduated and peed on the high school wall with an assembly of goofy punk rockers, Aunt May was diagnosed with cancer. There was nothing the doctors could do for her. Not at that age.

Regardless, it must have been rough receiving a death sentence, to be tapped on the shoulder and told "your time is up." Nothing can be done to stop it. How does one's ego handle such indifference? To know there is not always a tomorrow. Hard to criticize that kind of denial. Yet Aunt May was a responsible person. After the cancer diagnosis, she went to a lawyer to prepare a will and my grandmother was named the executor. Marie was also a beneficiary, though not for everything.

One of the reasons Marie was so cranky at graduation was that she was about to sell Aunt May's house, some old duplex she lived in for sixty some odd years in the Belmont area of Philadelphia. Marie inherited the house, as well as all the furniture left inside. She tried to sell some furniture to no avail, no one wanted it. She even tried to give some to Barbara, annoyed to find out she didn't want any of it either. Old became undesirable.

Marie did sell the house. I was not told for how much. Yet the problem was old Aunt May's other assets, somewhere in the tune of over one-hundred thousand dollars. That's what she had in her bank account at the time of her death. Chalk that up to a lifetime of no kids, no vacations, and not to mention being in a generation where a person could retire at a decent age. It must have been nice, however taken for granted. Quite like the Coyles on Browning Road way back when, and even having that much coin in the bank when it came time to die. Exasperatingly, Marie didn't see a dime of that money. Aunt May donated every dollar of it to the church down the street from her home.

Like everyone else in both families, my immediate ancestors were raised Catholic. All taught this particular religion when they were very young, and they often kept going to church every Sunday even well into adulthood. Then as time and generations went on, there was less worship. My own family generally only went to church at Christmas, and Joey and I did attend catechism classes after school until around the age of twelve or so. That was the religion we were brought up in. That was what was decided for us before we were even out of diapers. That was never spoken of either. Aunt May herself was apparently not that religious at all, having lapsed in her faith years before she died, if she ever had it to begin with. Her only affiliation with that church who got all her money was the fact that it was down the street from her.

"What the hell did they do with it?" I heard Marie complaining to Barbara about the rectory getting all that money. It was a good question, and a lot of money. Why give it to the church? All the more ironic, after everyone else refused to buy (or even accept as free) old Aunt May's furniture, Marie actually ended up donating all of that to her own local church. Mortality sells. Marie complained to everyone about this, even me. I thought she would have hated what I said regarding the matter, but then again, money talks and bullshit walks. Though that church did fairly well for all their bullshit.

"She tried to buy her way into heaven," I said, honestly, certainly, but in near shock someone in my family actually agreed with me for a change.

Marie nodded and said, "No kidding, that's exactly why she gave them all of it," while Barbara slinked away from the both of us. Criticizing the "boss" again. That always brings out the fear. It never fails, and is all too obvious to ignore. Aunt May was already well into her eighties, and with the cancer diagnosis, there was simply nothing for it. She could have donated that money to anywhere, those estate lawyers deal with it all the time. They could have provided her with lists of all kinds of charities to donate to, be they animal welfare, education, anything. Hell, many people dying from cancer will often donate money to cancer research charities in the hopes of finding a cure, and perhaps for others not to suffer the same fate. Marie didn't get a single dime of that treasure. She could have. No. The church got it. One cannot help but to question their own existence, and Marie was whatever hell her old aunt evidently saved herself from.

Aunt May was not a particularly religious person, raised that way, yes, but how effective can those stories really be compared to any other? Be it as it may have been, she decided to make a deal, and did a "good deed" by donating every bloody cent to the church down the street. Charlatans know their game well. Yet I doubt the rectory was really that surprised to receive that check. They very likely never even knew who Aunt May was. Did her donation grant her entry into "heaven," if she even really believed in it at all? We often just believe what we are told, and people will do anything if they are afraid.

Aunt May was gone right before graduation, and I hardly knew her. She was part of my family's old world, gone but clearly not forgotten. They were all raised Catholic. Christian. That meant a lot more to the time when my parents were children themselves, more so probably when Marie was young. Would the man known as Jesus of Nazareth behave the way that my family had behaved, and have continued to do so long after their white flight from Pennsauken?

I never accepted the stories and false promises, but even if Jesus was real, and not entirely a composite of prior myths and historical distortion over two thousand years, I will admit that at least on paper, the Jesus way is not the worst idea. Contrary to how we so often, if not always, behave. He was supposed to be better than all this. That character laid on that hippy peace, love, and sharing motif pretty thick. Conveniently, he later became an overseeing babysitter for when one's parents were not there, or when they didn't want to be. A boogeyman in the guise of a loving father who demands you fear him. Malleable purposes.

I doubt that Jesus, whatever he may have been, would say "don't sell to no blacks," or "money talks and bullshit walks," or "look in the mirror." Any of it. All the fear, all the competition, all the mistrust, most certainly all the denial, the lies and manipulation; it was not at all "Christian." Why was I treated the way I was the day Barbara broke her arm? Why was I told to 'forget it' when I would not ever? Why was it never mentioned again, and left unresolved? All that abuse, the fear, those memories; I never wanted it, but I was always a bad liar. Not religious, and frankly proud of that, but is any of what I was or am, "Christian?" We still don't talk about it, and if we do, more often than not, it doesn't last. Sensitivity. Or perception again.

Speaking of denial, why was denial a thing? All the Joey crap alone is hardly worth another mention to them. I suppose that is the whole idea. There is more power and advantages in silence. Maybe that was a religious byproduct, but being forced to love someone whom you also fear is impossible. It's sadomasochism at best.

On religious upbringing, I used to believe until all too recently, that the nuns or priests or whoever were my family's teachers back then actually pulled young people like Barbara and old Joe aside after their graduation and said something along the lines of, "Okay, you graduated and now you go forth in the world. Just know that it was all bullshit, and you are to despise and fear black people and they are not to walk in your neighborhood. You are to obey capitalism, in that while the rest of the business world is not tax free like ours, money is still king, and all that Jesus shit was made up to make us look good. It's all a trick. 'God' is whatever we say he is, and he said whatever we say he said. Bullshit is the real religion. We are the real 'gods.'" Understand this well and enjoy."

That was a rather funny albeit unpleasant thought, yet all the same, it's not the truth. The truth is, Christian kids growing up like my family were never told it was all bullshit, nor were they told to be racist. But they were expected to understand it regardless. Most of them "got it." They fit in well. Expectations were to not ask any questions. Any questions at all were insubordinate. They love Jesus but they hate black people, and are perfectly comfortable using a certain word to describe them. As long as it is behind closed doors, of course. People do not care about what offends you as much as others seem to expect. That was my family. Essentially all of Browning Road back then. They understood the game and liked it. They got it. I didn't get it. That caused a few problems down the line.

As for my hometown of Pennsauken, I often wondered why the racist, invisible man worshiping "Christians" would even move there in the first place. The Pszcynacks arrived there in the mid-seventies. They raised children there, and directly abused at least one over accidents, attention, disappointment, malcontent, and perception of all of the above; not to mention his complete lack of ability to deny, to play the game the way they wanted and needed him to play it. That was not in their interests.

Why move to that town in the first place? It's right on the edge of Camden, New Jersey, which was poor, rough, and predominantly black even in the seventies. Why not move to Moorestown before having children? Or Mt. Laurel, New Jersey, or any other town that is still now relatively white? Seems to make sense given how racist they really were. It's okay to be full of shit as long as everyone else is.

The initial move to Pennsauken was partly (perhaps mostly) that my family was cheap. Money hurts. Just look at that little house in Moorestown they moved to. Pennsauken was cheaper to live in, more so than those other predominantly white towns of the time, even in the seventies when home prices and mortgage rates were significantly less than they are now. Boomer privilege. So what if Pennsauken was adjacent to rough neighborhoods? Barbara and old Joe grew up in Philadelphia. The city. They grew up adjacent to black neighborhoods all their lives. But back in the apparent glory days, there was an understanding. Black people did not ever wander into white neighborhoods and vice versa. Never could they move into a white neighborhood, that was unheard of. Impossible. It was all understood without even once having to explain it to anyone. That's the ideal understanding, immature as it all was.

Even when the Civil Rights Act passed in 1964, outlawing discrimination on race and color and everything else that mattered so much in the United States; even after that, it was still unspoken that black people and white people would keep to their own, and neighborhoods did not and apparently never would mesh. It was all understood. Then things changed. Times changed. Black people started to move into Pennsauken in the eighties, ever closer and eventually into the neighborhoods where they were not previously allowed. Don't sell to no blacks. Eventually, someone did. Worse yet, white kids such as Matt Del began playing football in the streets with black kids, and with far less stigma. Unheard of. The understanding was gone. The world was changing, and my family, along with so many other white flighters on Browning Road in Pennsauken couldn't handle it, even by implication; and so began the exodus.

As for why all the racism to begin with, well there is a reason for that too. It was never as simple as that guy over there has darker skin, so therefore I hate him. It's easy to say when describing racists that they really are as simple as disliking the "other" simply for being of a different race, color, or what have you. Easy answers like that are always wrong. No one talks as much, especially older generations, of our vast differences in class. They won't speak of the greater issue here. The issue that obsessions with race and other immutable features keeps us from ever really discussing. That, unfortunately, is still very much an understanding. It's exactly what they want. They, up there.

No one likes to talk about wealth inequality. The fear, again. It's how my family, certainly how entire generations were raised. It's what they were taught, however indirectly. They were taught not to question authority. To accept it all without explanation. They were taught not to "punch up." Though punching down, that was just fine. The more we obsess and divide over race, gender, or any immutable characteristic we may have, the less we talk about the ever-widening gap between those that are wealthy, or at least well off, and everyone who is not. "Authority" likes that just fine.

We have to feel superior to someone. My father, old Joe Pszcynack, and even old Aunt May, along with everyone else, were not rich people. They were well off middle class at a time it was easier to be well off, but they knew they were not rich, and they knew not to criticize their "betters." But old Joe and his incessant racism, along with just about everyone else on Browning Road, they could feel superior to black people. The idea in their thinking (if it's even fair to call it thought) is: "I am not rich, and I won't be. What I have is good, but this is still the best I am ever going to get in life. This is it. I won't question or dare defy the 'bosses,' simply because the bosses told me not to, and we don't get rich in life by criticizing the rich. So, I will be 'superior' to these people over here. Black people, specifically. I am better than them. I am superior, and they are inferior. They can't have what I have, even if it's not really that much. I hate them for that reason."

Denial as a machine has many moving parts. A monitored and well-oiled machine. That machine is precious, sad as that is. Grandmother Marie was still fuming about Aunt May's death and the accounts of her will when my graduation day came along, even while Xonxe, myself, and the rest of the punk rockers were peeing on the high school's front wall. I saw my family again in the parking lot after that. As they were getting into their car, Marie came up to me alone.

"I am proud of you, Jack. You graduated from a good school, congratulations," she said while squeezing my hand. Thankfully not giving me that grandmother kiss on the cheek in front of my terrifying punk rock friends.

"And your father is proud of you," she said while wagging her finger down at me.

That finger. That's how I knew it was a lie. Punching down indeed. Old Joe was there at graduation, but he never said a word to me. He didn't need to, and it was no different that day than any other. It was better that he didn't say anything. He was probably complaining to Barbara about the amount of black people at the graduation ceremony, however few in comparison. Insatiable.

What anyone else and less so I thought just didn't matter. As long as the lie was said and received, it not being the truth was of little consequence. They left. The guys and I ended up smoking weed all night out at the old train bridge where the cops would never bother to go. Later we had a late-night band practice in Ian's basement, and that was essentially how my time in Moorestown ended.

The band had a lot of shows that summer afterwards. Even still, it was another end. The band was never going to last past the coming Fall. Ian went out to California for college that August. Rob went to the local community school for less than a semester, before he dropped out entirely. I was going away too. Craig was left alone in town for a time with his drugs, which for him, only got worse as years went by. It happens so often we almost expect things to get worse than they are or were. How could any of it ever get better? How could any of this have ever really worked? It couldn't. I just didn't see it then.

Time wrecks us more than anything else in this world. Life afterwards didn't always go too well. I still lost friends, always losing more than I found, or so it often seemed. Ian all but disappeared in the following years. I heard he never finished college, but got into motorcycles and cross-country road trips, working occasionally as a motorcycle mechanic. Trust fund rich kids. That is real privilege, and they didn't work any harder than anyone. We so often love to piss in each other's pockets and tell them it's raining.

Rob got involved with another girlfriend shortly after he stopped taking classes. Naturally, he disappeared. No need for friends in such a scenario. No need for us. I think he knew I despised that about him, as with so many others. His girlfriend eventually went back to school on a scholarship all the way down in Florida. Rob followed her down there and worked as a waiter, of all things. He must have cut his hair and lost the fork bracelet. He eventually split up with that girl as well, and she returned to New Jersey. He's still down there in Florida, as far as I know. Dubious relocation, but maybe he likes it there.

Craig and I continued to hang out a lot, becoming one of my very good friends in life but scaring the hell out of all the "normal" friends I made in college and thereafter. Despite all the ridiculous fun and crazy music, I actually always wanted to be normal, whatever normal was. Well and beyond out of my reach, long before I ever realized it.

After a while, I turned myself off of the punk rock music. I tried to move ahead and beyond, as if I wanted to mature and be that other guy I never was. Times change, though I sometimes listen to a good Ramones or Misfits song in the car or at home. They were still great bands, and I was happy I met Craig and all the guys to be exposed to it. A bizarrely positive take away from that bygone era.

For Craig himself, the drug habits grew far and beyond casual weed smoking, getting to the point where he would not want to do a thing with anyone unless he was high on something first. No longer just weed. Nothing in moderation with him. I got sick of the drugs and aloof attitude to any point to the contrary, and we eventually grew apart. He never really understood why. All that mattered was the drugs anyway. He certainly was a character. But everyone has their limits. I still think about him and laugh all the time.

The harsh truth of the punk rock, or the Moorestown era friends that they were; is that I never fit in with them at all, and never felt completely accepted by any of those guys. Same as never being completely part of the Michael clique in Pennsauken. I was gone and didn't really arrive anywhere. The outsider. No hometown for me. No consistency. Incongruous everywhere I went; and with whomever I met. Always displaced. How things turn out. That was the consequence of the white flight from Browning Road all those years ago. This was the result.

I still continued my trips past the house on Browning Road, though as time went on, those trips were getting much more few and far between. Once a year, maybe. Mostly only when I was feeling nostalgic, so often enough. Sometimes I would even visit the Longfellow School website, just to see pictures of the inside of my old haunts. It got ridiculous after a while; the kids there now have absolutely nothing to do with me. But then again, if the information is available, why not take advantage of it? That's where social media came into play. It's where you can see what a casual acquaintance you had in grammar school ate for lunch just the other day, even decades after the fact.

Sometimes I even wound up "cyber-stalking," or just spending time seeing where old friends and yes, even those casual acquaintances wound up. There was something wrong about knowing all that. Something inconsistent and against the natural flow of time. Almost as if I shouldn't know. Pennsauken was a graveyard, to me anyway. Yet I could never really let it go. That would be giving in. Or maybe I really missed it. However, the online exchanges were another way to connect to that era. It's how I started to talk to Damon Bailey again. It's how I learned how he was doing and made a friend all over again. It's how I helped Damon's nephew out on a history of Pennsauken project he was working on for school. Damon's nephew now lived on Browning Road. That is how I was finally able to go home.

Chapter Nineteen

TOBACCO POUCH

Twenty-five years have passed since I graduated high school and violated the school's front wall with the punk rock jokers. Well, about that much time has passed, I think. I find I am keeping track of all the time far less than ever before. Just a couple of months ago and completely on a whim, or perhaps a desperate feeling to reach out to just anyone these days, I contacted Damon Bailey through the internet. He immediately "friended" me and we started talking again. He and I didn't part on bad terms, and I was more than elated for the chance to speak and hang out with him again. Damon was above cliques, and somehow, I always knew that. It didn't make me feel better about some of the choices I had made. I wish I had stayed in touch with him. The roads we take.

Damon spent his whole life in Pennsauken. Now he lived in a house by himself, not far from his parents who were also still in town. I could not believe it when I met him for drinks. Not that he still lived in Pennsauken, but just how professional and exceptionally well dressed he was when he went out on the town. I actually felt underdressed by comparison, maybe even a little jealous. We are both in our early forties now, and he looks like a bald Luther Vandross; clean cut, nice gray and blue suit, shiny shoes, bling, cologne, all of it. The man has more than just some class.

Damon is now a real estate manager, taking care of a number of apartment buildings and other rental properties in the area. Neither of us ever became rich, but Damon reached a point in life where the clothes would almost make the man, at least enough to always dress well wherever he went. I need to ask him to take me shopping. It turned out Damon never completed college, yet wanted to go back again just to say he finished. That just had to be accomplished, his words. Damon's face lit up when I told him I was a college English professor, maybe he would have to take one of my classes. I wouldn't go easy on him because we were friends. I'd probably have trouble with all the college girls keeping their eyes on him, and not the lesson plans I was teaching that week.

We talked all night, mostly catching each other up on everything since we were freshman in high school, where it all was and what has become of it. Damon said he knew I used to hang out with Michael, and he knew I briefly dated Wendy Eastman, only being one of her many boyfriends around that time. Bad memories. It still kind of hurt but that was always the kind of guy I was. Honest. Especially to myself. Damon confirmed that Michael and the crew were considered snobby and exclusive for the sake of shutting others out, as if to somehow be cool that way. That's the point of a clique. All they ended up doing was alienating everyone but themselves and apparently, none of those guys even talk to each other any longer, according to legend. It really makes one question what the big deal surrounding cliques were in the first place. Time burns it all away.

Michael did have some nameless girlfriend himself during his exclusive senior year. He got her pregnant right before college began and broke up with her as a consequence. Both his family and hers guilted the hell out of him not to run away. So he didn't go to college at all apparently, and went right to work to support his new family. No one knows what has happened to him since. His kids are probably over twenty-one years old by now.

Damon laughed his head off when I told him I used to be in a punk rock band in my other high school. He said the punk thing didn't seem to match who I was then, and less so now being the "upstanding" intelligent college professor I happened to be employed as. I told him he really had no idea how angry I was back then. I suppose no one did. As for the "intelligent" professor vibe, well, I told Damon to his face I didn't dress half as well as him and he was making me a little uncomfortable. Damon always had his way with the opposite sex, probably more so even now. The man smiled more than me. He had been married twice in the intervening years. Life takes us where it wants, not where we would like it to take us; one way or another.

Damon also let me know that his cousin Coletta, herself only a year older than us, was a grandmother now. She didn't work and relied entirely on government assistance to take care of her family alone. Rough times. I honestly felt kind of bad, and maybe even a little worse for that part of me who once felt she deserved it. She was a bully. Unpardonable even at that age, if not more so. This was indirect justice. But we were kids. Times had changed, and I hoped she was okay. I always liked kids, and never had any of my own. I just wished everyone didn't respect Coletta the way they did back then for the way she behaved. We so often do not take any thought for tomorrow.

All of that was far less difficult than catching Damon up on what happened to my family after Aunt May died. Barbara and old Joe still live in that little house. They are getting up there in age, and the house, the glorified trailer, it's more or less falling apart. I keep asking them to sell the house and move into a retirement community. That is always met with turned heads, and even more silence.

Perhaps they do not want to hear my sigh of relief when that house and town are finally in the past. Perhaps selling and leaving the little house would be admitting a mistake. All it took to leave last time was black kids playing in the street. History does not always repeat itself. Barbara still shows off her rage if it's even implied that the house is as small as it is. Some days I call it the "dead horse." Consequences. We don't talk as much these days anyway. My former wife once said to me said to me, "Your family does not like you." It hurt hearing that, even though I knew more than anyone she was right. Yet to actually hear it.

To their credit, my parents never got rid of the dog. However, Christy did pass away at around the age of fifteen, which was rather old in basset hound dog years. She died in her sleep one night, well fed and rested. I was saddened yet not too surprised to hear of her passing. Both of my parents cried that day. Yes, even old Joe. The house is less charming without the dog. At least there are still scratch marks on the windowsill from when she would go berserk at the mailman visits. That dog was good for the Pszcynacks, probably the only good thing, and she was the only family member to love everyone and do so without condition, without unspoken rules, needs to be met, only then to be punished for those failures. Of course no one would ever admit it, but Christy was the only reason we all didn't end up killing each other. I will always remember her and smile.

Grandmother Marie is still alive, very late eighties at this point. Still doing well, she's tough, that is for certain. She spends most of her time coddling Barbara, trying to convince her she didn't make any mistakes, and that the fact that I don't talk to them much is somehow not an indication that things had just gone horribly wrong over the years.

Not easy getting old though. Everyone always praises the very elderly for living so long, I suppose they should, but no one seems to ever mention how being that old must really be awful. I am guilty of not taking much thought for when my own body will eventually betray and give out on me, and I fear for who may not be there for me when it does. I don't want Marie to go, but it will happen at some point, unfortunately. I wonder how much money she will donate to her church then, if any. I wonder what they will do with it, and why. I wonder if they are waiting.

Joey died in his early forties, not too long ago. It was sudden, I couldn't believe it when I got the call. He had a good job selling sheet rock for a while, then got laid off during one of the many housing crises. Coming of age in the modern economy. I've lost track of how many recessions there have been recently and there will be more. He took it hard. I realized more by then exactly how much he wanted to emulate old Joe, as if there was any reason to emulate him.

Joey lived in the past. He hated technology, would not use a cell phone, he had to ask me to write him a resume to find another job because he didn't know what a resume was. He didn't even have an email address because he just didn't want to live past the seventies. I suppose we were indirectly alike in that manner. He became less violent after Tina, that was true, but nothing really changed about him. He would drop the "N" word almost as much as his father. He really liked him, and wanted to emulate him. I had to look at myself sometimes. The true path. Night and day.

Alas, Joey died alone. Separated, basically a single dad, no job and a couple of D. U. I. 's on his record. None of that killed him. Whatever his health issues, he somehow developed a blood clot in his leg. It was quite painful, yet being the stubborn ass that he was, he refused to obey doctor's orders by wearing a compression stocking, especially overnight. No doctor was going to tell him what to do. The clot killed him in his sleep.

That was rough on everyone, and everyone knew he and I never got along. Harder still, they were right. No psychology. He could have been treated by a therapist but the madness continued unabated. Just forget about it. I didn't. That was real. "Real" was the experience of living in fear. Abused. Forgotten, or at least brushed aside when necessary. That was often. Worst of all of it, what of reputation. The Pszcynacks were perceived in their loss. Any further grief mattered little, at least by comparison.

Even still, Joey's passing was hard to take in. I spent a lot of time with his daughter after that. I always felt slightly bad for feeling good about that in turn. I was happy to fill in, so to speak, as her dad. We always got along well, and it is wonderful watching her grow up into the positive person she always was, even as far back as a little girl. Remarkable, given her roots. She always makes me smile, alight at her presence, or even a thought. Quite the opposite of all the abuse and negativity from when her father was her age, even younger. Times changed. At least for that, that is something, and it is good. Sometimes the sun rises, even if we don't always notice.

Barbara was rightly upset at Joey's passing, and didn't get into the "what will the neighbors think of me" routine nearly as much as she would have had it been any other occurrence. What could she do? None of her girlfriends lost their children. None of them. I hope that wasn't as much of an issue for her, but I see little reason for such confidence. But we all did what we had to do and buried him. No church service. Less weight on my own heart, though I know that is selfish, however true. My niece was glad I was there. That's what really mattered.

Damon told me he was sorry I lost my brother, telling me a loss of family still matters, even if we didn't get along. That was an understatement. I hated being part of it because understatements were part of the bullshit my entire family built their kingdom on. Denial. Downplaying. Outright lies. "Just forget about it." Dishonesty. That was something I could never really be, and being the bad guy for it made it all the worse.

Damon's jaw did drop a bit when I told him about that Moorestown fight that broke out over a dog growl. He still didn't understand why Tina was dating him and continued to do so after that nightmare. He was right to at least question it. I had more concrete ideas as to why. I remembered everything. Despite the comic books, marijuana, and punk rock in those days, I always wanted to be normal. We are what circumstances make of us. That's easier said than lived with.

I do not see or visit my family much, at least not my parents at the little house. Bad memories, and somehow it becomes more uncomfortable and confining every single time I am there. They never act the way they are when my niece is there, but somehow, even over a quarter of a century after that panicked white flight from Browning Road, they are more racist than ever before. Old Joe, specifically. How could it get worse? They moved. Isn't that enough? Whatever it is, they are not getting over it. But how can anyone get over inferiority? They would have to get over themselves. For far too many, that god in the mirror.

Old Joe still drops that infamous word "nigger" in nearly every context of conversation. Name it: sports, politics, college, work, entertainment, everything. It's almost as if they never left their former home. They brought it with them. The inferiority complex. Incidentally, old Joe continued his near daily trips to Philadelphia to drink at the bar he did back when he was young. I swear, that guy was never once a kid. He didn't ever have the maturity to be even that.

It all eventually came to an end, though. The journeys to Philadelphia that is, not the drinking. The trips over the bridge to the city continued unabated for years until one final evening, old Joe was pulled over by a cop for a depleted taillight. He didn't get busted for drinking and driving, yet he was furious over being ticketed and never went back to Philly again as a consequence. This was because the cop was black.

A black cop pulled over old Joe Pszcynack. Who knows if that officer had that appalling cop ego. In this case, I really hope he did. Old Joe couldn't handle it. Apparently black cops were not allowed to pull over old white men. I was not aware of this law, yet old Joe was fairly confident it was true. Confidence. It's appealing to the wrong kind of person.

Sitting there and enjoying conversation with Damon, I realized again that the Pszcynacks, that family that lived on Browning Road in Pennsauken, they were just not normal. Whatever normal may be. Just like anyone else who lived on that street, we could be dangerous, ignorant, even criminal; sometimes violent, and most consistently in denial about any and all of the above. Since I was around three I have been responsible for all of it. Why are you hitting yourself, Jack? The playground. The truth is rather easy to deny when one is not at all interested in truth whatsoever. Easy as breathing. Only outweighed by their own sensitivity, or insecurity. Both, really.

In one of my last visits to the Moorestown trailer several months ago, Barbara played me a short video from her sixty-year anniversary party of all of her friends' first meeting, way back when they were in first grade or whenever they all met. It was cute, showing pictures from when they were all little girls, then teenagers, then older, families and kids, and now grandkids of their own. They had a huge gala that was catered somewhere to celebrate this inadvertently dubious milestone.

They know what they are. They do not think of it. Would they? Even still, I was always impressed with Barbara and the other old girls' ability to remain friends for that length of time. Looking back and even then, it really was what hurt about losing Michael Del as a friend. He was to be my friend for life that I knew since I was about six. An overestimation, yet I suppose that expectation was based on Barbara Pszcynack's success before, and after. Michael is alive and well out there, yet long gone. What could have been can always hurt.

Something that Barbara said to me afterwards ultimately took most of the wind out of those sails, however. The nostalgia video ended and the credits rolled, thanking some of their parents who had since passed away over the years. Again, nice touch but then I was reminded of what smoke and mirrors can be.

"We were together for that long," Barbara said, turning off the T.V. "We are all still friends. All of us. Look at that last photo of everyone. All those years. No divorces."

Smug comment. Then again, if one spends a lifetime denying, deceiving and even cheating to "stay ahead" in life, one somehow should be allowed to take their victory lap. All of this for how she was perceived by a clique of girlfriends that I hardly even knew and now wanted to know even less. Perception. Even at the cost of abuse.

Barbara bragging about how she never got a divorce is like an anorexic bragging about how thin she is. The purpose of the goal was accomplished, yes, yet look at how much you hurt yourself, how much you hurt others, and how dishonest your victory actually is. It is nothing to brag about. I realized very long ago that my parents not getting a divorce was likely the root of all the psychological issues we had with one another. All of them. There was no release. Never.

To this day, my parents generally ignore each other, old Joe still spends his free time drinking (and he's long retired), they have taken separate vacations for decades and have mastered the art of quiet des-peration in that, no, their marriage did not come to such an end. Yet for all their boasting of that never happening, they took no thought for what consequences that farce actually had. All for an apparent competition with a clique of girls from a bygone, albeit better, era that has lasted over sixty years and counting. For them.

By divorcing only in their hearts, and quietly in their minds, I realize what my parents created in their home, in Joey's behavior, and even my own disagreeable experiences. Their decisions, and whenever convenient lack thereof had all been a questionable, destructive, and sometimes even violent pressure cooker created for all of us to live in. That's what started that fight before I entered Moorestown High School. That fight was plain and clear evidence that this family was by no means stable, I dare say not even loving. Not even close.

We did not love one another, and the more that selfishness was challenged, or even implied to be, the worse it got. What more evidence was needed? There was an abundance of additional evidence, and to spare. Speaking of, or apparently even thinking of, any of this was completely against the narrative that somehow, everything in the little homestead was exactly the opposite to any truth at all. The sky wasn't blue, and the sun revolved around the earth. No such criticism was acceptable of any of it. The show had to go on, even if Joey had killed me that night. It would have gone on.

By not divorcing, or at least by never really speaking in any adult sense of the issues that were about us, that created an atmosphere of mistrust, contempt, suspicion, uncertainty, and oftentimes outright hate that underlined my entire upbringing within those four walls. Small price to pay for not being perceived as a failure when you most certainly were. I never had any vested interest in any of this farce. They did. I was always off the deep end, even among them. Especially among them. Brushed aside and expected to accept it. Removed and expected not to notice. No.

We can't go through childhood twice. We cannot have the opportunity to grow up again. It's all hard to digest whenever I actually think about it, and I think a whole awful lot. For all their bravado, for all my own resentment, for all my being younger than they were; they were not adults. Never once. We are only as good as our word, and if those words are drenched in deceit, racism, ageism, preaching, and just all-around willful ignorance that provides a certain level of bliss (presuming that sufficient denial is provided in turn) then I suppose they will be content with all of it. I was not them.

I sure sound confident. I am. Though that doesn't mean that it all doesn't hurt like burning hell, and always has. I didn't grow up well. I have to live with that. They didn't know what they were doing, only how they were (apparently) being perceived. The truth be damned. Not for me. Denial was never on the menu, difficult as that really was, and always has been. Unwelcome. That's an understatement.

There are good people in this world. Yet they are a dying breed. That's not as cynical as they want me to believe. At best what they have is faith. Not fact. Important distinction. All the same, I was happy to reconnect with Damon again, I hope it's not for selfish reasons. I hope he knows I care about what friends are even if separated by so much time. He did want to talk to me about his nephew's project. Jamal Bailey and his parents actually moved to Browning Road after the white flight era. Some years after I left, his family moved into the Myers' house, two houses down from my home, and right next door to the naked break in house with Mr. Graff that night. A lifetime ago. It turns out Jamal was working on a history of Pennsauken project for one of his classes in middle school.

I recall having such lessons back at Longfellow and after, history of the United States, history of New Jersey, and even history of the little town called Pennsauken. Just like nearly every single other town in the country, the area where Jamal and I grew up was originally occupied by native Americans. This land of what was to be southern New Jersey, and outlying areas, was the home of the Leni Lenape and the very word "Pennsauken" is believed to be derived from the Lenape word for "tobacco pouch." Better times.

Those people who once called my hometown home were eventually run off by the United States government in the nineteenth century, and most of them settled in what is now modern-day Oklahoma. Part of me always wanted to meet them, and I wondered what Browning Road looked like, and how its people were some hundreds of years before my parents initiated the historical white flight. It wasn't even a road then. But the road was history.

White flight. That was Pennsauken history too. Jamal Bailey knew that his town's history, indeed his own neighborhood's history, was not limited to Native Americans meeting European settlers and later being driven off from their homelands. That history should be taught and learned by every kid in that town. All towns. Jamal is a smart kid, and he wanted something a little different for his history project. Something else. Damon gave him the idea of interviewing me.

Jamal was always fascinated with the block he lived on, and who lived there before him, what it was like and how it became what it is. Good or bad. All that racism, that was history too. All the fear, then tensions, even the crimes; all of it, history. Teach that in schools. Who said it all had to be pretty? Who presumed it was? It's not outrageous to say that history is not often kind, seldom as though we tend to disparage such a notion. We all have our motives.

I was reluctant to participate at first. To be honest, I was a little embarrassed. If I were to tell Jamal the truth of all the crap that happened leading up to the Pszcynacks and everyone else's departure over twenty-five years ago, I'm not sure such a story would be too appreciated, and I am a bad liar. Even still, Damon was able to convince me to be interviewed, and that it was okay. Jamal wanted to know about the white flight era of Pennsauken. It's not as if anyone else would tell him. History.

I relented. After hearing only a little bit of my story from Damon, there was no way Jamal would let me say no, so that was it. He and Damon actually delighted, and at the same time terrified me, with the prospect of meeting with Rosie Quann, still occupying the very same house she shrewdly bought from my frantic parents so long ago. All three of us would be meeting with her to catch up on and discuss Browning Road history right there in her home. My home. I could go back, if only briefly.

I knew it was Rosie's house now, and had been since my family left. Yet part of me was still there. I have no shame in it. Nonetheless, I had no idea what the hell Rosie would think of any of this. A history project, sure. But this white kid from the past would be travelling through time to discuss the ins and outs of racism and a changing neighborhood decades after the fact. Rosie agreed to this insanity, understanding at least that I once lived there and could visit. My hands were shaking to the point of running away, but I could never resist such an opportunity. I had to go back. I hoped she would truly understand. Jamal was a good kid.

What I really hoped would not happen is that Rosie may have found my wedding ring lying on her front lawn and might ask me what that was all about. Truth is, I had actually "visited" Rosie's house about a year before reconnecting with Damon. That was after I went through a divorce. I thought I had experienced everything before, and was somehow ready for anything life could throw at me. Yet nothing could quite prepare me for the pain, cruelty, and altogether indifference by design that abused my life by that of my own failed marriage. It was beyond terrible. Ignorant. Immature. Evil. It still is. Memory. That never goes away.

But it happened. After all was said and done, I had moved out of the home I shared with my wife and now live on my own. Starting over, but not knowing how. I still have memories lying about; bookshelves, kitchen tools, random furniture, all things that were once part of a life now gone. Reminders. I had no idea what to do with my wedding ring once the divorce had gone through, and had no courage or presence of mind to sell it.

That's when I got the idea to throw the ring right on the front lawn of my former home on Browning Road. After all, that's where all this nonsense began. All the anger, constant mistrust, and daily abuse began at that house; and it could have that particular memento of such a failure. It belonged there. So I drove down Browning Road one day, not getting out of the car, and tossed the ring into Rosie's front yard and then drove off hoping no one would notice. It appears no one did. Sorry about that, Rosie. But you did buy that house, and here we are.

I didn't think it would come up as a subject, but I was not returning to the house to find the ring. Let it stay there. I did arrive and met with Damon at the Myer's, pardon me, Jamal's house, and we were to take the minute long walk to Rosie's. No inclination for sitting still. I liked Jamal, he looked almost exactly like Damon did when we were kids, and was just as friendly. Part of me wanted to take a walk to Westfield Avenue with him and buy some comics. That wasn't happening. It is alright. My life was my own, and some memories are good, and always will be.

But I am back, physically standing on Browning Road in Pennsauken, New Jersey. My home town. It's all admittedly surreal, and my heart is racing as we walk down to my old house where I can see Rosie standing at the door, waiting for us. She looks exactly the same as the day she finagled my parents when they were desperate to leave and I was desperate to stay. She hasn't aged a single day. Her dress is bright red, as colorful as her personality. We would probably never actually get along if everything is still "blessed" but she is something else.

Here I am. Unbelievable. Rosie does have an awkward look on her face. As if this was the most ridiculous idea anyone has ever had. Who is this guy I barely remember and was fifteen the last time I saw him? I mattered more back then than you could ever have imagined, Rosie. Though I am sorry. It's almost wrong. If this was an intrusion, well, who could blame her?

Rosie appeared to be alone. I don't know who else has been living there. She painted the house a new color, it's now a yellow hue, not what it is supposed to be, damn it. It should be a light green house, with white shutters adorning the windows. That has changed too. Some of the bushes in front of the windows look exactly as they always did, once snow covered on Christmas morning when everything was better. Squirrels and birds still roamed the area. Animals. Flora and fauna. Life immune to all the abuse and racism, really, all of it. Probably better for them. Hopefully they will be here long after we are all gone.

Some trees I used to climb in the yard were no longer there, nothing but unsightly dirt patches left where they once towered. Half of me expected to see Barbara on the phone talking with her friends, and Christy running to the door to greet us. Some eighties music playing in the background. Michael coming to the door to ask if I could come out and play. None of that was actually happening.

I still miss my old room, and seriously doubt that I will resist asking Rosie to see it just one last time. I knew I was here for Jamal. I wonder if he or Damon can see how ridiculously nervous I am. This was my town. My block. My house. No, it was ours. That is the truth of it. Even still, I cannot help but look up at that bedroom window. The three of us walk up the house's concrete path. It is ravaged by time, cracked and weather stained but still the path that was there when I was only just a kid. We are closer. I can hear waves of voices, friends long gone, screams and berating tones from ages past. The way the wind blows across the lawn. I can't get enough of it. I am sweating, in fact, barely breathing. Trying to control it all in the seconds I have left. Rosie looks a bit bizarrely at us as we approach, probably more at me, I don't know. She beckons us to come in, Damon is smiling and waving at her as we move closer. I can see the stairway inside the house now. It leads to the above. I walked through the door.

ACKNOWLEDGEMENTS

We don't often get to choose our experiences. This book was quite a ride to even think about, let alone to write, but I am grateful for the opportunity to complete a second novel, and cannot begin to thank everyone who inspired me to write this story, and helped bring this all about, for better or the worse for it. I have to give great thanks to Sanjay for encouraging me to continue writing, and for remaining a friend during the roughest and craziest times imaginable. Friends matter, thank you for not forgetting. As well as the last, this book is made possible by my niece, Brooke Denshuick, who can often handle life's turbulences far better than I, and I remain joyful and privileged to call her family. This book had far more than one inspiration. History is history, even the unpleasant things. Unpleasant is part of life, sometimes all too predominantly. Cynicism is often honesty. Honesty being the more offensive term. The worst thing we can do is succumb to denial, or not ask questions when it's all questionable. Memories are what will be left of all family, of all friendships, so I suppose there's no shame in having a good recollection. Thank you for reading.

9 781735 891736